the star attraction

the star

HYPERION
NEW YORK

attraction

a novel

ALISON SWEENEY

Library of Congress Cataloging-in-Publication Data

Sweeney, Alison.
 The star attraction : a novel / by Alison Sweeney.
  p. cm.
 ISBN 978-1-4013-1104-9
 1. Single women—Fiction. 2. Investment bankers—Fiction. 3. Motion picture actors and actresses—Fiction. 4. Man-woman relationships—Fiction. I. Title.
 PS3619.W4424S73 2013
 813'.6—dc23
   2012031087

Book design by Karen Minster

FIRST EDITION

10 9 8 7 6 5 4 3 2 1

THIS LABEL APPLIES TO TEXT STOCK

We try to produce the most beautiful books possible, and we are also extremely concerned about the impact of our manufacturing process on the forests of the world and the environment as a whole. Accordingly, we've made sure that all of the paper we use has been certified as coming from forests that are managed, to ensure the protection of the people and wildlife dependent upon them.

For Carrie and Steph.

I couldn't ask for better friends.

the star attraction

prologue

I CAN'T HIDE IN HERE FOREVER.

But I don't know what waits beyond the other side of the door.

Catching my reflection, I barely recognize myself in the bathroom mirror. What happened to Miss Perfect? Okay, never Miss Perfect, but I was perfectly happy. Everything I've worked for—my job, my relationship, my *identity*—is up in the air. Or destroyed.

And it's all my fault.

Three Weeks Earlier

BASICALLY, I AM A THIRTY-ONE-YEAR-OLD GLORIFIED BABY-sitter. The elegant business cards I carry read: SOPHIE ATWATER, PERSONAL PUBLICIST, but really, it boils down to the same babysitting skills I began honing in the seventh grade. Only now instead of making sure homework is done and bedtimes are observed, I arrange "playdates" with my celebrity clients and the media. And trust me, knowing how to wrangle the occasional spoiled brat or princess still comes in handy.

Don't get me wrong—I love my job and its enviable upsides. It can feel exciting and glamorous to be in the know—even surreal, like when I'm at a checkout line and know for a fact where the line of truth falls on a tabloid cover. And no day is ever the same, so I can't get bored. I'm not the type of person who could handle sitting behind a desk all day, shuffling reports and getting excited about the 4 P.M. microwave popcorn break. I get squirmy just sitting in a theater seat for more than a couple of hours. Plus, you certainly can't dismiss the really cool perks, like when high-end or über-trendy designers send over free samples of clothes and makeup hoping to get them in the hands of our highly visible clients. Or simply court favor with us gatekeepers. With clients' closets often overstuffed, I'm happy to carry home what's left behind or "re-gifted" to me. Who would refuse "free"? Although, lately the reflection in my dressing mirror has been somewhat sobering . . . and now I find the trendiest looks better suited to fearless twenty-somethings.

But the very best thing about my job is that I am in charge of my own destiny. After starting as a lowly assistant—where fetch, copy, and collate were the sum of my responsibilities— more than seven years ago, I'm now pretty successful in my chosen field, and there is a certain satisfaction in knowing I worked damn hard to earn my status and reputation. And I work for Bennett/Peters, one of the most elite boutique PR firms in the industry. The boldfaced names you see regularly on "Page Six" or Perez Hilton? We represent most of them.

And it certainly isn't a *downside* that I get to work with gorgeous men all day, and tell them what to do.

Ow!

Someone just kicked me softly in the shin under the conference room table. I look up to find my assistant, Tru, *Hello Kitty* notepad at the ready, giving me wide eyes.

"Sophie?"

Elle, my boss, is seated at the head of the table. From the tone of her distinct New York accent, it's safe to guess this isn't the original query.

"Yes?" I reply confidently, tidying my notes as if I had been strategizing instead of zoning out as a couple of junior agents exhaustively detailed their upcoming events. Every Wednesday morning the entire department gathers around the long table with bullet-pointed lists and *venti*-sized Starbucks cups in hand for a major staff meeting.

"I wanted to be sure you are free first thing tomorrow morning," Elle continues, "because I've set up an important meet-and-greet with a potential new client: Billy Fox."

Now she's got my complete attention.

Mind you, I already represent more celebs than anyone else at my firm except Elle herself. But it is a compliment that she thinks I can secure this particular client better than any of the other publicists.

Billy Fox is a star.

Taking the Brad Pitt in *Thelma & Louise* route, Billy seduced audiences and critics alike with his brief yet undeniably charismatic debut as a sweet-talking, golden-haired con man in a Quentin Tarantino ensemble heist film. Since his breakout role (and Golden Globe nomination), Billy has gone on to become a versatile leading man in films ranging from a high-grossing romantic comedy to a high-adrenaline legal thriller to a surprising choice of role in a risky indie costume drama. After just a half dozen films, Billy Fox is widely considered one of the elite, bankable A-list actors—and fodder for women's fantasies across the globe. Signing him to Bennett/Peters would be a major coup.

I knew his former publicist, an amazing woman. Really, a Norma Rae in the PR world. But she retired, incredibly wealthy and on some tropical island from what I hear, and now he and his manager are looking for another firm to represent him. Obviously, Bennett/Peters wants this account and wants it bad. Elle wants this for the firm, for her career. I want it, I mean him, I mean *this account* for her, for the company, but also because it would totally cement my reputation with the firm for literally ever.

"Definitely," I say. "Count me in. I'll prepare for the meeting this afternoon. And thanks. You won't be—"

"With all due respect," interrupts my coworker Priscilla Hasley, in her smooth, Gwyneth Paltrow–like inflection, "don't you think I'd be the most appropriate choice? His prior publicist and I run in the same social circles. It might aid the transition."

No she didn't. Unbelievable. As if I'd be booking Billy while getting pedicures and deep-tissue massages at exclusive country clubs.

In truth, I shouldn't have been surprised. It's typical Priscilla. I hate the way she speaks—especially because her polished voice, chic auburn bob, and ridiculously perfect body disguise her total ineptitude and appalling work ethic. Not only is Priscilla a lousy publicist, she is a complete and utter bitch. I consider myself to be a pretty open-minded person, but having seen Priscilla in action for three-and-a-half years now, I think I have enough to base my judgment on. Though she's never crossed me (other than just now boldly stepping on my toes), I've observed how she treats the assistants and junior publicists. Just last week she took a long look at one of Tru's more colorful ensembles and snidely asked aloud if we'd taken on Barnum & Bailey as a new client. I couldn't help but notice that usually confident Tru wore her jacket inside for the rest of the day. And Priscilla infamously sent a former assistant she felt had crossed her back to the drugstore to return a defective yeast infection test—which was humiliating enough for the poor girl without it being in *used* condition.

Now all of us in the room seem to be holding our breath, awaiting Elle's response.

Elle is by general consensus a great boss, except when it comes to Priscilla. She is completely blind to how inept Priscilla is. Everyone knows Priscilla got the job only because her dad is the publisher of a very snazzy magazine. So far I have managed to steer clear of her, but her attitude of superiority grates on my nerves. The weird thing is, she is Elle's "pet project."

For the most part, everyone tries to ignore it when Priscilla gets great assignments or fun responsibilities like managing the "loot locker," the storage room of random gifts—from luxuries to personal electronics to board games—we routinely receive from companies or events, for our clients. But there are the inevitable eye rolls when Elle dismisses obvious mistakes Priscilla makes or covers for her by buying into Priscilla's attempts to pass blame to someone else in the department.

Thankfully Elle is clearheaded today. "I appreciate your enthusiasm, Priscilla, but Sophie is the best fit and my choice for Mr. Fox. Moving on . . ."

It takes all my adult self-control to refrain from smirking.

As soon as the meeting wraps, Tru and I regroup in my glass-walled office. I wish I could brag that it's a super-stylish workstation, but in all the years since I graduated from a cubicle, I still haven't gotten around to decorating it with many personal touches. Yet after so many long hours hosting my ambition, it comfortably feels like home. And besides, my job is just as much on the road anyway, whether it's shuttling clients to the gated studios and backlots of Burbank or Hollywood, attending press circuits (aka media musical chairs—new face, same short list of questions) in plush hotel suites, overseeing corner-booth interviews at West Hollywood's Chateau Marmont, or dodging the "Fashion Police" on red carpets when a client's wardrobe choices were annihilated the year before. "For tomorrow's meeting," I instruct Tru, "we need to research everything Billy Fox. I'm talking career, press, personal life . . . the works. Get Googling."

My quirky yet highly capable assistant of the past eighteen months may not look like the usual blond and polished LA publicist, but I wouldn't trade her selfless Midwestern drive and resourcefulness for anything.

Hours later I'm sifting through an impressive pile of clippings—from deals and box office numbers in the *Hollywood Reporter* and *Variety* to far more gossipy items in *TMZ* and *Star* magazine. *Entertainment Weekly* gushingly crowned Billy "Hollywood's Next Golden Boy." And with that notoriety, his personal life has been equally public. He'd been dating this pop star for a while, actually, especially by Hollywood standards, and their breakup saw major tabloid coverage for weeks. In fact the pop star's latest single is rumored to be a thinly veiled critique of their relationship.

That's got to suck. Breakups are bad enough without the court of public opinion.

After checking off another day's to-do list and gathering my notes for tomorrow, it's time to hit the road home. Pulling out of the office's underground parking, I wave good-bye to the familiar, rotating security guard (tonight it's Latin-Big-Flirt-with-Soul-Patch on duty) and ease into the evening traffic. In some cities families are already clearing the dinner dishes, but here in LA, seven-thirty is still peak rush hour. As long as it's just the usual crawling traffic ahead, the commute from

Century City to Brentwood should get me home by eight-fifteen or so. My iPod lights up as I blast the new Killers album through my BMW's stereo system. With the office shrinking from sight in the rearview mirror, I take my first deep breath of the day.

I can't lie, I am a little stressed out. The days are rewarding but draining. There are a lot of egos, overbooked schedules, and periods of necessary hand-holding—and that's just over lunch. Yesterday, for instance, I half-listened to a nineteen-year-old actress client (one of Nickelodeon's fresh-faced ingénues) babble on and on about how the show's director insisted everyone's lunch break be shortened to forty-five minutes to help pick up the schedule. "But it's called a lunch *hour* for a reason," she vented to me over the phone as I tried to ignore my own stomach's growling. "Do you know how long it takes to prepare 'raw'?! It's not just slicing up carrots, you know." Never mind that I rarely find *fifteen minutes* to duck out for a bite or must ask Tru to pick up some sad salad for me to scarf down as I mute my end of a conference call.

But honestly, it comes with the territory. I wouldn't trade my career—and it isn't just about the hot guys and the swag. I appreciate the challenge of raising someone's profile or working out a campaign for a client's new independent film. Photo shoots, press junkets, launch parties, premieres . . . nothing is more exciting for me than taking a hardworking actor and turning him or her into a star. At this stage in my career I have earned the right to pick and choose my clients. So, for the most part, though they can be demanding, I really like and admire the people I work with. Celebrities are generally fun to hang out with because when you're with them they treat you like you're their best friend, and your opinion is gold. It's those damn managers you have to watch out for—they can be so bitchy. One wrong move and they'll yank your star client right out from under you. But that hasn't happened to me in a long time.

Outside Hollywood—or "the business" as it's aptly called in LA—people may not know my name, but they certainly recognize my clients. And that's in large part due to my hard work in getting their names and faces out there. I've even been mentioned in the gossip columns. Okay, well, not by name, but when you read "so-and-so's representative was not available for comment"—that's me! And the "unavailable" part? Completely untrue. I am *always* available for work. But sometimes the best defense for a client's sticky situation is to pretend it doesn't exist and wait for someone else to screw up and grab the spotlight.

Thank you, America's short attention span.

I hear my BlackBerry pinging from its perch on the passenger seat and resist the urge to pick it up. Okay, so I am a BlackBerry addict. I know that's a cliché even by LA standards, but I admit that I get a bit shaky if the little black box isn't within my line of sight. I've burned through the keypads of two BlackBerrys already. The tech guys at Bennett/Peters didn't even know that was possible until I came along. After the first incident (where I practically had a panic attack), I keep my I.T. person on speed dial. BlackBerry #3 was in my restless hands within only a few—but seemingly infinite—hours. This may seem a bit workaholic psycho, but to me, it's normal. It's business. Sophie Atwater is available by email or cell phone 24/7.

It will probably say that on my tombstone.

Not that I *can't* take a vacation when I want to . . . but the few times my boyfriend, Jacob, and I have tried to go away for weekends, to Santa Barbara or San Diego, I was still returning calls and constantly emailing people. Jacob likes to half-joke about throwing my BlackBerry out the window as we sit in traffic on the 101, but he would never really do it. And it's not like he can talk. He brings his laptop everywhere, and his nose is always buried in the newspaper. And not just the *Los Angeles Times*—he reads *all of them*. I'm talking the *Wall Street Journal*, the *New York Times*, and even Washington and Chicago papers. At first I was impressed. I bragged to all my girlfriends how intelligent and informed he was (he doesn't even skim the Entertainment section). But like discovering news-ink stains on your fingers, it is pretty annoying to find stack upon stack of previously read papers in your breakfast nook. I own a less than sprawling one-bedroom condo. I'm lucky to *have* a "breakfast nook," and I don't always feel like pushing aside a foot-high pile of last week's news just to sit down while I power through my bowl of Cheerios.

At a red light on Wilshire (home to the longest red lights on the planet), I sneak a look at the incoming emails—nothing urgent—and get in a quick text to Jacob to say I'm almost there. As you might have guessed by his non-*Variety* or *Hollywood Reporter* reading habits, he's not an actor. That is always the first question people ask me. I suppose given that I spend seemingly twenty-three hours a day with actors it is an obvious assumption. But dating clients is strictly forbidden at Bennett/Peters, and for anyone with an ounce of common sense, not a good idea.

Nope, Jacob R. Sloane is not in the industry at all, actually.

He's an investment banker. Don't ask me what that means because, honestly, I have no idea. Except that it does have a sexy, grown-up sound to it. He's gamely explained to me a couple times what he does, and I go out with him and his work buddies occasionally, but when they're talking about "lenders" and "portfolios" and whatnot, I can't help but tune it all out. And inevitably, I have several pending emails I should be replying to anyway. Sometimes I sip my wine and scroll through my inbox and let Jacob's low, growly voice wash over me, trying to ignore the occasional frown I see on his forehead when he catches me discreetly, or not so discreetly, tapping away on the keyboard.

Finally I park my car in another underground garage and drag my overstuffed Louis Vuitton shoulder bag and exhausted self up the steps to my condo on the third floor. Home is my favorite retreat. Once inside my door, I let out a sigh of relief as I kick the four-inch Jimmy Choo stilettos off my screaming-red, swollen feet. I'm only five-foot-three, so I always go for the highest shoes possible. Not just to keep up with the supermodels, but because nearly everyone I work with is taller than me. I like to even the playing field as much as possible, and for the most part I am very good at walking in high heels, but today has been a really long day. I carefully replace my Choos in their tissue-lined box of honor in my closet. The relieved sigh turns into a groan of pleasure as I replace my suck-in-the-stomach black pencil skirt with a pair of Juicy sweats and my favorite bunny slippers. Now, I don't want to lead you on with all this "Jimmy Choo" and "L.V." talk. I do a good job of giving the impression amongst my peers that I am well off, but aside from the money I put toward my mortgage, it's a month-to-month existence I've got going here. I indulge in my "taste for the finer things" because when you're standing next to Anne Hathaway on a red carpet, you feel bad enough about yourself as it is. At least when I'm clutching my Chloé bag I can hold my head up. Besides, if my boss, Elle, saw me show up at the office in my favorite Gap jeans, she'd never let me live it down.

The phone rings, and I have a Pavlov's dog–type instantaneous reaction. It's nearly impossible to turn off the adrenaline rush of crisis management. But the call is only Jacob signaling his arrival with our much-needed take-out BBQ. We're on a mission to find the best of every type of food in LA. It's a "travel escape" via cuisine. Right now, we're working on Texas barbeque (you know, spare ribs, pulled pork, and all things good and heart attack), but frankly, we've been pretty disappointed so far. I was in Nashville last month with a client, and he took me to some delicious hole-in-the-wall place where the tea was sweet and the food perfection. I've been craving it ever since, but nothing local is living up to that memory. Still, we haven't given up trying.

My kitchen is primarily used as a morning coffee station.

Jacob strides in—looking the part of athletic, former frat boy turned respectable businessman in a sharp suit and Italian leather shoes—and flashes a broad smile as he drops the aromatic bag of food on the kitchen counter.

I want to say it's because I am an intoxicating vision of beauty tonight. But I have some idea what my hair must look like: dirty-blond straw. I have stick-straight, relatively healthy, down-to-my-shoulders locks, which can actually be blown out to look quite pretty when I bother. But this morning was too damn early, and I'm not the one on TV anyway. So the best I could do was a tight ponytail, which gives a finished appearance but at this point in the day is no longer tolerable. I now have the ponytail holder around my wrist, and self-consciously, I tuck the man-made lighter blond highlights behind my ears as I return to flipping through our viewing options.

I don't remember when I stopped checking the mirror before Jacob's arrival, but I did.

"Hi, babe." He leans over the couch and gives me a quick upside-down kiss. His chestnut-brown bangs tickle my chin. And I get a note of his warm, earthy cologne. "I got baby back ribs, smoked chicken, and corn bread. How was your day?" He disappears into the adjoining kitchen.

"Good and exhausting. We might be signing Billy Fox as a new client tomorrow. And Elle chose me to win him over."

"The actor, right?" Jacob's voice floats in from the kitchen along with the sound of drawers and the refrigerator door opening and closing. "You're a pro. I'm sure you'll wow him."

That's so Jacob—supportive of my career yet rarely starstruck. It's an endearing trait and a retreat from my celebrity-saturated world. "Thanks for the vote of confidence," I say, hoping he's right. "Oh, Julie at *Hollywood Tonight* says hi. She's the one who got smashed at the Sunset Room last week, remember?"

"How could I forget?" Jacob reappears juggling a Sierra Nevada for himself and the rest of an already open bottle of wine for me, along with plates, napkins, and utensils. "She serenaded the entire bar with three choruses of 'I Will Survive.' Too bad she couldn't remember the verses. And there you were cheering her on!" He chuckles, organizing everything in front of us.

We exchange the ritual small talk as we set up dinner on the small square coffee table in front of my fifty-inch flat-screen, an unexpected client gift from Christmas. Now I would dearly love to impress you with the list of highbrow shows I watch, but while Jacob "season passes" shows like *The O'Reilly Factor* and *Meet the Press*, I am addicted to guilty pleasures. I consider them a present to myself for when I get home at night and find my brain on standby. Aside from keeping up with the standard reality TV fare, I am still attached to the soap my Theta sorority sisters got me hooked on—*Days of Our Lives*. Some people even say I resemble the longtime character Sami, which is up for debate, but I'll take it as a compliment. And whenever I'm feeling really down, good old-fashioned *90210* (the original) and *Dawson's Creek* repeats are the best antidotes.

But beyond the girly stuff, Jacob and I appreciate a lot of the same shows.

Our absolute favorite is *Survivor*. Seriously, it is such good TV and a useful reminder that even on my toughest days I've at least got takeout on speed-dial, a hot shower, and Jacob's alliance to keep me sane. I'm no prima donna, but honestly, I'd be the first to vote myself off the island. Jacob and I have a pact that no matter how tempted, we won't watch our favorite show without the other person. In fact, one time we got in a huge two-day fight because I thought he'd watched it without me and so I started viewing the recorded episode before he arrived.

So there we were, both ridiculously furious at each other for watching *Survivor* without the other. At some point, while I was still good and riled up, he just grabbed me and kissed me hard on the mouth. After that it was pretty difficult to stay mad at him. I don't know why, but there are times when I'm simply in the mood for a good fight, and Jacob just isn't like that. He's Mr. Steady. Mostly, though, I do appreciate how even-tempered Jacob is, and I love that our relationship isn't built on drama. I get enough drama with my clients.

When we first started dating, I used to think of Jacob as "Jake" and even teasingly call him that to be sexy. You see, the first time I laid eyes on Jacob, he totally reminded me of dreamy "Jake Ryan" from *Sixteen Candles*, a preteen crush that I never outgrew. Both certainly fit "tall, dark, and handsome." Plus he's preppy and conservative. Not that he's a prude. I mean, we met at a trendy Hollywood bar, not in the Elizabethan poetry section of the library, and he had definitely been drinking. I recall he was holding a bottled beer in his left hand when he shook my hand with his right. His smile, loosened by the alcohol into a very compelling grin, gave away that he was attracted to me too.

The second we officially met, I doubly pictured that hunk in John Hughes's movie. And not only because of his name. Jacob had this way about him that reminded me of how cool "Jake" was, how he went his own way, liking Molly Ringwald instead of the vapid popular blond girl. We too were at a party, not a wild high-school rager with Long Duk Dong, but basically its adult equivalent. A Theta sister from USC was throwing a party for her thirtieth at the Saddle Ranch on Sunset, home to one very feisty mechanical bull. Trust me, I've found that out the hard way. There we all were, drinking sour apple martinis and making fools of ourselves, which is not exactly the position you want to find yourself in when you meet a guy you want to have a real (read successful) relationship with. But Jacob was different. He spotted something special in me, something that inspired him to make it through the dense crowd and introduce himself.

He left with my number. I left unable to shake the thought of him.

The very next day he called and asked me out. Less than a month later, my Facebook relationship status was officially changed, and, well, here we are, together for almost two years now.

"Babe—your hands are clean, hit fast-forward, will you?" Jacob interrupts my reverie, reminding me of my remote-control responsibilities. A weird side effect of my job is that I am a really fast eater, so I'd already devoured my chicken and irresistible side of sweet corn bread. Ever the boy, Jacob's fingers remain covered in BBQ sauce. He flashes an adorably greasy smile that moves me to lean in and kiss him. I giggle as I skip past the commercials to the Immunity Challenge, happy that we have our own ritual retreat and that we have a pretty good alliance.

Sometimes I think Jacob and I could contentedly spend every night like this for the rest of our lives, which is new ground for me. I always thought of myself as a tough, independent girl. With every guy I've dated, I've kept my own place, and I've never really been tempted to move in with anyone. But I can't help loving the way Jacob pulls my body up against his as I'm falling asleep. And the thought of waking to his broad arms around me each—well, at least *weekend*—morning doesn't feel like it would be a compromise or surrender. Two years together is pretty much a record for me. And for once, the idea of settling down doesn't feel suffocating. But what and when exactly *is* the next step? Moving in together? And does Jacob want the same thing?

All I know is I'm ready for more.

MY ALARM is blaring the Black Eyed Peas at 8:05 Thursday morning. As I dive for the snooze button, I can smell the coffee Jacob brewed wafting into the bedroom. It's nice to lie still, breathing in dark Italian roast, and picture Jacob quietly setting the high-tech coffee machine for me. It's the kind of sweet and considerate thing he is so good at. I hate that he's not here in bed with me though. When he stays over, he wakes up super-early to hit the gym before heading to his office downtown. It's hard not to feel guilty whenever I think about the extra commute he puts up with just to spend the night with me. But not so guilty I want him to stop.

Now if we *lived* together . . .

Glancing over at the clock, I am horrified to discover that almost fifteen minutes have gone by while I daydreamed about Jacob. My morning routine is timed down to the last minute, and now—if I don't seriously scramble—I'm going to be late. Damn it.

I wasn't always a late riser. Before Jacob, I was seeing this bleach-blond surfer boy named Zach. He miraculously had me in a wet suit before 6 A.M., trying to catch waves. My inner

Gidget phase didn't last long though. I'm not much for working out in the morning, much less in the cold ocean waters. Looking back, sports always seem to have been embedded in my relationships, as if the spark is actually competition. Before Zach, there was Chad. Tennis was our game. Chad was one of those ultra-preppy frat boys who didn't realize Lacoste had come back in style, because for him and his habitually upturned collar, it had never gone out. Alas, a shared appreciation for styling mousse and winter tans wasn't enough, and like the sport, our "love" became synonymous with zero.

The guy I dated for two semesters in college was really into Tae Kwon Do. It was my *Karate Kid* phase, and I totally wanted to be Elisabeth Shue. But he was no Daniel-san, so we broke up before I got my yellow belt. I even fell for this kickboxer—"the sport of the future"—because I couldn't get John Cusack out of my head. I think I could blame all those classic eighties movies for my love life.

Other than the occasional round of golf, Jacob simply goes to the gym like regular people. In fact, I don't work out with him at all. We kind of have our separate routines and then do stuff together when we can. Personally I think that's why we've lasted so much longer than my previous relationships. We're not living in each other's pocket.

And he brews a mean pot of coffee.

Requisite caffeine boost in hand, I lean against the sliding doors of my closet to choose an outfit for the day. I wish I could be one of those people who pick out their clothes the night before and have them all laid out for the morning next to the perfect shoes and accessories. But really, I am just not that organized in my personal life. There's no time for indecision today, so I simply grab a flattering skirt and a favorite top, jump in the shower, and pull myself together with an anxious eye always on the time.

Grabbing my bag and keys, I dart down to my car. I'm freaking out not because I'm nervous or star-struck to meet Billy Fox, but because I'm supposed to be sitting in our conference room in, *oh my God*, forty minutes. If I show up late, Elle will be understandably upset. *Thirty-nine minutes. Argh!* I love Elle, and she loves me, but *no one* wants to see Elle when she's angry.

All I can do now is pray to the traffic gods.

9:27 A.M.—the elevator is taking *forever*. And, of course, it's filled with people who are getting off on every floor between here and the thirtieth. Our offices take up two floors, twenty-nine and thirty, in one of Century City's biggest buildings. My personal office is on twenty-nine, but a furtive glance at my watch confirms that Billy Fox and his "team" are probably already walking into Elle's upper-floor office as we speak, so I figure I'll stake out the conference room. Be there waiting when they arrive.

This meeting would normally be a breeze, except that Billy's manager can be a complete bitch. Her name is Wanda von Kingstead—it even sounds snotty. But I don't think I'll have any trouble with Wanda; she's warmed to me ever since I sweet-talked *Us Weekly* into pulling a disgusting (but true) story about one of her clients. It bears mentioning that Wanda admitted to me in a panicked too-sober voice during a 1 A.M. phone call that *perhaps* she might have revealed this secret to a one-night stand whose name is well known on the gossip circuit. Since I represent this celeb, it was in my best interest to do as much damage control as possible. I still can't believe I got out of that one by giving a good tip as to where a certain reality show judge takes her handsome young would-be stars for a night on the town.

You may think that cold and cutthroat, but, hey, I didn't create the system. I just make it work for me. Believe me, never trust a publicist with your secrets—we'd sell out our own mother to protect a client.

Either way, knowing Wanda is going to be present forces me to elevate my game a little. But meeting hunky stars is not all it's cracked up to be. Inevitably I find myself let down a little; some of them don't even shower unless they're required to on a set. As any makeup artist will tell you—some guys, you have to trim their nose hairs for them. Or they're shockingly dull. Hygiene and personality shortcomings aside, I've had my share of favorite movies ruined forever by the actors being such utter bastards off-camera. I'm very curious to see what Billy Fox is like.

Yes! The conference room is still empty. I scoot around to the far side of the table, take a seat in an emerald-green rolling chair, and triumphantly help myself to a pitcher of ice water.

"Oh, Sophie! There you are." Elle's sweet-but-professional voice in the conference room doorway catches me off-guard and I involuntarily jump, spilling the entire cup of chilled water into my lap.

Fuck!

"Your assistant didn't know where you'd disappeared to,"

Elle breezily continues with no idea that my crotch has reached arctic temperatures. "Of course you know Wanda." Smothering a groan, I try and compensate with an overly bright smile showing too many teeth.

"Good morning, Elle. Wanda!" I fake like I'm going to stand up, but carefully keep my soaking wet lap hidden behind the conference table.

"And this is none other than Billy Fox," Elle says, giving me an odd look before choosing a chair at the head of the long oval table. I realize how rude my behavior must seem at this point. Luckily I quickly preoccupy my hands with paperwork and my now-empty cup so as to appear completely unable to rise to politely greet Billy.

"A pleasure. I'm Sophie." I strive for a slightly harried and yet completely capable tone.

"Sophie, it's nice to meet you," Billy says in a soft Texan accent as he leans over the table and helps me "gather" my papers. He takes my reluctant hand in his and holds eye contact a moment longer than necessary. In that instant I see what has captivated women worldwide. This man is utterly gorgeous. And his pale blue eyes have this adorable crinkly smile. *Yikes, Sophie, pull it together.*

"Billy. Nice to meet you too." For a second I forget the mini icebergs I still have in my lap and start to rise again. The quiet thud of the ice cubes hitting the carpet brings me to my senses, thank God, and I ungracefully slam my butt back in the chair. It is a relief to have the freezing element removed from my thighs. Now I just look like I've peed myself. Great. That's a confidence booster.

Now clearly I should just tell them what happened. With a disarming laugh, I could confess, "Oops! Silly me, I spilled ice water on my silk skirt," and it would be no big deal. Well, it was too late. I started a lie, and to come clean at this point would make me look like a fool as well as a klutz. Hopefully, my skirt will be dry by the end of the meeting.

"Well, let's get started, shall we?" Elle clears her throat, and I recognize my cue to launch into our well-rehearsed but seemingly spontaneous explanation of the advantages of signing with Bennett/Peters.

"To begin, we'd like to hear from you and your team," I say, gesturing toward Wanda since often the manager takes the lead at this point, speaking on behalf of the client. A lot of "creative types" sit back, not bothering to hide their boredom, and let their managers decide the major aspects of their careers. "Tell us what Bennett/Peters can do for you."

Without hesitation Billy speaks up. "I want to make some changes. Wanda and I have gone over this, with my agents too. I want to continue to find new roles. Different characters to play. Now is the time to step up my game as an actor. And I think the best way to get those roles is to change my image."

Now, clearly, we are not in the business of casting movies, but Billy isn't the first person to come through our doors hoping to land a different role with our help. The idea is that public perception can definitely impact how an actor is perceived by casting directors, directors, and producers. Sometimes they need a little push to see an actor in a new light . . . to be willing to take a chance on him. And we can help with that.

Billy continued. "When I first started out, I was getting

more variety than I see now. The last ten scripts I've seen were exactly the same. The same character, the same romantic comedy, I'm always offered the same role—a copycat of Hugh Grant from *Bridget Jones*. Look, I know which film of mine made the most money . . . but I don't want to be pigeonholed."

"We can absolutely help reshape your image," I confidently say. "And help you better control how the public—and therefore the industry—sees you." As part of the meeting prep, I collected all his recent tabloid mentions, and I start spreading them out on the table. For a while he was practically neck and neck with Kim Kardashian for coverage. "Frankly, there are some simple steps we can take to help make quick changes. If you're on board, and willing . . . that's the easy part. The harder part would be to reboot public perception of you into something else. How do you see yourself? In our experience, sticking closer to the truth is always easier . . . to establish and maintain."

"I understand what you're saying," Billy says, totally focused on the discussion. "I'm not trying to make people think I'm someone I'm not. I just want to be taken seriously. Like Johnny Depp, for example. I want that. I can do mainstream *and* have indie cred. I appreciate art and culture. I mean, if they're going to peg me as a playboy, why can't it be the George Clooney type?"

"For a lot of reasons." I look him in the eye. "First of all, George has a few more years on him. But it's also the way he escorts the appropriately dressed women he dates. He takes them to international film festivals, where he's been nominated. Not out to Hollywood clubs. He brings them to his villa in Lake Como. Which just *sounds* good. He's an Academy Award winner, and he acts like it."

"Exactly!" Now Billy lights up. "I'm not saying I expect to win an Oscar, but I want those roles. I know I can tackle them if serious directors will just give me that chance. I don't care about the clubs, or the girls. I will totally follow your lead here. If we can get me back on track and off TMZ's Most Wanted."

Elle, sensing a meeting of the minds, wraps things up. "It sounds like we are all on the same page then. Billy, it seems to me that you and Sophie have a clear understanding of how this is going to work. Sign with Bennett/Peters and I will make her your direct contact. You are aware of our monthly rate. Take your time, discuss things with your team, and get back to us?" Elle rises and hands her card to Wanda.

The Billy Fox meeting wraps up around 10:15 A.M. Is my skirt dry? Not enough for me to confidently stroll out with the group. The water stain alone is sure to be hideous. Trying to seem as inconspicuous as possible, I wait for the rest of the group to get distracted gathering their things, and I rise with my files and bag strategically located in front of me. I follow everyone to the door, and after our good-byes—which include an ever-so-charming kiss on the cheek from Billy—I duck down a side corridor to the ladies' room to inspect the damage to my skirt and pride.

Smooth one, Sophie. Real smooth.

AS MENTIONED EARLIER, lunchtime is always a hectic affair. Unless you're meeting someone for a business lunch, the team at Bennett/Peters, as an unspoken rule, doesn't take much time to eat. Three hours after the Billy Fox meeting I am at my desk, snacking on sushi that Monica, one of the interns, ran out to get for us. And I'm finally comfy, thanks to my Rock & Republic jeans that I found in my emergency-staying-over-at-Jacob's bag. Life is good. I've even finished typing a thorough email to Wanda, reiterating our delight and intended plans with representation. Despite my initial social awkwardness, Bennett/Peters was well represented. I know I did my best. Fingers crossed, we've just landed another major client to add to the roster. *And* I managed to secure two long-lead magazine covers for some up-and-coming starlets that Elle is pushing. So, all in all, a good day.

By the time I'm wrapping things up, it's already past 7 P.M. Again.

Usually Jacob and I have dinner plans either Thursday or Friday night, but the last couple weeks, I've had to bail out at the last minute. I'm just too exhausted for anything more than a bath and my pillow. Lame but true. Jacob understands—he has to work late too sometimes, but I hate being the bad guy. With a final glance at the bottom corner clock on my computer screen, I sheepishly call Jacob's cell, relieved to get his voice-mail, and leave a message.

"Jacob, it's Sophie. It's seven-fifteen and I just wanted to let you know I don't think I can come out tonight. Prep for the big meeting wiped me out, and now that it's over, I just want to head home and crash. But first I'm going to still be here for at least another twenty minutes or so. Let me know what your Friday night and weekend look like. I could come over to your place, or something, tomorrow. Shall I pick anything up on the way?"

I try to keep my voice peppy though I know I'll be asleep within twenty minutes after I get home.

As I finish typing up another email, the phone rings. I see the caller ID and pick it up before Monica can—yep, she's still here too, paying her intern dues.

"Hey."

"Hi, babe." Jacob sounds tired. Or maybe disappointed?

"So, I'm almost done now. I really am too tired to go out, but if I can rally a second wind perhaps we can camp out on one or the other's couch and watch Netflix?" I'm not *that* tired, I try to convince myself. And curling up beside Jacob sounds good, even if I am sure to nod off in the first act of whatever movie we decide to stream. That's why I had to quit going out to movies after work—nothing is more embarrassing than falling asleep in a movie theater. (And worse, I sometimes snore.)

"No, Sophie. Remember? We were supposed to go to the committee meeting tonight."

Oh fuck! I forgot about that.

Jacob's mom had a breast cancer scare ten months ago, though she was very lucky and they caught it early and now she is in the clear. But ever since, Jacob has been an active member of Tribe of Hope, an organization that raises awareness and money for research. It's so like Jacob—he's not always good at the emotive side, but he can "help." It's been his role ever since being caught in the middle of his parents' messy divorce while still a kid. Whether it's fund-raising or organizing, Jacob's your man. It's the mushy stuff of commitment he has trouble expressing. Tonight is the kickoff meeting to begin planning the annual gala, and I promised Jacob I would also help.

"I'm sorry. I really am. I had a million things to do today and I just completely spaced. Even if I left now, with traffic, I would be at least an hour late." Honesty is always best with Jacob. If I made up excuses he would know. "Take good notes for me, okay? I swear I'll make the next one."

"Yeah, okay." He still sounds kind of quiet. From anyone else it would be censure, but Jacob isn't the guilt-tripping sort.

"I'll make it up to you tomorrow night, I promise." I try to put a little Demi Moore throaty sexiness to my voice, but I probably just sound sick.

"It's okay." Now Jacob sounds like he's holding back a laugh. "I did get that Hitchcock film we added to our queue. How 'bout it?"

"I'll bring the takeout. Ready to tackle Indian?"

"Sounds good. Always up for a spicy evening with you."

It is my turn to suppress a giggle.

"Well, I've gotta run to make the meeting," Jacob says. "Miss you."

"Hey, wait!" I say. "You never asked how my meeting with Billy Fox went."

"Oh yeah. Sorry. So . . . ?" I imagine him standing there clutching his briefcase and car key, monitoring the time. Unlike me, Jacob is always punctual.

"Pretty good, I think." And pray. "It's wait and see now."

"That's my girl."

We hang up. I love that we're at the comfortable point in our relationship. I can just show up on his doorstep without having to dress up or reapply makeup. I can be tired, sloppy, and simply ready for some Netflix. Yet sometimes I do miss the thrill of putting on a sexy dress and having a guy unable to take his eyes off me. And then, without pausing to consider why, I absent-mindedly raise a hand to my cheek and gently touch the spot Billy Fox's lips graced only hours ago.

2:47PM

Izzy12242: so . . . ? how'd it go with Billy yesterday?
PRCHICK78: really well. I think.
PRCHICK78: trying to stay calm and positive.
would be a major coup.
Izzy12242: HUGE ☺
PRCHICK78: but what if we didn't wow him?
PRCHICK78: I was kinda a hot mess at first.
or rather cold.
Izzy12242: ?
PRCHICK78: never mind. long story.
Izzy12242: S, of course you wowed him.
but what's he *like*???

Izzy has been my best friend since grade school. If anyone knows me best, it's her. She gave me my now well-worn bunny slippers in high school as an inside joke because I would always "hop on over" to her house. From slumber parties to high school keggers, we were inseparable until Izzy was accepted at Brown and left West LA for the east coast. We still saw each other during holidays and summers, but to be separated during such a defining period of our lives inevitably led us to drift apart. We reconnected by chance a few years ago, through the biz of all things, when Izzy started working at *Vintage*, a fabulous, glossy wine magazine in New York, and her familiar name caught my eye on its masthead. From there we picked up where we left off after college and now email or IM every day as if we're still passing notes or procrastinating about homework.

There is no stress in my friendship with Izzy. Maybe it's because she's in New York and I'm in LA, so we're not in each other's life too much—though we always wish we saw each other more. Or maybe it's because she's now married, settled down, and always provides a different perspective on my issues. The bottom line is Izzy is once again the coolest chick I know.

Izzy12242: tell me EVERYTHING! I've been dying here.
Izzy12242: I walk by his latest billboard every day.
PRCHICK78: walking??? I thought you were on an I'm-a-New-Yorker-and-New-Yorkers-take-the-subway kick?
Izzy12242: can't handle the smell anymore.
plus I need the exercise.
Izzy12242: AND I get to see Billy Fox's beautiful face every morning.
PRCHICK78: lol. all good reasons
Izzy12242: Yeah, Simon is very impressed that I have stuck to walking every day this month. lol. I don't think I've mentioned the billboard to him.

Simon is Izzy's fabulous husband and a talented graphic designer. They met while both working at the same magazine and were mutually happy to make the relationship official after months of water cooler flirtation and near-daily shared lunches in Central Park. No one at the workplace was surprised by the good news. I don't say this about a lot of couples—mostly because I don't want to jinx it for them—but I think Simon and Izzy are meant to be together. And you can't hate them for it. They are smitten and couple-y without being smug or obnoxious. And I never feel like the third wheel when I'm with them. Without fail, whenever I get to New York, Simon and Izzy always treat me to dinner, whether sharing their new favorite haunt or remarkably whipping up a huge feast out of their tiny Manhattan-sized kitchen. And I love that Simon is as much involved and a part of the conversation as Izzy is.

> **Izzy12242:** Now, tell me everything about Billy Fox.
> I want details.
> **PRCHICK78:** Okay okay! He's hot.
> **PRCHICK78:** Hotter in person than on-screen.
> **Izzy12242:** that's not possible
> **PRCHICK78:** believe me. You shake his hand and he looks in your eyes and your heart sort of goes . . . crazy for a second.

As I'm typing this, I realize it's true. I didn't really want to admit it, but Billy did wow me a bit. And I really don't know what to think about that.

> **Izzy12242:** Does he have an accent?
> **PRCHICK78:** Not really. I mean, there was a hint of a drawl on a few words, but for the most part he sounded normal.
> **Izzy12242:** Normal? Billy Fox could never sound normal!
> **Izzy12242:** What did he wear? Did he seem smart? Smell good?

PRCHICK78: yeah. he was definitely smart. and he seemed nice too.
PRCHICK78: not all full of himself. He wore slacks and a casual button up shirt.

How refreshing. An actor who actually dresses appropriately for a business meeting. Usually, unless they know there's a camera present, the celebrities who come through our doors dress like they live underneath a freeway overpass. Not that you'd expect them to be always close-up perfect, but most dress for the PR firm like it's a milk run or a trip to Target.

Izzy12242: I am so swooning over here. I can't believe you met him.
PRCHICK78: it was kind of
Izzy12242: ?
PRCHICK78: BRB—on phone with Elle
Izzy12242: no prob
Izzy12242: la da di
Izzy12242: la da da
PRCHICK78: so . . . you're talking to Billy Fox's new publicist!
PRCHICK78: it's official. we literally just landed him ☺
Izzy12242: WOOT!!!!!!!!!!!!!!
Izzy12242: I mean, congratulations! ;)
PRCHICK78: and there's more. guess who's coming to NYC next month?

Yep, as I explain to Izzy, I'm going to be in Manhattan next month, escorting Billy Fox on the press junket for the premiere of his latest movie. And wouldn't you know it, "The

Boss" added another NYC night to his concert tour that falls
smack down when I'm in town. Simon and I are both lifelong
Bruce Springsteen fans. Izzy—who still mourns the closing of
legendary punk and New Wave venue CBGB—not so much. But
she totally doesn't care that Simon and I will go together without her.

> **PRCHICK78:** tell Simon I think I've got an in for tix at the
> Meadowlands
> **Izzy12242:** he's going to FREAK out! ☺ You're the best.
> **Izzy12242:** I can't wait to see you!
> **Izzy12242:** Do you think Billy would want to do something
> for the magazine?

As a senior editor at *Vintage*, Izzy occasionally interviews
celebs, but only when they really know their wine or buy a vine-
yard or something. And then *Vintage* runs a one-page Q & A
about the star's favorite wines or obscure spa getaway. I suppose it could seem like a conflict of interest. And I'm not going
to lie, Izzy and I definitely mix business with our personal
lives. But she can get celebs without me, so when we help each
other out, we're not crossing any boundaries. And, let's face it,
there are much worse examples of nepotism in Hollywood. At
least we're both good at our jobs.

You wouldn't believe the number of assistants and junior
publicists I have to deal with every year here who are the kids of
celebs or investors or whoever. They march around with their
venti Starbucks and size 0 Seven jeans and act so entitled. This
one recent grad, Denise, is a perfect example. I don't think I
saw her answer the phone once the whole time she "worked" at

Bennett/Peters. It got so bad that Elle finally had to put her well-heeled foot down and remind the assistants pool to stop flipping through *Glamour* and *Vogue* and actually *assist* the publicists. Denise left less than two weeks later for medical "exhaustion" reasons, surely disillusioned that her life wasn't turning into a *The Hills*–like fantasy.

PRCHICK78: I don't know if Billy likes wine. But I'll ask.
Izzy12242: Whenever. We just closed the September issue.
Izzy12242: I am so exhausted and need a break.
Izzy12242: Luckily the in-laws invited us to their place in the Hamptons for the weekend. We're leaving after work today. Grandparents are thrilled to see the little guy.
PRCHICK78: And how is little Charlie?
Izzy12242: In truth, not so little anymore. You'll be shocked to see how much he's grown.

Charlie is their two-year-old son. He is the cutest kid ever. Like ready for his own Gap Kids ad adorable. Yes, sometimes Izzy's luck makes me a little jealous—envious, I mean. It's just that when Izzy and I were in eighth grade, we shared a plan as to how our lives would unfold. We'd each meet a great guy, get married in front of all our friends and family, and then give birth to a boy first, followed by a girl. We were going to live next door to each other and our kids were going to be best friends. It seems a little naïve now, but to a couple of close twelve-year-olds, it was our blueprint to happiness.

My competitive side uncomfortably rears its ugly head occasionally to remind me that I am the one who is behind. I mean, I'm totally happy with my life, and with Jacob. He *is* that "great guy" I envisioned years ago over tall glasses of Sunny Delight. But it's been two years, and he has never brought up the M word. It's beginning to feel like a problem—as if this is it, prepare to settle or move on. Yes, I'm guilty too of falling into an easy rut, and I am still girly enough to want Jacob to make the next move. Or maybe I'm just lazy.

Or scared.

Izzy, per usual, is an apparent mind reader.

> **Izzy12242:** so, how is Jacob?
> PRCHICK78: good
> **Izzy12242:** uh huh . . .
> PRCHICK78: what does that mean?
> **Izzy12242:** nothing. just that you haven't said anything about him in a couple days.
> PRCHICK78: and?
> **Izzy12242:** come on, Sophie . . . I just wondered what's up with you two.
> PRCHICK78: nothing. Nothing is going on . . . literally nothing.
> **Izzy12242:** Sorry, hon. He hasn't said anything about going away again?

Ahh, I wish Izzy would let this go. Like six months ago, Jacob planned this awesome weekend for us. We flew up to San Francisco, saw Dave Matthews Band in concert, and did all the San Francisco touristy things, like riding the trolleys and visiting the sea lions off Fisherman's Wharf. Even though I'm a California girl, I'd never truly explored the Bay Area. It was a really fun weekend, packed with postcard views and insanely delicious meals. Except that both nights, I got all dressed up thinking that this whole trip was a big buildup to a proposal. I even secretly called Izzy from the hotel bathroom, telling her how he was behaving and all the romantic plans he'd made. We whispered and giggled over what the ring would look like and what he would say. I had a $100 bet that he would go down on one knee. That's the kind of guy Jacob is—very traditional.

Except that he didn't propose.

And after all the effort he put into the trip, I couldn't exactly behave like I was upset about it. It took me two days to call Izzy back because I was so embarrassed. I knew I didn't have to tell her—I mean, if he *had* proposed, I would have called her the second I could to give her the good news. She knew he hadn't and I just didn't have the courage to talk about it.

PRCHICK78: No. We've both been really busy with work and stuff.
PRCHICK78: Things are pretty much the same as always.
Izzy12242: Don't give up on him, Sophie. He loves you. I know he does.
Izzy12242: Sophie?
PRCHICK78: Yeah. I know.
PRCHICK78: Listen, I've got a ton still to do today. Gotta get back to work.
Izzy12242: Okay hon. Email me later if you want.
PRCHICK78: Enjoy the Hamptons. xoxo
Izzy12242: xxoo

Even when instant messaging, Izzy is a very perceptive person. Sometimes it's frustrating because I can never get anything past her, but the opposite is true too. She knows when to back off and give me my space. I'm the first to admit that I don't have the best track record with men. When the going gets tough, I'm usually the first to pull the parachute. But only because I don't want to listen to some pathetic excuse the guy will come up with to break up with me.

Being with Jacob is the first time I don't feel in control. And it's a little unsettling to feel the old—if dysfunctional—dynamic shift. Izzy assures me it's a sign of maturity; that a little vulnerability and trust in the unknown is a positive thing in a relationship. I'm cautiously optimistic but still need (or want) to know where the parachute is hidden.

3

WEEKENDS ARE NEVER LONG ENOUGH. SATURDAY MORNING
is often dedicated to sleeping in or nursing the hangover I've
earned on more sociable Friday nights, so forget working out
or attempting anything productive until after noon. Then the
rest of the day is spent catching up on stuff I can't get done during the week, like errands and paying bills, and Sunday is
practically ruined from the beginning because *tomorrow* I have
to go back to work. I remember this particular TV show that
aired when I was beginning high school. It was about a girl who
could stop time by clapping her hands together. Now, *that* is a
superpower I could get into. I would go nuts with a gift like
that, freezing time to think up a clever retort or witty joke. But
mostly I'd freeze time so I could sleep in as long as I wanted.

Tonight Jacob and I are meeting his best friends, Damon
and Travis, for sushi at Katsuya. I had the fortitude to make the
reservation for a party of six because last time we all got together at a trendy restaurant, we waited an extra half hour
while the annoyed hostess found us a bigger table for Damon's
last-minute arm candy, an unbelievably bitchy former Playmate. I was starving by the time we got seated, and *perhaps* a
little affected by the apple martinis I'd consumed on an empty

stomach while waiting at the bar, and therefore a tad bitchy and more forthright than usual myself. So you can just imagine how the evening escalated. Jacob almost choked on his bacon-wrapped date when I asked Ms. Playmate how difficult it was to move past her career working "the pole." How was I supposed to know it was true?! She screamed at Damon for telling us how they met and stormed out. Needless to say, that's why we're at a new venue tonight. I doubt they would even let us in the door again at the other spot after that scene.

Damon may be Jacob's buddy since far back in high school, but it's no secret that he gets under my skin. We didn't get off to a good start. I'll never forget hearing the way he mercilessly teased Jacob for not still playing the field after we first met—preciously calling me "the Little Woman" and always undermining the emerging relationship. I swear, it was like he was threatened or something. With Jacob as our mutual bond, we're forced to share tables and play nice. But neither of us is exactly volunteering to chair the other's fan club.

In sharp contrast, as much as I loathe Damon, I adore Travis. He reminds me of the carefree frat boys I used to hang out with in college. He's still living the frat life; only now, he owns his "frat house" and prefers imported or craft beer over a keg of Milwaukee's Best. Jacob and Travis met as associates at the same investment banking firm. It's funny to me that Jacob and Travis instantly bonded—in that weird way that guys "bond"—because from Travis's now-long surfer-boy sandy hair to his Harley-Davidson motorcycle, he is seemingly Jacob's polar opposite.

I walk into the restaurant and check my watch. Okay, I'm

only ten minutes late. That's actually pretty good for me. I hate that I'm late all the time. I know it's so rude, but no matter what I do, it seems I can't get anywhere on time. Case in point, the Billy Fox meeting last week.

As I bypass the leggy hostess and start weaving through the tables toward the back, looking for Jacob and friends, I am spotted by a client. I've represented Kimberly Galando for a couple years, since her first feature movie, and now here she is eating with Sarah Michelle Gellar. SMG is repped by the competition. Some publicists get all weird and competitive about stuff like that, but bottom line, I'm just too busy to be that way. And anyway, Sarah's got a great publicist. She and I have lunch from time to time . . . she's tough but good. The publicist, I mean, not Sarah. I don't know Sarah that well, but I stop by their table to say hi to Kimberly.

They are cute and all, but being late I can't truly focus on more than pleasantries. I haven't spotted Jacob yet, but it's a sure bet that he was on time, and I can practically feel his eyes on my back. Finally I tear myself away from the starlets and find Jacob, Travis, Damon, and an unknown blonde sitting at a table just next to the patio. By the time I rush over, Travis has already stood up to attack me with one of his patented bear hugs. He's a big guy, and I disappear in the folds of his shirt.

"Hi, everyone." I pull free, laughing, and turn to notice that Damon has remained seated. No surprise there. Jacob stands silently at my side, his hand on my lower back. "I'm so sorry I'm late. I'm glad I got a bigger table." I reach forward to shake Blondie's hand. "Hi, I'm Sophie."

"Sophie, this is Juliet. Juliet, Sophie," Damon says, his arm behind Juliet's chair, and still makes no effort to stand up. Juliet reaches forward and we shake hands. She seems cool. We make brief small talk as I sit. I can't help but feel embarrassed by Damon's cold-shoulder routine. We've never been "friendly," but lately it seems that he is edging toward hostile. It feels like the only time Damon speaks directly to me is to comment on my blood-alcohol level. I honestly plan to drink less at the start of every meal with him so that he can't criticize me, but that never lasts because I need at least two drinks to relax enough to enjoy myself when he's around.

A quick glance toward Jacob confirms that he and Travis are in the middle of a work-related story. Either he didn't notice Damon's behavior, or he's chosen to ignore it. I'm not sure which I'd rather imagine at this point. While I would never want Jacob to have to choose between Damon and me, I can't help but wish he would stand up for me. A little knight-on-the-white-horse action never hurts.

With the exception of my awkward entrance, dinner goes fairly well. I actually enjoy chatting with Juliet (a makeup artist over at Warner Bros.) and Travis keeps us laughing most of the evening. It's always fun for Jacob and me to live vicariously through free-spirited Travis. He has such crazy stories and leads a ridiculously cool life. But it also seems exhausting, so not the kind of lifestyle a regular person (such as myself) would ever really lead, but the kind I unabashedly admire.

As the server brings out the dessert menus, and a delicious chocolate martini for me, the evening becomes pleasantly blurred. But I mainly attribute feeling all nice and fuzzy inside

to the fact that Jacob reaches out and holds my hand underneath the table.

And I get this warm feeling, which could be the vodka, but
is mainly the dawning certainty that this is the person I want to
spend the rest of my life with.

But Izzy's innocent inquiry from earlier today is still knock-
ing around in my mind. I can't resist thinking, *When is Jacob
going to show me he feels the same?*

SUNDAYS I USUALLY GO to my parents' house for dinner. I am
the only child of Dennis and Jeanne Atwater and as such have
an open invitation. They each came from large families, so I
have tons of cousins, but for whatever reason (which changes
depending on their mood when anyone asks), they decided not
to give me siblings. Apparently I asked for one once, when I was
five. They got me a goldfish instead, and I was satisfied and
never brought up the subject again.

Personally, I find the only-child stereotypes in general to
be insulting. Like most stereotypes (except those about actors
and musicians, I've discovered) they are the uneducated babble of closed-minded idiots. I am who I am. Of course it's possible I'd be different if I'd had a big brother to roughhouse with
or a little sister to tease or compete with for my parents' attention. But I was never lonely—and rarely spoiled. I have fantastic
memories of brutal games of touch football on Thanksgivings
with my cousins and plenty of lakeside summer reunions. All
in all, I had a great childhood.

My dad is in real estate. He owns apartment buildings and small commercial properties around LA and rents them out. He's not Donald Trump or anything, but we were always well enough off as I was growing up. And finding my first apartment was a no-brainer.

Right now my mom co-owns an independent bookshop, the Reading Room. It's one of my favorite places to retreat, getting lost in its stacks and petting Libro, the resident tawny cat, who likes his belly rubbed as he soaks up the front bay window's sunshine, oblivious to any comings and goings. My mom and her friend started the cozy venture together about five years ago and have been doing gangbusters business ever since, despite the presence of e-readers and larger—if diminishing— mega-chains. Of course it's like my mom's fourth career. She was a concert violinist when she met my dad, but she quit when I was born. Mom is such a perfectionist that if she couldn't practice and play 24/7, she'd rather quit. So that was that. When I was about ten, she began dabbling in accounting. She's one of those people who succeed at everything they try, and I am sure it was from her that I got my competitive spirit.

Both my mom and my dad contributed to my ambition, but given that they are still in their first marriage, and met at the age of twenty-six and twenty-eight respectively, neither can figure out how I got to thirty-one never having been in a successful long-term relationship.

And thus we arrive at the main reason I dread coming to my parents' house. I may not be *single*, but sometimes I still feel very much the old maid.

Jacob's joined me on a few Sunday evenings when he was

able, but he usually has his own weekly rituals to accomplish. And with the expectant looks my mother embarrassingly hands out, I can't entirely blame him.

Ready or not, my car pulls into the driveway of my childhood home in West LA. The two-story, traditional forties house with its front planters and brick walkway brings back instant memories. I get out and walk by the spot where I used to set up my lemonade stand. I made good money in front of our house. Beside the avocado tree, laden with fruit, the side entrance door is unlocked as always.

I call out as I throw my bag onto the kitchen counter.

"Mom! Dad! I'm home." No matter how old I get, it's still *home*. Mostly because it looks exactly the same as it did when I started high school.

But just like in my high school days, there is no human response to my yell. But the *tap tap tap* of canine nails on the hardwood floor signals Lizzie is waddling in to sniff her greeting. "Hi, Lizzie. Hi, little puppy dog." I bury my face in her now graying fur and scratch behind her ears. Lizzie's tail is furiously wagging and she gets more animated than I've seen her in years. The homeowners' association in my building forbids dogs, and even older Rottweilers need space to run anyway, but that doesn't stop me from feeling guilty. You see, Lizzie is *my* dog. I picked her out the summer before I started high school. I took care of her for four years and then on every break when I was home from USC. Lizzie would wake me up by sticking her damp nose in my face until I finally would agree to take her on a run. She was my indulgent chick-flick partner, always ready to curl up next to me when I felt like watching *Sixteen Candles* for the umpteenth time.

Now Lizzie rolls over for a little belly rub, and I oblige as I realize I still haven't heard from my parents. I know they're home, but my dad is most certainly holed up in his should-be-on-*Hoarders* office, only to emerge when one of us draws him out with dinner. I move over to the stove and take a deep breath, inhaling the rich, delicious scent of my mom's cooking. Yet another reason I brave visiting my parents each week. My mom could have added gourmet chef to her long list of credentials. Not that she studied professionally or anything; it's just that she effortlessly whips up incredible meals that make it impossible to stick to a diet. Of course, she doesn't let it stop her from critiquing my weight.

I poke my head into my dad's office. "Cluttered" doesn't even begin to describe the state of his desk or the piles surrounding it like some kids' idea of a play fort. He and Jacob share housekeeping traits. Dad's juggling his cell phone and the landline on either ear. He nods at me and smiles, then gestures to the phones like I don't get it that he's otherwise occupied.

"Where's Mom?" I mouth silently. He points vaguely in the direction of the rest of the house and all their property. I head off to hunt down my mother. There's some faint noise from the patio, so I head through the family room out into the backyard.

"Mom? I'm home. Where are you?"

"Sophie! I'm here." Her voice floats to me from her side herb garden. As I follow the sound, she appears around the corner, her hands filled with fresh-cut herbs and kitchen shears.

"Hi. Can I help?"

"No, darling. I've got it covered. Dinner's almost ready."

She ushers me in the kitchen door and immediately heads

to the fridge, where an open bottle of champagne sits waiting. I'm still nursing a small hangover after the night at Katsuya but believe in "hair of the dog" and all. She pulls out two flutes from an upper cabinet, and no words are necessary as we clink glasses and take our first crisp sip. Mother-daughter bonding, Atwater style. Gotta love it.

"So, how's the shop these days?" I ask.

"Wonderful. Did you get the books I sent you? What are you reading for your book club?" Yes, I'm part of a book club. And even if I wasn't, I'd *say* I was to get my mother off my back. But my "book club" is more like a group of girlfriends who like to read chick lit and then sit around and gossip over wine roughly every couple months. Sometimes we discuss the book, sometimes not. I choose not to explain this to my mother, who even with all her careers somehow missed her calling as a college Lit professor. She has very highbrow taste in books, and sometimes she'll "lend" me volumes that make me feel like I am still in high school with my summer reading list. I do love to read, so it's normally not a chore, but *Fifty Shades of Grey* is on my Kindle just like it's on the tablet of every other woman I know. Meanwhile my mom doesn't embrace romance unless it's tortured and Tolstoy.

There was no question of whether or not I was going to be a reader in some form. My father, being in business, reads the paper like Jacob does, cover to cover. But other than the newspaper and a few real estate and business journals, that's it. I don't think I've ever seen him crack a Clive Cussler for fun.

Work is fun for my dad. Go figure.

Mom pads around the kitchen, doing a million things at

once. She reminds me of those unflappable chefs on the Food Network who can concoct magic out of any ingredients. The fresh herbs she collected get perfectly chopped or chiffonaded and stirred into the pot simmering on the stovetop. She has tried to teach me to cook countless times, but aside from your basic pasta with marinara (from a jar) and one ridiculously easy roasted chicken dish, I really can't cook at all. Clearly I didn't inherit the patience, instinct, or sense of timing necessary to get a proper meal on the table. Hence my addiction to takeout. Luckily Jacob is simpatico about ordering in, and he has actually made dinner for us a couple of times. But neither of us is big on cleanup, so we don't do it that often.

"How's Jacob?"

I love my mom and all, but we don't really have a close girlfriend-type relationship. I definitely don't fill her in on all the nuances of my roller-coaster love life. So this could have been a completely innocent question. And yet I'm still immediately defensive.

"He's great. We're great. Never better."

"Oh good." But I can hear in her voice the question . . . the hopeful suspicion. Ever since I crossed the thirty mark and started seeing Jacob, I think my mom saw the opportunity to see her daughter settled, permanently. Lately, her hints have become less subtle, or maybe I was just too obtuse to pick up on them before. Yeah right. But what am I supposed to do, buy *him* a ring?

"Don't you two have an anniversary coming up?" she adds oh-so-innocently.

As if to the rescue, my dad appears in the doorway, his pale blue Oxford shirt a bit wrinkled but still tucked into his khakis.

"Hi, Dad." I step over Lizzie, who has laid herself at my feet, and give my dad a hug. He kisses both my cheeks and smiles down at me with affection. I am a pretty solid mix of both my parents. Though if you told them I said that, I'd deny it. Nowadays we get on pretty well. We're not the family that talks every day or anything like that, but we email all the time, and our mostly weekly dinners are rarely strained.

We settle into another delicious meal—a fresh vegetable risotto with chicken, and a simple micro-greens salad with backyard cherry tomatoes and lemon thyme vinaigrette to start. I plan to focus on the veggies and chicken, trying not to chow on the risotto, but inevitably, the delicious starch finds its way onto my fork. The conversation flows as I fill my dad in on my work. He loves to hear the minute details and all the office politics. As my mom adds a warm loaf of crusty bread to the table (sealing my willpower's defeat), I tell my parents the good news about landing Billy Fox. Leaving out the embarrassing ice-in-lap incident. My mom refills my flute as she asks how I'm going to handle another major client without the others suffering.

"Jeanne, leave her alone. You don't know what you're talking about." My dad throws the jibe at my mom to get her off my back. But, of course, now I have to defend her.

"No, Dad, she's right. I am going to talk to Elle about it next week. I need to figure out which client I can give up, and who should take over for me."

"Are you sure you want to do that? You don't want Elle to think you aren't capable of handling the work." And he's right too, hypothetically. Obviously, in normal business offices around the world I'm sure that logic applies. But in my crazy world, it's just not like that. But how do I explain that to my commonsense dad? I take a gulp of champagne to buy time.

"Dad, it's just different in Hollywood. I totally understand what you mean. And I'll be careful how I talk to Elle about it. But she knows that each client requires personal attention, and so I'll offer her some options of my lower-profile clients that could easily go to newer publicists. That's the way it works—it gives the junior publicists a chance to prove themselves."

"So you can be a mentor—you can inspire a young publicist, just as you were by Elle. That's an exciting prospect, isn't it?" When Mom gets all wistful and pensive—often timed with her second glass—my dad sends me an eye roll and just disregards her comment entirely.

"Well, you're going about it the right way, Sophie. Just be sure you're prepared with an answer for any questions she may have for you. Just like I taught you, right? Never point out a problem unless you have a solution ready to offer." That is true. I gotta give him credit. There are universal business guidelines that my dad has instilled in me since I can remember that have played a major role in my success at Bennett/Peters.

"You're totally right, Dad. I'm just going to be, like, ready with all the options of which of my clients could go—and which other publicists would fit best with them."

"Don't say 'like,' dear," my mom interjects.

I down the rest of my champagne in one gulp.

4

AFTER HAVING OFFICIALLY TAKEN ON BILLY FOX AS A CLIENT,
I am determined to kick ass for him, proving he and Wanda
made the right choice. What's a million more phone calls to
make? Over the next workweek I focus on lining up some long-
lead magazine features, including a couple of guaranteed covers. Of course Billy is not my *only* client. As much as I'd like to
sit at my desk and pitch him all day, I'm still running around to
premieres, interviews, and talk shows for my other clients. By
Friday night I am exhausted and relish my plan—or rather, *no
plans*—for a lazy weekend spent catching up on TiVo and sleep.

But first I have an obligation to fulfill—a Saturday afternoon meeting for the Tribe of Hope organization. It's the second gala planning meeting, and I am still feeling a tad guilty
for missing the first one. Even though the last thing I need is
one more thing on my plate. But it's a cause important to Jacob,
and a good one on its own, so the least I can do is donate my
time—and my skills.

I love that Jacob selflessly contributes to their fund-raising
efforts. It's really noble and sweet of him to help in any way he
can. It's also clear that he does it because he can't feel helpless
in a situation, no matter what it is—there is always something

he can do to make it better. When my dad once stayed over-night in the hospital for an angioplasty, all I could think to do was bring him his newspaper, and three business books on tape. I knew my mom wouldn't think of it, because she is defi-nitely the panic-first-ask-questions-later type.

So here I am at the planning meeting for this celebrity gala event, alone, while Jacob is out of town on business. To be fair, it's not his fault he couldn't be here. As he pointed out, my business has plenty of last-minute items that pull me away from events. Once in a while, so does his.

The committee is made up of young executives from around LA, in all different fields—a few agents, some technology types, and banking people like Jacob. We spend the afternoon orga-nizing the events for the gala and assigning tasks. Like who's in charge of the silent auction and who is going to handle pub-licity. Ha. I see where this is going. All eyes look to me, and I take my cue to offer up my skills to help the organization. Look, I realize I sound totally obnoxious. I really do appreciate good charities . . . but I'd rather write them a check.

By the end of the meeting we have all the tasks assigned and I realize that I have my work cut out for me. As the most sea-soned publicist, I am heading up the subcommittee to promote the event. There are two WME agents on the committee who offered up a few of their clients to give the event cachet, and I plan to ask a few of our clients to attend as well. We agree to ap-proach some A-list talent we know to "host" the event. Mean-ing they only have to attend and graciously let us use their names on the invite. In the end I leave with a list of things to do, fifteen email addresses to cc on each update, and the belief (I would never voice) that Jacob owes me big-time.

ON MONDAY Elle calls an unanticipated staff meeting to discuss everyone's upcoming events. As a department, the general rule is we help one another out when appropriate or possible. But always, your own clients come first. So, while everyone else at Bennett/Peters would have loved the chance to help me with Billy Fox, I knew the second I walked into that pitch meeting that he would ultimately be *my* responsibility. It's like that "promise" one makes with one's parents at age eight:

"But Mommy, I *want* a puppy! Yes, Daddy, of course I'll take care of it. And feed it! Yes, *every* morning!"

Ha! And then, of course, a week later, there are Mom and Dad up at the crack of dawn feeding "your" dog and taking it for walks. But Billy is a multimillion-dollar client, not a scruffy shelter dog, so I will need to make sure his coat shines, keep his nails clipped, and, of course, clean the dog run every day— well, the publicist's equivalent of all that at least.

I give the team an update on all my projects, which are under control as usual. Then Elle's attention turns to the other publicists. There's been some shuffling since my pregnant co-worker Melissa has been out the last few days. Junior publicists eagerly step up, happy to score more direct contact with bigger clients.

But now that we've moved past my projects, my mind is admittedly elsewhere. I miss Jacob when he's gone. He'll be back tomorrow from a retreat hosted by some small company that is trying to get his business. Or something like that. Anyway, he is in Alaska of all places—salmon fishing. I never really considered where salmon comes from or how difficult it is to fish, until he excitedly called me on Saturday night to share the whole story of how he'd caught this huge fish. He's never done anything resembling fishing in his life; in fact, he went to Sport Chalet to buy a DVD on fishing as homework before the trip. But he was so proud of his "catch." His enthusiasm was incredibly cute, but picturing Jacob all Eddie Bauer out on the river just made me miss him, and our weekend routine, more. And then just as I was falling asleep that night, a secret place in the self-loathing part of my brain questioned if spouses had been invited.

I lay in bed staring at the ceiling for roughly an hour after that, trying to fathom how I could get Jacob to admit to purposely not inviting me along. Is he ashamed of me? Embarrassed? Finally I convinced myself that I was being absurd, took a for-emergencies-only Ambien, and fell asleep.

But there is a weight in the pit of my stomach that won't fade away this morning. And I just can't figure out how to ask Jacob where we stand on this—our future as a couple—without putting him on the spot. I have never pressured him. I'm not the kind of girl who carries around in her wallet a picture of the engagement ring she wants (true story). Or the girlfriend who demands marriage or it's over. Principles like that are all well and good on paper but feel doomed in real life. Yet lately it's just been more and more on my mind. It seems like after we exchanged keys, there was no forward movement in our relationship, and Jacob is okay with that. And the key thing was a *year ago*! I don't know what to think. Am I overreacting? Or am I afraid of how he might respond if I rock the boat?

"Sophie?"

Elle's impatient tone slices through the mental cobwebs.

"Yes?" I reply with what I hope is a commanding, totally involved, I-was-just-considering-before-responding definitive response, with a hint of question just in case.

"Good. That's settled." *What? What's settled?* Now would be the right moment for a go-back-in-time superpower. Elle continues in a perkier voice, "And for a fun announcement: our very own Sara Garman is engaged! Congratulations, dear!" Squeals and applause from all the girls, and I watch Sara, a junior publicist, fake modesty as she flashes at least a two-carat rock. She's all of twenty-three. Here I am at thirty-one, with not even a hint of an engagement in my future, while everyone in the office is fawning over the latest bubbly cheerleader who is getting married next fall. I realize how jealous I sound. And bottom line, I *am* jealous. But I am not going to let anyone know it. That would be unprofessional, but also completely humiliating.

Standing at the back of the group peppering Sara with questions, I smile and nod appropriately and even take a turn examining her ring. It is large but tasteful, and fits her hand perfectly. Just as I'm starting to feel that a quick exit is my only option, Elle catches my eye and motions me over to her as she finishes up her conversation with Jeff, a young, black, nattily dressed associate.

"Sophie, are you all set for tomorrow, or do you want Jeff to back you up?" Tomorrow is one of my first events with Billy. He's hosting a charity auction at this black-tie affair in Hollywood. It's part of our campaign to give Billy's image a little shine. Not that he's Charlie Sheen or anything, but still, a worthwhile cause is always a good PR move.

"No, thanks. I've got it covered." I see the enthusiasm fade from Jeff's face. Jeff's been a fast-learning junior publicist for almost a year now. He's what my parents would call a "go-getter" and is next on the list for a promotion. I think he's been a great addition to our firm. Not just because I found him, either. His evident ambition and hard work remind me of myself years ago. For Elle's benefit, I add, "The hospital is so thrilled that Billy wanted to participate in the event. The press release went out yesterday and they emailed me a PDF of the program, which looks great. The actual event is the easy part."

"Excellent. Then I won't worry about you taking over the Nintendo account and spearheading their new 3D system launch party next month. The executives are coming in for a status meeting on Thursday. At first I thought it might be too much, even for you, but you've clearly got things under control. Let me know what you need . . ." I think Elle keeps talking but . . . *What?!* When did I agree to take over the Nintendo account? That's a huge responsibility, and I have Billy's movie launch next month, not to mention all my regular clients. Nintendo is a major client, and I specialize in individual talent, not the corporate side.

"So I hope Melissa is going to be okay," Jeff says.

I come back to reality in time to hear the nails going into my proverbial coffin.

"Yeah, apparently her doctor had been concerned for a while and did more tests," Elle says. "The baby is going to be fine, but Melissa is going to be on bed rest for the remainder of her pregnancy."

"But that's three more months!" I exclaim. Melissa was going to take her maternity leave *after* the Nintendo launch.

"I know. Somehow staying in bed for three months seems more stressful than just taking it easy. Melissa even said her husband was only going to let her have her BlackBerry for an hour every day," Elle adds in a horrified whisper.

"She was joking," I say with certainty. Melissa is just like me, Elle, and everyone else in our industry. We wouldn't survive without our smartphones; I know I would have a visceral reaction to rival any drug withdrawal if I lost mine.

After properly dwelling on Melissa's three-month-plus exile, I speed back to my office, my mind going a million miles a minute. Here's the thing: I'm a good publicist, and I know what needs to be done for Nintendo, but with Billy's account (when did he become just "Billy" in my head?) and all the side planning for the Tribe of Hope event, not to mention my regular clients, the Nintendo thing—a launch for a couple hundred major gaming journalists and celebrity guests, complete with food and entertainment, that should be exciting enough for celebrities to actually *stay at* till the end—is a major overload for one person to handle. There are just not enough hours in the day. But as the daughter of Dennis and

Jeanne Atwater, I am not someone who backs down from a challenge.

Yes, I considered talking to Elle earlier, but there was never a good time. Plus I hate to ask for help. I can do this. Somehow it always works out.

Following an emergency strategy meeting with Tru—and a plaintive message left on Jacob's voicemail with a brief run-down of my new "client" and the fresh drain on my free time—I sit down at my computer. And without another thought to my personal life, I hunker down to get things moving forward for Billy Fox, Nintendo, and everyone but myself on the list.

I COME UP FOR AIR around 8:30 P.M. when the cleaning lady knocks politely on my office door to empty the wastebasket. The office is almost spookily quiet, deserted by all but the few working with me on my projects.

"Tru?!" I yell out my door from behind my desk. She leans back in her chair from her cubicle across the hall and raises her bohemian-thick eyebrows in question. I see the telltale white earbuds peeking out from behind her wavy brown hair and raise my voice. "Go home. We'll get caught up with all this stuff tomorrow. Okay?"

Then I see Jeff walking around the corner with a stack of press clippings. "Jeff, you too. Go home. Thanks again for your help with this." Seriously, he didn't have to help with the Nintendo campaign, but he knows a good opportunity when he sees one. I would've done the exact same thing in his shoes. Besides, I'm grateful. Finally, I see everyone out and am beginning to wrap up the remaining open files on my desktop when a new email pops into my inbox.

From: Fox, Billy

To: Sophie.Atwater@bennettpeters-la.com

Subject:

Sophie,

What's the deal for tomorrow?

B

I try to contain my immediate panic. Did I overlook something so important? I search my outbox to review the email I sent Billy at 1 P.M. this afternoon with his itinerary for tomorrow's charity event. It shows that the email was sent. Talent are notorious for ignoring petty things such as memos no matter what format you send them in.

With a copy of the itinerary and the original email printing out in hard copy (rule number one: Always cover your ass), I hit reply.

From: Sophie.Atwater@bennettpeters-la.com

To: Fox, Billy

Subject: tomorrow's charity event

Billy,

I'm so sorry for the confusion. I sent you an email earlier today with your itinerary in a Word doc attachment. I am

resending it to you now. If I don't hear back that you got
this, I will have a hard copy messengered to you first
thing in the morning.

Thanks again for doing this event.

Sophie

There. That sounded professional but still friendly. But it is
a little disappointing that Billy Fox is like so many other stars
that need to have little things like travel details spoon-fed to
them.

If I had a dollar for every celebrity who's "misplaced" or
"didn't get" a memo I sent, well, I'd own Bennett/Peters. Seriously, I know they're "creative" people, but how hard is it to
keep track of a simple piece of paper with important information on it? Especially now that they all have an iPhone or a
Droid or whatever. And often even a personal assistant (or
three) to keep them updated. Read my emails! While I'm still
in the middle of my internal rant, my computer posts a new
email.

From: Fox, Billy
To: Sophie.Atwater@bennettpeters-la.com
Subject: re: tomorrow's charity event

Sophie,

Sorry, I did get your email. I meant what are *your* plans
for tomorrow night? Why don't I have the limo pick you

up, so that you can fill me in on the details on the way to the hotel? Does that work for you?

B

Hmm . . . My mistake. Billy, as it turns out, *is* the kind of guy who actually thinks about his publicist and appreciates the logistics of an evening. And now I imagine him on a date . . . with everything all perfectly planned out in advance. What girl doesn't love a take-charge kind of guy? I feel myself blushing and push all personal, ridiculous thoughts from my head.

From: Sophie.Atwater@bennettpeters-la.com
To: Fox, Billy
Subject: re: re: tomorrow's charity event

Billy,

If that's what you want, I can have the car pick me up on the way to you.

See you then.

And . . . thanks.

Sophie

I stare at the blinking cursor for a second before hitting send. I am proud of how I've managed to keep this exchange completely businesslike. The last thing I need is for Billy to pick up on the crazy fantasies that have been running around in my head.

But seriously, who could blame me? What's wrong with a few harmless fantasies? I mean, Billy Fox is fodder for women's dreams the world over. What's wrong with adding me to the list? It's not like I'll behave any differently toward him, as I have proven by maintaining a professional distance in person while still doing a spectacular job on his publicity. I can do this. You'll see.

And then, as if karmic reward, a text from Jacob appears.

The perfect reality check from the man I love. Hell, I might even surprise him with some sexting. I open it with renewed anticipation:

Be sure to clear room in your freezer for all the fish I'm shipping home. xo J

5

"GOOD MORNING, SOPHIE."

My assistant is at first glance wearing a potato sack. With geometric-patterned brown-and-orange tights and knee-high boots. Her hair is held back in a brightly colored tie—literally, a man's necktie.

Well, she is certainly an original spirit.

"Hi, Tru. Elle in yet?" Now that I'm almost at Tru's desk, I see that it is not in fact a potato sack, but some unidentifiable fabric that could easily be used to store russets if there was ever a sack shortage. As usual, I can't think of anything to say about what Tru is wearing that would sound like a sincere compliment, so I stick to business.

"Yeah, she came in early today. Lucas said she would be free for you until her ten A.M. appointment."

"Great. Thanks." I set my extra large Coffee Bean cup down on my desk, log in to the server, and pull up my email inbox. A cursory glance reveals nothing that can't wait until after I speak with Elle. I resignedly asked for an appointment so that we could discuss my current workload. Before going home last night I took another hard look at my to-do list and upcoming calendar. Since taking on Nintendo, as much as I hate to ever admit it, I have without question stretched myself too thin. Not one to give up, I still slept on it. But in the cold reality of a fresh day I know I'm fooling myself if I don't ask for *some* help. Given that I honestly care about my clients, not to mention my reputation, I feel it's in everyone's best interest if I work it out with Elle before something important falls through the cracks.

And if the solution makes Priscilla's life miserable, I consider that in everyone else's best interest too.

I thought there was nothing that would tarnish Priscilla's halo as far as Elle was concerned. That is until a few months ago, when Melissa, in a fit of new pregnancy hormones, lost it on Priscilla in between cubicles in front of Elle's office. Regrettably I was downstairs, in my office, but I heard later that Melissa was on fire. She tore Priscilla to shreds for completely flaking on one of Melissa's clients at a major red carpet event. Priscilla didn't even call another publicist to secure a replacement. So Melissa's irate client called Melissa to vent, and Melissa took her complaint straight to Elle. And she came armed—with printouts of the emails back and forth, wherein Priscilla had practically begged Melissa to allow her to cover the client. According to Lucas, whose cubicle was a front row seat to the wild scene, Melissa actually stuffed the pages down the front of Priscilla's perfectly tailored Armani jacket. *After* shoving them in her face close enough that Priscilla's lip gloss transferred to a page.

And all this occurred in the seconds it took Elle to get out of her office to break it up. Obviously no one else was interested in stopping Melissa's rampage—just about all the people there wished they had pregnancy hormones to blame so they too could lose it on Priscilla Hasley.

Anyway, Melissa saw a flicker of doubt cross Elle's usual composure as Priscilla tried to outtalk Melissa rather than accept any responsibility for her actions, despite the undeniable evidence. After that episode, Melissa and I hung on to the hope that Elle would one day *have* to face Priscilla's inadequacies. Believe me, I would never normally wish for someone to get in serious trouble, but Priscilla is the kind of serpent who literally drives you to extreme measures.

So, to that end, I am hoping I can use my new accounts to help Elle see how little Priscilla actually does for the company. Backup files in hand, I head toward the elevator bank. I know Elle's office is only one flight up, but very rarely am I motivated to take the stairs unless I'm hiding from someone.

"Elle?" I knock on her open door as I step in.

"Morning, Sophie. Come in." Behind an enormous Parsons-style white lacquered desk with its exotic potted orchid and mercury glass table lamp, Elle's facing her computer yet shoves away from the keyboard as she finishes her sentence. "What did you want to see me about?"

"I wanted to bring you up to speed on everything. With Billy Fox and the Nintendo launch."

"Excellent. I know it's a lot to have on your plate right now. But you can use as many assistants as you need, and I was thinking of officially assigning Jeff to you as well."

"That's exactly why I wanted to see you. I have some backup with the Nintendo account, and Billy Fox is keeping me busy, but I think it's going really well." Uh-huh. Like Dad says, always lead with the positive. "What I wanted to run by you was maybe reassigning one of my other clients until after the Nintendo launch. The United American Wrestling account in particular needs more maintenance than I can truly deliver right now. And, I was thinking . . . this might be the perfect opportunity for someone like Priscilla to get her feet wet handling a major client."

Or a rope long enough for her to hang herself.

"If she's up to the responsibility," I continue, "my contact with American Wrestling is great, and since it isn't a new account, Priscilla should be able to ease right into the day-to-day stuff."

There was a moment of silence.

Look, feelings aside, Priscilla was the obvious choice. She doesn't handle any big clients, but she's loosely considered my in-office peer. It's noticeable that she isn't as busy as the rest of us. In a fair world, she *should* do this.

But will Elle see it that way or continue to protect her?

"You're right, Sophie. I think Priscilla is ready to take on more clients." She leans across her desk to press the phone's intercom. "Lucas, is Priscilla in yet?" I covertly glance at my watch. It's now 9:50. If she *isn't* here yet, it would be so perfect. Another mark against her that Elle couldn't deny, since I was here to witness it. An evil fantasy spins through my mind, visions of Priscilla hours late, and Elle finally ripping into her the way everyone in the office has always yearned for.

"She's in her office," Lucas's voice interrupts to tell us. "Should I send her in?" Of course, my hopes are crushed. Back in reality, I realize that I should have been tipped off that today wasn't going to be that easy.

"Yes, please." Elle swivels in her executive chair to face me with her full attention. "Sophie, I'm so glad you thought of this. It'll give you the perfect chance to focus in on your new clients, and Priscilla can begin taking on more responsibilities."

"Happy to be a team player," I add, forcibly suppressing a smirk.

"Good. I'll tell her that your door is always open for any questions. Be sure she knows she can turn to you for help if she needs it."

Ah, the other shoe drops. Great. Now I'm going to be baby-sitting Miss Priss? And every screwup will be laid at my door because I'll be ultimately responsible. Not quite what I had in mind. Talk about karma for my plotting.

"Good morning, Elle." Priscilla's dulcet tones distract me from my defensive strategy. "Love that blouse. Isabel Marant, no? Exquisite taste." Somehow she manages to make the compliment seem so offhand that Elle doesn't see the brown-nosing. After a few words of idle small talk, during which I manage to remain polite, Elle finally brings up the matter at hand.

"Priscilla, Sophie has a lot on her plate right now, and I think it would be the ideal opportunity for you to take on a little more responsibility. We're handing you the Wrestling account."

Elle either ignores or doesn't see the brief look of unfiltered malice Priscilla shoots my way when the word "Wrestling" comes up. Frankly, this is the first time I've ever been on the receiving end of one of Priscilla's death stares, but they're infamous in the office.

I mean, I know it's not the hottest account at Bennett/Peters, but seriously? Who does Priscilla think she is? I was *psyched* to take on the major account—tights, costumes, and all—because it was a chance to prove myself. I'm shocked that even Priscilla could be so shortsighted. She should be nauseously kissing Elle's ass for the opportunity.

"Really? Elle, I too am very busy right now. Don't you think this is something Jeff could handle?" *A junior publicist? Is she kidding?*

"I would have thought you'd be jumping at the chance to step up."

Go, Elle! Way to call her out.

"I *am* stepping up. In fact I was just emailing you about the new strategy I've worked up for the Jones and Jones account. And I am trying to cross-promote—"

"I know everything you're working on, Priscilla. We're *all* busy here. I've discussed this with Sophie and you're going to handle American Wrestling. Sophie will fill you in on where the account stands today, and if you have any problems you can always ask her. But it's your responsibility now." Elle doesn't change her volume, but her tone tightens up and I'm glad she isn't looking at me. "Thank you, ladies." And we are dismissed.

Priscilla glides out the door ahead of me and struts to the elevator bank. I follow and automatically press the down arrow button even though it is already lit. We ride the elevator one floor down in silence. I'm not feeling triumphant exactly, but definitely vindicated. I replay Elle's words to Priscilla in my head as I stare blindly at the polished elevator doors. When the *ding* announces our arrival, my eyes refocus on Priscilla's reflection. I see complete and utter hatred in her eyes for the second before the doors open and her face disappears. It almost makes her unattractive.

The sheer venomous look catches me so off guard that I hesitate for a split second as Priscilla calmly steps off the elevator and disappears around the corner toward her office.

All of a sudden my self-preservation radar goes off. As I head back to my department, I do the math on everything I've heard about Priscilla and decide I'd better watch my back. Well, in the immortal words of Kirsten Dunst, *Bring It On*.

BILLY CLIMBS INTO the back of the stretch limo as I switch seats to give us a little distance. While I hire limos and car services for celeb clients all the time, I'm very rarely in them myself. It's a huge vehicle. An entire prom entourage could fit back here, but this ride it's simply Billy Fox and me. Tonight he looks the part of a movie star—perfect and absolutely gorgeous in a slim silhouette Paul Smith tuxedo. I had arranged with the Paul Smith people to lend him the suit for the benefit event, but knowing it was coming did nothing to prepare me for the full impact of Billy Fox in evening wear.

"Hi, Billy. You look great." *And the Understatement of the Year Award goes to . . . Sophie Atwater.* I clear my throat. "Everything go okay at the fitting this afternoon?"

Billy leans forward, and for a split second I hysterically think he's going to grab my shoulders and kiss me like in some old forties movie. But he doesn't. Instead I hear "Thanks" as he brushes his lips on my cheek, getting a corner of my mouth by accident, and then continues the forward motion to reach into the mini fridge for a bottle of water.

"It was easy. They had some great suits to choose from. I feel very Sean Connery in this." He offers me a bottle too, but I shake my head. Retreating back to his seat, he stretches his long legs out. I use this move as a desperate excuse to scoot farther back in my facing seat.

Swallowing a completely inappropriate giggle, I randomly remember a silly email forward that went around several years ago about which urinal in a row a guy should choose under different circumstances. Like if there's a guy already at one end, you have to take the farthest urinal away. Because guys don't want other guys to think they *want* to be near them. Or something weird like that. Anyway, that's how I feel in the back of this huge car. With all this empty space, I am obsessed with making sure Billy doesn't get the wrong impression about how I feel about him.

"Is it my breath or something?" Billy jokes, followed up with a test exhale against his cupped fingers. "Slide over to this side, will you?"

How can I refuse without looking even more like an idiot? I take his hand and cross over the divide, settling in beside him, but not too close.

"Um, how else was your day?" An inane question, I know, but the best I could come up with. The cheesy ambient "mood lighting" is making me a bit self-conscious. But maybe Billy doesn't notice. After all, celebrities are used to traveling in stretch limos; maybe it's always like this.

"It was fine. My agent gave me a new script to read. I really like it. It's a challenging character; I'd have to learn an accent. I'm kinda nervous about it actually."

Okay, wow, Billy Fox is opening up to me. Confiding in me. I can handle this.

"Sounds intriguing. What kind of accent? I thought your role in *Bonaparte* was pretty challenging. You played the villain well." And I'm not lying. For all his *People*'s Most Beautiful appeal, he's an equally fine actor. There's no need here for the often job-required flattery.

"Thanks. I couldn't wait to play bad. It was such a one-eighty from all I'd done before. But this is different . . . It's special." And as if proof I watch this look come over his face. The way you'd always want a guy to look when he's thinking of you, I guess. Thinking of what he loves. And clearly Billy *is* focusing on his one true love—acting. How can a girl compete with that?

And—yes, I'm aware—I'm taken. Why am I even wondering if a girl could compete with that? *I* certainly don't want to.

"Well, I can't wait to hear more about it. I mean, if you want to tell me . . ."

"I'd bore you to death on this one."

"No, really," I say, and again it's the truth. Don't get me wrong. I've suffered through a million actors waxing rhapsodic about the "craft" of acting. Detailing their characters' "backstory" and "subtext" until you need toothpicks to keep your eyes open. But as I listen to Billy explain the story of his probable next picture, his low, sexy voice describing his character's development, I am entranced.

We arrive at the hotel with no warning. One second Billy

has me in the imagined wilds of Africa, and the next, the doorman of the Beverly Hills Hotel is opening the car door. Thank
God Billy is closest to the exit, because I need the extra few
seconds to regroup.

"I'll tell you the rest on the way home. It gets really good
after that," Billy says, as he takes my hand and extricates me
from the back of the limo.

"I look forward to it," I think I reply as I find myself standing not four inches from Billy's face, looking up into his incredible ice-blue eyes. I can't back up . . . the limo is right
behind me. If anything, I should be moving forward to allow
the doorman to close the door. But I can't move forward, because Billy Fox is standing right in front of me, his hand holding mine, and he is *looking* at me.

"Billy! Billy, right this way." I recover from my momentary
trance and glance over Billy's shoulder to see Darren White
working his way through the crowd toward us.

Billy has seen him too, and the moment is gone.

"Billy, this is Darren White. He's in charge of the auction
this evening. Darren, this is—"

"Billy Fox, of course. It's a pleasure. Thank you so much for
hosting our charity event this evening." Darren places his arm
through Billy's and begins proudly escorting him toward the
paparazzi line. Gay men are equally entranced by Billy's charms.
I follow close behind, listening to Darren's rundown. For those
keeping score, my blood pressure has returned to normal, and
the faint crescent marks on my palms from my fingernails are
already fading.

"Sophie, where are you?" Billy turns around in the middle of Darren's recitation and draws me up beside him. "Thanks for the walk-through, Darren. We'll see you in the green room, then?" I watch Darren's face fall before he recovers, and now the three of us are walking toward the wall of press gathered at the edge of the red carpet. Obviously, I'm not the only one susceptible to fantasies when escorting Billy Fox. The Texan is a walking heartbreak.

"See you inside, then. Thanks, Sophie." Darren kisses both our cheeks and then disappears into the crowd.

"Okay, are you ready?" I give him a once-over to make sure he's camera-ready (it's a good habit—you don't want your talent stepping in front of a hundred cameras with a ketchup stain on the tie or an open fly) and approve him with a mental thumbs-up.

"As ready as always." Okay, so he's clearly not lacking in confidence, but that slight twang completely mitigates any hint of unattractive arrogance. Billy seems good-natured about running the gauntlet of international paparazzi and press. But as I guide him through the reporters with their camera crews and audio recorders, I see a different side of Billy. He's as polite and charming as always, but even more polished.

Billy definitely wins points with me as he smoothly handles each reporter with grace and skill, from answering questions about the hospital's charity—he's obviously done his homework—to subtly evading questions about his personal life.

"Billy Fox, man about town," a practiced female correspondent in a low-cut, sparkly evening gown says. "What brings you here tonight?"

"I'm here to support the amazing work the hospital does. I can't say enough about the work they do, not just for the children, but their families as well. When the hospital asked me to participate tonight, I couldn't say no . . . I am thrilled to support this hospital, and I encourage everyone watching to check out their website and, if you can, give a little something for a really worthy cause." Billy knew the statistics and supplied gossip-hungry reporters with enough personal stories, mixed in with the hospital's talking points I'd sent over to him earlier, to be sure they'd make it on air.

I found myself watching Billy in interview after interview put a different spin on each story, giving people a fresh, personalized version, with the same unflagging amount of charm as when we started. One thing's clear. He's an undeniable pro at delivering exactly what you might wish.

"Billy, thank you so much for your time," says the last reporter. That's my cue to pull Billy away from the press line and get him situated inside.

"Thank you, Shandra. Mitch." I wave to the producer on his cell phone behind the camera guy and then lead Billy through the behind-the-scenes crew to the green room. I flash our credentials, and we're in.

"Damn, there is a lot of press here tonight. That's it, though?" And then seeing the stern expression on my face, Billy immediately adds, "I mean . . . I could do more, I just . . ."

"No. I'm kidding. You did so great out there, I wondered if you're even human."

"Not human, huh?" Billy chuckled. Why did I try to tease him?

"I mean, you never seemed tired or unsure of yourself. I was just thinking you're the perfect client, and then you had to ruin everything by being normal!" Always go for the joke when you're about to totally embarrass yourself.

"What exactly is 'normal' in your world, Sophie?" Billy stands next to me, and the moment has become unexpectedly intimate. Or maybe I'm just paranoid.

"Well, my life is the *opposite* of normal. Just ask my boyfriend." Okay, okay, I know that wasn't the subtlest move in history. I panicked. A gorgeous movie star with I-want-to-run-my-fingers-through-it golden hair and a lanky cowboy frame flirts with you and see if you stay all calm and cool.

But Billy just lifts up the edges of his ridiculously beautiful lips and gives me a completely unfathomable look. I really don't know what might happen next. My mind is running through a million scenarios. But luckily, it doesn't matter what I might have done if Billy had kept looking at me in that inscrutable way. Because Darren saves the day, again.

"Billy, thank you again so much for doing this for us." Darren's entrance mercifully brings the air back into the room. "I was just speaking to the chairman of the hospital board, and he is—we are *all*—thrilled to have you here."

"I'm glad to do it," Billy says simply.

"Here is your script, a copy of tonight's silent auction items, and the *Playbill* we had made up for tonight. We also have a little thank-you gift." Darren is going a mile a minute, and then he stops, the gift bag held out in midair, as someone squawks in his earpiece. With an apologetic "I'm sorry" face, he darts off. I had managed to grab the script and glossy program from

Darren first and am juggling them with the surprisingly heavy gift bag when everything starts to slip from my hands. I awkwardly manage to secure a grip on the gift bag at the expense of all the papers, which fan out on the floor at my feet.

"Here, I got it." Billy hunches down and collects the papers before I can even kneel down next to him. He's putting the script back in order, but I can see the amused smirk on his face. *Nice moves, Ace.* Billy looks around the room. "Let's sit."

The "before you hurt yourself" hovers in the air unsaid.

As Billy flips through the program, reviewing the schedule for the evening, I pull out my BlackBerry. I check three voicemail messages . . . all work-related, nothing from Jacob . . . and then the emails. As I'm responding to a few, I glance up and see Billy concentrating on the script. He actually has a pen out and is marking a few changes. I keep being surprised by his depth and commitment. "You want something to eat? They have a buffet in the corner." I ask because I'm *starving* but I don't want to get up and go over there by myself. And aren't guys always hungry?

"Sure." Billy smiles and we go check out the spread. "Finger foods. My favorite." There is a lovely assortment of everything from egg rolls to chicken fingers. Billy and I load up a few tiny plates and juggle our drinks from the bar back to our seats. I'm having a Diet Coke, though I would dearly love to add some rum to it, just to take the edge off. But I don't see how to make that happen when Billy hasn't left my side since we arrived. Not that Billy seems the type to care, but drinking alcohol while on the job—especially in front of a client—is a PR 101 no-no.

As we feast, we chat about the people we see walking by, always easy conversation. And then Billy asks if this is my first time at the pink Beverly Hills Hotel with its iconic script signage.

"I've visited the Polo Lounge a couple of times. And I had a client in a fashion show here last year. They did a celebrity catwalk. It was a great event. Some real estate tycoon beat out Kobe Bryant in the auction for a Ferrari. This guy bid like half a million bucks on the thing or something. The whole crowd was going crazy."

"That's insane."

"I know. What are you auctioning this year?"

Billy looks back at the program. "A trip to Tahiti, someone's condo in Paris for Christmas, and check this out—access to a private jet."

"A *what*?!"

"Yeah . . . look." At this point we are both hunched over the program as Billy points to the picture of a state-of-the-art G5. "There's a time limit."

"No kidding. Still . . ."

"But it says to anywhere in the US. Now, *that's* first class."

I love that Billy is as impressed by the auction item as I am. I mean, let's be real here . . . Surely he's been in private jets before. He's worth millions. He could probably negotiate for a private jet at his disposal for his next movie project if he wanted. But like the rest of us, he still is "normal" about how cool it sounds.

I AM STANDING BACKSTAGE as Billy makes his opening remarks. I'm now holding another Diet Coke (with a well-disguised shot of rum because, basically, my work here is done). It's all up to Billy now. And I have this ridiculous sense of pride, especially considering I've only worked with him for two weeks now, as he gets a huge round of applause and even some hoots and hollers from the ladies—and a handful of guys—in the crowd. But Billy takes it all in stride and launches right into a real tug-on-your-heartstrings version of the speech the hospital's PR team had written for him. He tells a story about a kid he went to school with who died of leukemia. I have no idea if it's even true or not (actors make up stories all the time for talk show appearances and stuff), but it doesn't matter. I can practically hear the ladies whipping out their checkbooks. And then, with perfect timing, he lightens the mood and gets the crowd ready for what turns out to be a lively auction.

Billy clearly has a backup career if ever needed. He has an amazing talent for rallying all the wealthy patrons at their tables of ten into competing over who can give the most. He even uses my Kobe story to get a bidder all riled up so that he'll outbid everyone for the trip to Tahiti. Someone is spending more on a trip to Tahiti than I get paid in a year . . . but as Billy keeps pointing out, "It's for charity!"

Darren is rushing around behind me like a madman cueing people in the wings, arguing with the lighting guy, but Billy is on stage making everything go smoothly. He talks to the little girl who is this year's "poster patient" for the hospital, and has her giggling and telling adorable stories about her trip to Disneyland just like any other ten-year-old. But her present wheelchair and baldness tell a different, poignant story. The audience is wiping tears from their eyes. I make a mental note to log on to the hospital's website tomorrow to make my own donation.

"He's doing great. This is so fantastic!" Darren whispers in my ear, still for probably the first time all day. And we both just watch the magic play out on stage.

By the end of the evening I am, as always, wishing I wasn't so vain as to force my feet into high heels. No matter how much it hurts now, I know I'm going to slip into them next time, again thinking how perfect they look with this skirt. I lean pleasantly against the plush leather seats in the back of the limo and sigh with relief, knowing at least I don't have to drive myself home. The two rum and Diet Cokes I snuck backstage have left me feeling way more comfortable than I did on the way over.

Billy eases down next to me and I realize that I didn't slide in far enough to sit on the opposite or even sideways section of the car. Once again we're sitting right next to each other. Which, if we were in a normal car, would be no problem. It's just disconcerting to be right next to Billy in the back of this huge ten-person limousine, where you could easily stretch out and sleep on its buttery leather seats. But I can't move now; that would only call attention to the awkwardness of the moment. And for all I know, Billy isn't even aware of it, so why point it out?

He is the first to break the silence. "I had a good time tonight." He leans forward and helps himself to the limo bar setup, bypassing the bottled water.

"I'm glad. You did a killer job. The hospital is ecstatic. They don't have final numbers yet, but they think your auctioneering broke a record."

"Really? Cool." He seems content with that answer and

doesn't say anything else as he pops open a Red Bull and pours it into two glasses. He adds vodka and hands me a glass and then sits back next to me with a sigh. I think we're going to sit in silence for a while. Which I'm okay with; I certainly don't want to be all Chatty Cathy if he needs some downtime. I sip at my drink, and it helps me feel more comfortable in the quiet.

"So, what's your boyfriend like?"

Wow. A sucker punch right to the jaw. I did not see that coming.

"Uh, Jacob?" I stall . . . and take another sip.

"*Jacob*, huh? Not Jake?" I hear humor in his voice. Is he teasing me?

"Yeah, he likes to be called Jacob. He hates the name Jake." Really, he's not a big fan of nicknames in general, but I manage not to say that to the adult who still is going by Billy.

"So? What's he like?"

"He's a great guy. Really smart. He's in banking." It's not that I can't think of better things to say about Jacob, it's just that my mind is not actually functioning properly at this moment.

"How long have you been going out?"

"Two years." I am longing for this conversation to be over and hope my short answers help put me out of my misery.

"Are you living together?"

Since when did guys ask questions like this anyway? Maybe now is the time to go on the offensive.

"No. We're not. What about you? Girlfriend?"

"Nope. As the entire blogosphere knows, I broke up with

someone I'd been seeing for a while, and now I'm just, you know, laying low."

"Did you love her?" Now where the hell did *that* intrusive question come from? Sophie, shut up!

"I thought I did. We were really happy together, and we had a lot in common. But when we broke up, I guess I wasn't as upset as I thought I'd be. I realized that we were just going through the motions by the end. You know?"

I think about Jacob and me. After two years, are *we* just "going through the motions"? In some ways maybe we are. I don't know. And does Billy really care or is he just looking for empathy?

"What about you? Do you love him?" Billy asks.

"Yes. Of course I do." Did that sound too defensive? I can't tell.

"Okay. Sorry. I didn't mean to get too personal." He actually sounds a bit hurt.

"I didn't mean to snap at you. I guess I'm a little sensitive. About us. I mean, about him and me." Is that even proper English? I look for a place to rest my drink and really can't see how to get it back to the bar without showing Billy a healthy view of my backside. I know I'm not fat, but it's still not the most flattering angle.

"Why?" Oh sure, the one guy on the planet who actually wants to talk about relationships happens to be the hottest guy in Hollywood and is sitting a foot away from me in the dark backseat of a limo. *Danger, Will Robinson, danger.* I swallow the rest of my drink and just put the glass on the floor at my feet.

"I don't know. I guess it's awkward. Because we've been to-gether so long people ask when we're going to get engaged. And it *is* the next logical step, but I guess maybe I also worry that we are in a rut, or bored, or boring or something. I don't know." Yes, I know I said that twice. Because I really *don't know*. I don't know a lot of things, starting with why I'm opening up to Billy Fox about my relationship with Jacob.

I peer outside the window and watch as we merge onto the 10 freeway. No traffic at this hour, thank God. The limo is starting to feel very warm and claustrophobic.

"Do you want to get married? Does Jacob?"

For no reason, that I will admit to anyway, I find myself wanting to confide in him. You know how you can tell your manicurist anything? Or a friendly bartender. And it's okay because neither knows anything except your side of the story. And they won't meet any of the other people involved, right? So, that must be it. I'm overcome by that same compulsion to confess everything I've been stressing about to Billy Fox. Or maybe it's just because he's a good-looking guy who's asking me sensitive-sounding questions.

"We've been dating two years and he hasn't said anything about marriage. He doesn't bring it up and I'm not about to."

"Ah." The condescension is not difficult to sense.

"What?" I turn to look him in the eye, and our proximity makes my stomach do a flip-flop. But the smirk on his face man-ages to get my libido under control.

"Well, we're men, not mind readers. You can't expect him to just know what's going on inside your beautiful head." Save me from smooth-talking Southerners. His accent, usually so subtle, has become more pronounced as the evening has worn on. And the compliment, of course, counteracts the arrogance and his know-it-all attitude.

"For your information, I don't want Jacob to propose to me just because I want him to!" Maybe it's the Red Bull and vodka in my system, but now I'm riled. "It's supposed to be something couples do because it's what they *both* want. I'm not desperate for a ring. I just want to know where we stand. If *he* sees a future for us." Nice sidestepping. Very confident.

"You know what I think?" He is smiling, but I feel the intensity of his gaze as the limo pulls up in front of my building. I glance out the window as we stop, trying to think of something witty to say. In the end I just look back at him and our eyes lock. "I think you don't know what you want, Sophie Atwater. Not yet." I swallow.

And with perfect or horrible timing, depending on how you look at it, the car door opens beside Billy. The spell is broken as Billy throws me a killer smile before getting out of the car. He helps me to my feet with his perfect Southern manners, and the cold air shocks me back to reality. What the hell is going on with me?

"Good night, Sophie. Thank you for tonight." He leans down and kisses me on the cheek. I force myself not to think about how it feels.

"Good night, Billy."

He disappears back into the stretch behind tinted windows as I head to the front door of my building. The car idles there until I unlock the door and throw what I hope seems like a casual wave as I step inside.

My stomach is in knots as I slowly climb the stairs to my condo. In a daze, I go through the motions of getting ready for bed. It's only when I climb under the covers and lay my head on the pillow that I finally step back for some perspective. And one thought keeps running through my mind like a screen saver: *You are in big trouble, Sophie.*

6

MY HEAD WAS ALREADY RINGING WHEN THE ALARM CLOCK
joined in this morning. For the most part, my job allows me the
flexibility to roll in between 9 and 9:30 A.M. Nice, right? Well, it
makes up for the late nights I often work at red carpet events.
But occasionally, I am required to be up at the crack of dawn.
Like today. After a restless night of Billy-on-the-brain mini-
mal sleep, the 5:45 A.M. wake-up call was definitely unwelcome.

And here I am on the set of KTLA's morning news show.
They occasionally book celebrity guests to cohost the show
when one of the anchors is away. I scored my client Megan Keef
a spot this morning. It's pretty cool exposure for her; she's a
soap star who's about to break out of daytime. On *Black Mountain
Valley*, she plays Annabelle, the perfect, sweet heroine. In real
life, she's equally sweet and one of my favorite clients. There's
just one tiny issue I struggle to keep out of the tabloids. Megan
habitually "test drives" clothing and other small items from
boutiques and hotels . . . often without the establishment's
knowledge, much less consent. So far the kleptomania on my
watch has been kept to a few hotel spa robes, a pair of Gucci
sunglasses, two flatware settings, and some cashmere gloves

and hosiery that "accidentally" fell into her handbag, which I then discreetly returned with abundant apologies for the *oops!* The most random of all was when a hotel billed us for a Gideon Bible.

It's now 9 A.M. and—after two cups of coffee and a deeply satisfying eggs and bacon on a roll—my brain is finally starting to function properly. Once the show is over I'm heading straight to the office, which means I won't have time to change before I meet Billy Fox for a lunch interview with Lisha Hasbert. I would love to hold off seeing Billy again until I clear my head, but I still have a job to do. And there is no way I would let this particular reporter interview any of my clients alone. In journalist circles, Lisha is known as a pit viper, known for sensing weakness and going in for the kill. She's written up some pretty brutal—though probably honest—interviews with celebrities. Why then am I letting her interview him at all? It's going to be a *GQ* cover story. Like her or not, she writes a great interview, and the notable magazines—*People, GQ, Vanity Fair,* etc.—love her, specifically because she gets exclusive stories from big stars. My job is to make certain that she doesn't get anything out of Billy that he doesn't want to tell her.

But now I am stressing over the realization that I am not really dressed for a business lunch, never mind lunch with Billy Fox. Though I haven't been able to get him out of my head, or my imagination, since I met him, at 6 A.M. making a good impression didn't even cross my mind when I pulled on comfy jeans and UGGs. At least I'm wearing a flattering, semi-dressy black top—a slightly revealing V-neck, clingy (in the right places) knit sweater.

After I wrap things up with Megan and make sure she leaves with only what she brought with her, I check my voicemail on the way into the office. Already twelve messages. The rest of my morning will be dedicated to the Nintendo launch party. But as I cruise through our office doors and pass the interns' cubicles, all I notice are the fabulous shoes *everyone else* is wearing, not to mention that they are towering over me.

Argh. I need shoes!

I fantasize about my perfect pairs of Jimmy Choos lined up on a shelf back in my closet. Why couldn't I be one of those people who think ahead when their brain is still alert? If only I'd just brought shoes to change into for lunch.

"You have four messages. And Melissa called again," Tru says as I walk past her desk into my office. I'm so desperate at this point that I even eye Tru's shoes. I could so demand that she trade with me for my lunch, if we are the same size, and if she happens to have cool heels on. Sometimes she wears those ballet slippers that are in right now. While I would love to get on that bandwagon, my thighs need every extra inch we can pretend is there.

No luck. Tru is wearing Doc Martens. And purple leather knee-high boots with neon green laces, no less. Well, she has a look and she sticks to it. You've got to admire that. But now that the idea has struck, who else might have shoes I could borrow? For the rest of the morning I not so discreetly eye every assistant and junior publicist—even Jeff and the mailroom guy out of sheer habit—who comes by my office, in hopes of spotting a workable pair of heels. So far no luck. And there's likely a fresh rumor of my presumed foot fetish. I mentally start scrolling through the personnel on the floor above. I am deep into a shoe count when a knock at the door makes me lose my place.

"Sophie? I have a question." It's Jennifer, our newest assistant.

"Hi, what's up?" I keep a friendly tone but, Queen of Multitasking, turn back to my Outlook and continue prioritizing my emails. I like to make sure I get to East Coast people first, so they get what they need before the end of their day.

Jennifer needs to discuss the contract for Five-Alarm Blaze, a popular rap-rock band Bennett/Peters represents, which is going to perform at the Nintendo launch party. A little synergy for you. I help her decipher the band's rider. It's not until she turns to go that the flair of her skirt makes me notice her fabulous, perfect, similar size–looking shoes.

"Jennifer, wait." Okay, how do I ask this nicely? But she seems properly intimidated by me anyway, so maybe . . . "Hey listen, I have an important lunch meeting today, and I forgot to bring heels to change into. May I . . . borrow yours?" I try to deliver the question as nonchalantly as possible. As though it happens all the time. Wait and learn.

"Umm . . ." She seems hesitant. They *are* nice shoes. Laundry, I'm guessing.

"Let's just see if we share the same size, huh?" I smile confidently. She resignedly kicks off one three-inch heel as I pull my chunky boot off. We're not talking Cinderella magic or anything, but they fit okay. "You're an eight?"

"Yeah."

"Well, I'm a seven, so they're a little big." Great. Why not just call her Bigfoot. "But I can manage. If you don't mind."

From a sanitary perspective, I would so not do this if it weren't absolutely necessary. "I promise to take good care of them. And I'll owe you," I say assertively, the deal done.

"Okay." Jennifer smiles weakly, and I know I'm safe. "I'll come get them this afternoon?"

"Absolutely. I'll be back by two. Until then, we have some flip-flops from that Beach Bonanza event last summer in the loot locker. Tell Tru I said to get you a pair."

"Okay, thanks."

"No. Thank *you*!"

Thank God that's over. And the shoes look fabulous. Crisis averted. Nothing more could go wrong.

AS I DRIVE THROUGH downtown Beverly Hills, on my way to lunch, I can't help wondering where Jacob fits into all this desperate-for-sexy-shoes-to-see-Billy-Fox madness. Honestly, nowhere. And I don't intend that in a mean way. The way I see it, I'm just enjoying the fun of a little you-can't-even-call-it-a-crush crush on my gorgeous new client. He knows I have a boyfriend. And away from the dangerous dim-lit interior of limousines, we can realistically state that Billy would never be interested in someone like me anyway. So I'm having a little fun playing make-believe. It won't hurt anyone. Especially Jacob, who hasn't even called me back about watching *Survivor* tonight, so there.

Also, I'm bound to see a not-so-sexy side to Billy with all the time we're spending together, at which point my "crush" will be put out of its misery and I can go back to my regular life. It's not like I'm purposely ignoring Jacob or our relationship. I've got everything under control.

Unlike some clients who prefer meeting in notorious, paparazzi-lined scenes-to-be-seen-in like The Ivy's front patio, Billy asked for a more out-of-the-way, relaxed locale with the promise of great comfort food. As such, the interview lunch is being held at Off Vine, a cozy establishment in an adorable yellow-and-white-painted bungalow wrapped in hedges. Once I read about their famous dessert soufflés, I knew it was the perfect spot.

After leaving my car with the valet, I am relieved to see that I am actually the first to arrive. I like to be early to appointments like this because I don't trust reporters alone with my clients. And knowing Lisha, in ten minutes she could sweet talk Billy into going to a different restaurant or something and "forget" to leave word. She's like that.

Settled in our private room upstairs above the eaves, and waiting for Billy and Elvira, I mean *Lisha*, to join me, I pull out my BlackBerry to scan yet again through my emails. In the middle of trying to follow a long email chain Elle just cc'd me on, I hear:

"Hi beautiful." I look up, only to interrupt what was definitely meant to be a kiss on the cheek, but becomes lip-to-lip contact instead. I can't even enjoy the moment because I am panicking inside that he'll think I moved to kiss him on purpose. It lasts only a second before he takes a seat on the opposite side.

"Hi, Billy." I strive for a casual, I-kiss-movie-stars-on-the-lips-all-the-time type voice. "You found it okay?" I had

MapQuested the directions for him and attached it to his last email. Because I'm a type A publicist.

"Yeah, no problem. It was easy." He flashes his killer grin and announces, "I'm starving," and accordingly begins examining the menu. I take the opportunity to glance at my watch. Lisha should be here any second now. Billy, breaking celebrity rule number thirty-seven, was on time.

"You're always starving, aren't you?" I tease because I can't think of anything else to say.

"Pretty much. Especially here."

"I thought you hadn't been to Off Vine before."

"No, *here*," he says, waving his arms to indicate larger surroundings. "I'm never full in LA. Now, in Texas, they know how to feed a growing boy." He's obviously kidding because no one gets a body like his by eating Tex-Mex and barbeque all the time. But I smile and signal the waitress.

I'd like a gin and tonic please. I wish. I order an iced tea with lemon. Judging by Hi-my-name-is-Mandy-and-I'll-be-your-server-today's quick appearance, she already knows who is sitting with me, but she takes my drink order like I'm important too and proceeds to go through the tried-and-true "don't I know you from somewhere?" method of getting Billy to identify himself. Of course Billy is exceedingly charming and gracious to our waitress, and she is blushing by the time she remembers to go get our drinks.

"Aren't you a sight for sore eyes, Billy Fox!" Lisha appears next to Billy in a tight skirt, sheer blouse, and knee-high stiletto boots. She leans toward Billy, who rises to his feet like the Southern gentleman that he is, and she air-kisses both his cheeks. "Daaarling." Yes, she leans down to me, perhaps to give Billy a clear view of her perfect ass, and both sides of my face get "kissed" too. While I contemplate her intentions, she comes back to Billy's side of the table to chummily take the seat next to him.

Lisha and Billy proceed through standard actor/reporter chitchat ("Did you find the place okay?") as a conversation icebreaker, and mostly my job is just to listen and only interject if things get uncomfortable. Frankly, it's nice to be able to sit at the same table as the interview. Some magazines insist that the publicist not be present. As if I would let that happen. In those cases, we compromise, and I end up sitting at the next table over so that I can still hear the whole thing. Either way, I'm not supposed to be actively involved in the conversation (and my presence is duly omitted from the final profile).

I periodically check my BlackBerry, which is resting conspicuously next to my bread plate, so that I can appear distracted and therefore allow Lisha and Billy an opportunity to have a conversation without it being awkward that I'm sitting there being ignored. As Lisha settles into her warm-up questions, and Billy flows right into his comfortable, honest answers, my eyes lower to the device and I run my thumb over the wheel to scroll through the newest emails.

"Sophie? Do you know the London premiere date?" Billy is looking straight at me when I glance up, which sets my stomach aflutter. Lisha is also staring at me expectantly. Expecting me to butt out, I'm sure.

"I'll email Lisha the details."

"Perfect, darling," she purrs as she turns back to Billy and peppers him with another few questions about the six-month shooting schedule in Prague.

"I love traveling, seeing the world. It's tough on a shoot because you really don't have time while filming to see the sights, but I usually plan to stay at least a few weeks before or after to enjoy the locales."

"And? How was Prague? What did you see?"

Billy describes the romantic Czech Republic's capital city, and my emails remain unread as I am totally caught up in his obvious appreciation of its historic bridges and castles.

"Have you ever been?" Billy asks Lisha.

"I have traveled extensively through Eastern Europe, darling Billy. I love that we have traveled and seen so much of the same beauty in the world. Why I—"

"What about *you*, Sophie? Have you been?" I am so caught off-guard by his question that I don't even realize that he totally interrupted Lisha in mid-sentence. But her shocked look and the death laser she shoots me make her unhappiness transparent.

"I once saw a little of Europe backpacking with my best friend from high school, but we weren't brave enough to tackle Eastern Europe." A simple but specific answer, calculated so that he'll go back to his interview and stop talking to me. I stare directly at Billy in what I hope is a meaningful way. He knows his media training—he's doing this on purpose. He can't quite hide his smirk as he takes a sip of water. And the interview continues.

But by the time the hour-plus of our meal is up I have lost track of the number of times that Billy has caught my eye to share a private smile or include me in the discussion. He never crossed the line of making me speak again, but his mannerisms made it clear that he was speaking to me as well. Not just for the reporter or the tape recorder. He is sharing his stories and his life with me. And I just don't know what to make of that.

Lisha pays the bill on her corporate AmEx and appears satisfied with the interview. We maintain small talk as we exit the restaurant and approach the valet. Lisha sticks close to Billy's side, leaning against him with each laugh. She's just a schmoozer. I know she wouldn't really make a pass at my client. Certainly not in front of me. But it's still awkward to watch her nestle up to him for a friendly yet non–air kiss good-bye before she disappears into her huge Lexus sedan.

With Lisha's departure and life back off-record, I can feel my shoulders relax. "That went great. Sorry Lisha can be such a . . . so . . . affectionate." I laugh to show that I'm not jealous or anything absurd like that but am trying to sympathize with him.

"It's no problem. She's fine, really. It was an easy interview—it went well, right?"

The valet next pulls my car up. I drag myself from Billy's company to deposit my heavy shoulder bag in the backseat. I feel Billy following me and am suddenly all a-tingly inside as my "good-bye" kiss takes over my imagination. And then, *wham*. My heel misses the curb and I can already feel my knees scraping the pavement when Billy's arms wrap around my waist and pull me up against his body.

"Oh God. Sorry! I'm such a klutz." I am seriously mortified by my stumble, and the fact that I can still feel the warmth of

Billy's body pressed up against mine. He lowers me back to my feet slowly and I desperately find my footing. Granted, I'm no ballerina, but why am I so clumsy around this man? Well, it also doesn't help, I suppose, that I am wearing shoes a size too big.

"What are you, a buck ten? It was no problem," he says, smiling. And seemingly sincere. I haven't seen 110 pounds since high school, so his offhand compliment thrills me to my toes. He ushers me into the front seat of my car and chivalrously shuts the door for me. He remains looking into my eyes through the driver's side window until the valet distracts him. Billy glances back one more time, waves, and then heads toward his sleek navy Porsche. I still have this ridiculous grin on my face as I drive away.

ALL AFTERNOON I can't focus. I am seriously giddy thinking about Billy. Which is now, officially, not okay. At one point I was tempted to call or instant message Izzy about the butterflies in my stomach. But what would I say? How could I admit that I am insanely attracted to my new client? First of all, who isn't? Every woman in America is in love with Billy Fox. But I'm the one spending all day working with him, and when I'm not actually with him, I'm thinking about him, planning his days. And, I'll be honest, having the occasional fantasy.

But I can already anticipate Izzy's response: "What about Jacob?" And what can I say except "I don't know!" And I don't. I mean, I love Jacob. I do. And it's not like I want to have these feelings for Billy. But I do, so I have to figure out what that means. I can't just ignore it. Besides, confiding to Izzy would only have her wisely recommend that I pass Billy on to someone else, which I'm not ready to do.

For now, I need to figure this out on my own.

In the memo section of my BlackBerry I've even started a reminder list of all the sweet little reasons I love Jacob:

✓ *Lets me have the last bite of any dessert we share.*

✓ *Remembers his friends' birthdays even though he's a dude.*

✓ *Always puts my phone in the charger for me if I fall asleep and forget.*

✓ *Never—*

Tru interrupts me with the one thing that I can't put on hold.

"Sophie? It's Priscilla on line two." I wonder if Priscilla is calling to thank me for the extremely detailed email I sent her with the wrestling account's entire background. I was extra-diligent and included every aspect of the relationship, because I refuse to give Priscilla any excuse for not doing a good job. I grab for my headset.

"Priscilla. What's up?" No point in small talk.

"I just have a couple questions about dealing with Brandon Falken."

"Brandon Falken?" Mr. Falken *owns* United American Wrestling, and if anyone interacts with him, it would be Elle. "What happened to Christine? She's the PR contact. Why would you be dealing directly with Mr. Falken?" Oh my God. Seriously? I can't leave Priscilla alone with this account for a day before she's ruining relationships I've spent years developing?

"No, no. Christine and I are getting along great." Maybe Priscilla finally has learned to hear the nuances of stress in my voice, but whatever the reason, I am relieved to hear her explanation. Maybe she's not entirely incompetent. "Christine and I are working on some big concept pitches. That's all. And I know that you've done some big projects with the account, so I wanted to chat with you about what Brandon is like. What he wants to hear." Of course she's already on a first-name basis with the mogul. Priscilla proceeds to ask some absurdly basic questions about the account, and I do my best to maintain my strategy: give her every piece of advice I can, so she can either prove herself—or prove that I've been right about her all along. Eventually it becomes impossible not to tune out her irritatingly cultured tone of voice, rattling off mundane details I already know about the client.

The other half of my mind drifts back to the Billy/Jacob situation.

I suppose it seems awfully arrogant and perhaps a tad presumptuous to think of it as Billy vs. Jacob. Billy hasn't exactly proclaimed himself, but he has certainly been flirtatious. And am I seriously even considering breaking up with Jacob, a totally great guy, for what will likely be a short-term fling with a movie star? I'm not naïve. But maybe if I'm even having these feelings, it's a sign and I owe it to Jacob to be honest with him about it?

It's so easy to give other people advice, but when it's actually happening to you, the right answer isn't so obvious.

Priscilla seems blissfully unaware that I am barely hanging on to our conversation. She keeps prattling away at such a chatty pace that for a second I wonder *why* she is being so agreeable with me all of a sudden. And then the thought disappears when the caller ID shows an incoming call on line one.

Jacob.

". . . so, when I realized that Christine and I were thinking so similarly, it occurred to me—"

"Priscilla. I'm sorry but I have to take my other line. Let's talk later. Or better yet, email me." I disconnect with her and grab Jacob's call before Tru can pick up the line.

"Hi," I say, followed by an awkward pause. And I'm not usually one for awkward pauses.

"Sophie. Sorry I couldn't call sooner. I've been swamped all day." Jacob's voice seems completely unaware of the tension on my half of this phone call. "So, what's for dinner? I'm dying to find out who gets into that fight they teased on last week's *Survivor*."

Crazy thoughts circle my head. *This* is the romance in my life? I feel righteously indignant and entitled to an emphatic silence at the very least.

"Sophie? Are you there?" Even when you're not on a cell phone it's become an instinctive question nowadays.

"Yes. Yes, I'm here." I flick a pen back and forth on my desk like a teeter-totter.

"What's wrong?" Jacob is a cut-to-the-chase kind of guy.

"Jacob, it's six-twenty P.M. You haven't called all day. Actually, it's been nearly two days since we last spoke. I didn't know if you were even coming over tonight. You can't make assumptions." All of a sudden Jacob's minor inattention is a problem the size of the Grand Canyon. As if I was waiting all day for a personal email that never came. And now here he is, and he doesn't even know how he's ignoring me! Izzy's faint rational voice whispers in my head, *Passive-aggressive much?*

"Sophie, I said I wouldn't be able to talk yesterday because we were dealing with the bigwigs from New York all day then and today. Remember? I promised you I'd be up for air to watch *Survivor* together and I am keeping my promise. I'm sorry, okay? You know what it's like."

Oh, yeah. He *did* mention that his bosses' bosses were coming into town and that he'd be incommunicado. My haughty tone evaporates in my throat as I also remember why *I* was distracted over the last few days too. God, why am I behaving like such a shrew?

"I'm sorry too." I know I owe him more than a begrudging apology but I still can't seem to swallow my pride all the way. "See you at eight?"

"Yeah, okay. What about dinner? Are we still on Indian or how 'bout we revisit Mexican?" Still caught up in my own head-drama, I barely register the kindness and genuine forgiveness in Jacob's tone.

"I'm really not in the mood for Mexican. Let's just get some sandwiches from Westies." It's a café literally around the corner from my condo. All organic foods, but not über-healthy. And it's close and easy. No fuss.

"Sounds good."

"See you."

"Love you."

"Love you too." I hang up, but it takes me a while to look away from the receiver.

JACOB HASN'T BEEN at my condo four minutes and already I'm annoyed.

"I didn't pick up the food, Jacob, because *I didn't know what you wanted.*"

"Okay, Sophie. Don't snap at me. I just asked if the food was here because I'm starving. I wasn't attacking you." Jacob puts his briefcase down next to the wine I opened and left on the counter. He draws me in and offers a peacemaking kiss.

"Well, it felt like you had expected me to read your mind or something." In my head it was intended as a slightly pointed joke. The reality was much more sharp and bitter. But, unwilling to take it back, I just step aside and refill my glass as Jacob shrugs out of his suit jacket and drapes it over the seat of one of my counter bar stools. I walk away, waiting for him to respond. Am I hoping for a fight here?

"Do you want to walk over there or shall we have them send it up?" Clearly Jacob is an expert in taking the high road and I'm not going to get him off it.

"We'll walk over, but I have a menu. We can call down so we're not waiting." We go through the paces of selecting entrees and calling in the order. By the time I've finished explaining to the waiter the specifics of what I *don't* want on my salad, Jacob has removed his shoes and tie, and has a bunch of newspapers folded on his lap. He is already engrossed in something on the front page.

"So, I guess *I'll* go get the food?" I ask, annoyed again that he's just assumed I would do it.

"No, Sophie. I'll go. But it won't be ready for another couple of minutes yet." He goes back to his article, the crinkling of the paper on my nerves. I look at my watch and stew. This is so like him, I think, as I sip more Shiraz. Cramming in one more article before dinner. It's frustrating because I would just go to the restaurant. In fact, I'd rather wait there to make sure I get the food as soon as it's made rather than imagine it sitting in a bag on the counter for ten minutes while I read the freakin' paper.

"I'll just go. Obviously, you still have work to do." I don't play the martyr well, but it doesn't stop me from trying. But this is a pretty obvious bluff. All Jacob would have to do is look up from his paper and see the old, ripped sweats and the stretched T-shirt to know that there's no way I'd show my face in public like this. But he doesn't look up, and in fact doesn't seem at all motivated to get up from the couch. Or perhaps he just won't take my childish bait.

"Sophie, the food can wait a second. I'll go get it if you'll let me finish this one article. Take a seat and relax." How did he get so engrossed in an article that he just *had* to finish it before we could eat? And the underlying message that I just don't understand how important his work is didn't escape me. Jacob always claims he sees the importance of my job and values how difficult my career is. But in moments like these, I get the sense that he doesn't feel that way at all. That secretly he thinks his job carries more weight than mine, and his way of proving that is by reminding us both that the world's news matters, before generously tossing me the Entertainment section.

At least another five minutes pass while Jacob calmly finishes the article he was so set on reading. He puts his hand on my shoulder as he passes my position on the perpendicular sofa. "I'll be back in five." As he walks out the door, I put down the book I was only pretending to read and close my eyes.

It is impossible for me to ignore the fact that I've turned into a raving bitch, not to mention a lunatic, in the last four hours. I know I'm behaving in a completely irrational way toward Jacob, and his composed reactions are only aggravating me more.

By the time Jacob gets back with our food, I have polished off the rest of my generous wine pour and am working on a third. Without saying anything, he starts setting up our meal on the coffee table. And yes, our food looks perfectly fresh, and his side soup is even still hot, steam rising from its open lid. I watch him work without really seeing his actions. Just clinical, unemotional movements and the crinkling of wax paper.

He doesn't comment on my wine, and I suppose I am grateful. I can't stand when he gets all judgmental—it's not like he's some teetotaler, for God's sake. But it's hard to be indignant and self-righteous when you're the one getting drunk and you know that your reactions are probably not as levelheaded as you would like. Nonetheless, a disapproving attitude is rolling off Jacob in waves, threatening to drown me, and I intentionally reach for my wineglass to take another gulp in defiance of his obvious censure. What an ass . . . This is my home and I am entitled to get trashed every night if I want. It's not like I'm driving or anything.

Jeff Probst begins explaining the "reward" challenge, and I get caught up in the "real" world of *Survivor*, eager to leave the lonely island of my own making.

7

THE BLACK CROWS' "HARD TO HANDLE" IS ANNOYINGLY
blasting from far away. *Turn it down, asshole*, I groggily think
from beneath the covers of my soft bed. *Trying to sleep here.* Even
with the ceaseless guitars, exhaustion wins, pulling me back
under its comfortable embrace. Happy happy sleep. My fingers
curl around the edge of the . . . sheet? Instead of the familiar
smooth Egyptian cotton, I detect soft knit wool. *Huh?*

My eyes open and reluctantly focus. I'm curled in a fetal
position on the living room couch. The wool throw from atop
the adjacent armchair has been draped over me.

Jacob.

I must have passed out. The empty wineglass on the coffee
table reminds me why.

A never-ending soundtrack is coming from my bedroom
down the hall.

My alarm clock.

Oh crap.

I jerk upright, and quickly regret the sudden movement.
What time is it? Clutching my head, I check the cable box display. It's 9:20 A.M. I am supposed to be meeting with Elle and

the Nintendo people *in ten minutes*. How long has that damn
alarm been going off?

There's no time for a shower. I splash some water on my
face, quickly brush my teeth (ugh, cotton mouth), and throw on
a Nanette Lepore dress. My hair is its bedhead best, but all I
can do is pull it back in a ponytail. Grabbing heels and my
makeup bag, I race down to my car. As I stop at red lights along
Wilshire, I apply mascara and lip gloss and slip my heels on,
trying to look semi-presentable. I am desperately scrolling
through my BlackBerry as I finally pull into the office building. Tru should be in the office by now, and hopefully she'll be
able to forward me some notes from my desktop when she gets
my panicked email, but for right now, I'm winging it.

As much as I wish to ignore them, my mom's words come
back to haunt me: *Don't bite off more than you can chew.* I am *so*
not prepared for this meeting. Whereas getting Billy Fox to
sign with us was the well-rehearsed song and dance with a personal touch, the more formal Nintendo agenda requires concrete details for their upcoming launch party and media
rollout. I had planned to review all the consolidated info and
get fully prepared last night. And I totally passed out. I seriously don't know what happened. In business at least, I'm never
a flake. And yet twice in two weeks I'm racing to an important
work meeting. I used to only have nightmares about sleeping
through my alarm clock and missing my final exams or an important interview. Now I am living them.

Riding up in the elevator, I focus on everything I know
about the Nintendo launch. The venue logistics. Jennifer's

work with the band. The confirmed guest list. Melissa left me her notes on the project, but we hadn't truly discussed it yet. She steered our few short phone calls—technically forbidden as part of her mandated stress-free bedrest—toward office gossip and other business that the fellow workaholic greatly missed. My later attempt to connect found us in a frustrating game of phone tag. And because of yesterday's distracting Billy/Jacob agitation, I totally forgot to call Melissa back in time. Now, on the spot, I have a ton of unanswered thoughts about the plans, but I need to check with Melissa before I pitch anything new to the Nintendo team in front of Elle. If Melissa already went over it, I'll just look foolish, and worse, the company will look incompetent. When you're the switch point person on a client, the transition has to be seamless. That's the difference between Bennett/Peters and the competition. I know that, and I fear I'm not going to be able to deliver today.

As I walk up to the glassed-in conference room—*dead publicist walking*—I catch Elle's tight expression and her sharp glance toward the clock. Mortified, I check it myself. 9:50. I'm twenty minutes late. Since no excuse will justify twenty minutes, I decide that as they all look up at me I will simply apologize and move past it.

"Everyone, this is Sophie. She's been handling the campaign since Melissa had to leave." Elle masks her disappointment, making introductions around the room in a friendly, business-as-usual tone. I feel myself begin to sweat.

"I'm so sorry to be late." True. "It was unavoidable." Not true. "I know Melissa wishes she could have stayed on the cam-

paign until the launch, but she is staying in touch—we exchange emails and phone calls daily." Sort of true, minus the
phone calls . . . and the daily. "Well, I definitely don't want to
waste everyone's time bringing me up to speed," I say, taking a
seat beside Elle, "so let's continue, shall we?"

Forget my wish to get Priscilla fired. I'm doing a fine job
putting myself out the door first.

PING. The instant messenger box pops up in the center of the
notes I am drafting on what I did and didn't screw up in the
Nintendo meeting. Right now the lists seem distressingly even.

> **Izzy12242:** how was your meeting?
> **PRCHICK78:** how did you know about that fiasco?
> **Izzy12242:** didn't know it was a fiasco. what happened?
> **PRCHICK78:** wait. Then why did you know to ask?
> **Izzy12242:** What do you mean? I called your office.
> Tru said you were in a meeting.
> **Izzy12242:** I just saw that you were back online.
> Are you upset? You seem very uptight.

Only Izzy could get away with saying that to me right now.

> **PRCHICK78:** I am uptight! I was 20 MINUTES late for my
> meeting with the Nintendo people. And Elle was not
> amused.
> **Izzy12242:** holy crap!
> **PRCHICK78:** I fell asleep on the sofa, and didn't hear the
> alarm.
> **PRCHICK78:** Elle's face = if looks could kill!!!!

Izzy12242: Yeah, I can imagine. So . . . what'd you do?

PRCHICK78: Some major tap dancing. I felt like Richard Gere in Chicago. Only I was definitely not as good.

Izzy12242: well he had months to practice and professional choreography

PRCHICK78: haha

Izzy12242: Seriously . . . what happened? Is everything okay?

PRCHICK78: Yeah, Izzy, yeah. I'm fine. just had a long day yesterday, and I was so psyched to unwind with a bottle of wine, and the next thing I know, I wake up on the sofa, late for work.

Izzy12242: But, wasn't Jacob with you?

PRCHICK78: Yeah. He was there; we watched Survivor.

Izzy12242: But he didn't stay over?

PRCHICK78: Nope

Izzy12242: "Nope"? Are you guys fighting? What's going on?

PRCHICK78: I don't know. We're not fighting, it's just tense and weird. He was all lame about the takeout, and I didn't really want him to stay over, and I guess he left.

Izzy12242: You guess?

PRCHICK: Well I sort of passed out.

Izzy12242: Oh Soph. Have you talked to him since?

PRCHICK78: Not yet.

Izzy12242: Call me. I've got a few minutes free.

PRCHICK78: Actually, I gotta get back to work—make up for what happened this morning. Call you later, okay?

Izzy12242: Sure, call me anytime. xoxo

PRCHICK78: xxoo

I *am* busy, but I also really don't want to talk about this with Izzy right now. I mean, what am I going to say? That I've turned into a lunatic I barely recognize? And frankly, I am still reeling from the barely disguised disaster that was my morning. My head is throbbing and I am staring at the untouched turkey wrap sandwich in front of me, wondering how I expected to choke down this food. I should have just ordered fries with extra grease and been done with it. I hear Tru answer my line as I pick up the pickle lying alongside my sandwich and am about to take the plunge when she buzzes me.

"It's Jeff."

I take it. "Jeff. What's up?" Anything to distract me from my thoughts.

"Emergency. Code red. Orlando is sick. He has to cancel the *Tonight Show* booking."

"Oh, God. When's he supposed to be on?"

"*Today!* He's supposed to be getting into the car in less than three hours. Jesus. Who can we offer them? Help save my ass." Now, obviously, the producers understand that people get sick. It happens. And certainly Orlando Bloom will be forgiven under such circumstances . . . but the firm doesn't want to risk our relationship with the "late night leader" by not at least offering them another excellent guest. It's only good business.

"Give me ten minutes." And I hang up. Now it's time to cross my fingers. I dial, and pray.

"Hello?"

"Billy? It's Sophie." Thank God he answered. That's the first hurdle. "I know this sounds crazy, but I'm wondering if you're free this afternoon to do a guest appearance on *The Tonight Show*."

"What, like *today*?"

"Yes, in a couple hours actually. You'd need to be there at

four for the taping at five. Orlando Bloom—another one of our clients—just got ill and had to cancel last-minute. And so Leno is in a bit of a bind. We'd love to offer them a replacement that's, you know . . . on the same . . . level. You'd be doing me a huge favor." Oh God . . . what was I saying? I should definitely shut up now.

"Um . . . yeah sure, I can do it."

"That's fantastic. You're actually doing us *all* a huge favor. The show will love you for it too."

"Yeah. No problem."

"Okay. Thank you so much, Billy. You're a lifesaver."

"Well, *you'll* be there, right? You want to grab a drink or bite afterwards?" The warmth in his tone, the suggestion, makes my stomach do a triple somersault.

"I'd love to but . . ." *I have a boyfriend. I'm in enough trouble as it is.*

"You'd deny the request of a 'lifesaver'?" Billy teases.

He's right. I do owe him a little. And it's just a bite. Only my overheated imagination needs a chaperone. "All right. You win. I know a fabulous French bistro practically across the street from the studio."

"Perfect." And he is gone. A deep breath, and then I am back on the phone.

"Jeff. We're golden. Billy Fox is available tonight for Leno. Do you want me to make the call?"

"No. With good news like that to soften the blow, is it okay if I do it?" I love this kid and his can-do attitude. And Jeff's right. He needs to get comfortable doing the dirty work too. And as far as an "I've got bad news and good news" kind of call goes, this one has a happy ending. So it's the perfect chance to let him get his feet wet.

"Call me back. Let me know what they say."

"You bet."

With another disaster averted, I lean back and consider an email to Elle. Bottom line, I owe her an apology. Big-time. And even though I ultimately rallied and left the Nintendo folk smiling, I am going to have to eat some major humble pie to get her to forget about this morning. Securing Billy Fox to step in last second isn't even going to win a half smile out of her. An email isn't enough. And flowers are too kiss-ass. What can I do?

My thoughts are interrupted by an email.

From: Jacob R. Sloane

To: Sophie

Subject: call me

No note, nothing. Somehow the succinct email feels very ominous, but then Jacob can be curt in emails without the intent. Maybe I'm reading too much into it. My normal "when in trouble" response is to delay . . . and spend hours dreading the inevitable. But right now, I'm in a "rip the bandage off" mood. So I dial his work line.

"It's Sophie," I say when he answers. The less I say the better.

"Sophie. What happened last night?" He doesn't *sound* mad. I sense a trap.

"What do you mean? Nothing happened." I wouldn't say it was the most romantic date or anything, but still . . . it's not like we had a raging fight either.

"You passed out on your sofa . . . Before the show was even over."

"I saw it. I was just so tired I couldn't keep my eyes open." I can sense denial's armor springing up all around me.

"Sophie, you were drunk. You passed out cold."

I am so glad he's on the phone because this conversation face-to-face would be unbearable.

"So? I had a bad day and I wanted some wine. I was not *drunk*."

"I just hate when we fight, and I have to tell you, we seem to always argue when you're drinking too much."

"Since when did you become such a prude?"

"God, Sophie. I have tried really hard not to say anything, but last night has happened a few too many times lately. And I just wanted to discuss it with you—when we can both be rational."

"Well, now's actually not a good time for me. I've been putting out fires all day, and I just found out that I have to head over to *The Tonight Show*."

"I think this is important." The sensitivity in his voice makes it sound extra grave, but I ignore the shivers it sends down my spine.

"Well I guess I'm just not in the mood to be 'rational' right now. I've got a lot going on, and working through my presumed shortcomings is going to have to go to the bottom of the list."

"We were supposed to go over paperwork for the Tribe of Hope committee last night. That deadline is coming up."

Of course the Tribe of Hope committee takes center stage again. I return the turkey wrap and pickle to its original bag and toss it all in the trash can. I've lost whatever appetite I had.

"I *know* what the deadlines are, and I've been working on the guest list and have some other publicists lined up to help us."

"Well, Sophie, that's what we needed to go over last night. It's great that you have it all organized, I don't underestimate you, but we need to get that info to them so the whole event is set up right."

"So you only came over because of the event. Not to see me?" When did I become my mother? And can crucifying him for changing the subject make me any more of a hypocrite?

"You know it's not like that." I'd finally shaken his calm demeanor, but just barely.

"Then what *is* it like, Jacob?!" Tru leans back in her chair to catch my eye through the doorway. She makes a "cool it" gesture, which is a gentle warning that my rising voice is carrying into the hall.

"Never mind, Sophie. Just forget it."

"Already forgotten." And I honestly don't know who has hung up on whom.

THE *TONIGHT SHOW* taping provides the perfect opportunity to leave the office early and head home to shower and regroup before the show. The retreat is doubly welcome, as I am still so agitated by my conversation with Jacob that I doubt I could focus on much else behind my desk. And Tru needs to witness no more meltdowns.

Refreshed, I arrive at the NBC studios in Burbank right as Billy is being escorted into his dressing room. He is already out of hair and makeup and appears charged for this last-minute appearance, as if it has been scheduled for weeks.

"How's it going?" I ask. "Are you all ready?"

"Yeah. I was telling the producer some of my stories of growing up in Texas, and she loved it."

"Perfect. I spoke with the film's PR department. They are thrilled for you to talk about shooting in Prague, but they don't have any clips we can use. I got a few behind-the-scenes photos."

"Yeah, I can wing that. We had some pretty crazy fight scenes that were tough to shoot." This is my first big show appearance with Billy. And I am relieved to see that he seems very comfortable. There are some extremely successful and famous actors who freeze up with anxiety before live audience appearances. They're totally fine in front of a TV or film camera, shooting something that millions of people will see, but not in front of a studio audience of two hundred and fifty tourists. Honestly, I couldn't do either. I get stage fright making a toast at Thanksgiving.

Jay Leno himself knocks and comes in to chat with Billy before the interview. We've met a few times, but it's always nice to see how friendly he is, and I think it sets so many people at ease to have them meet or catch up with him informally first. Billy immediately reminds Jay of his last appearance here, when apparently a wildlife trainer's Amazonian snake got out of hand while Billy was still on the sofa. They laugh over the unscripted comedy that followed and then talk cars a bit before Jay goes to finish getting ready for the show.

Now that it's clear Billy is not stressed or unprepared for the interview, I head out to schmooze with the other publicists and talent bookers I recognize in the green room. Also, I must confess that Billy looks incredible in slim, black trousers and a sea-blue shirt that highlights his eyes. My mouth is literally watering. And it doesn't help that he kept glancing at me and sharing all these private looks. Believe me, I am *not* making that part up. He is definitely flirting with me tonight.

Finally having run out of safe people to make small talk with, I head back to the danger zone—I mean Billy's dressing room. I walk in as he's getting his mic put on. Which means his shirt is pulled up as the technician strings the wired mic up under the shirt to discreetly clip it on his collar. And the glimpse of his gorgeous abs makes the temperature in the room go up ten degrees.

"Looks good," the audio guy says before heading out. *You have no idea.*

I must have kept staring, because when Billy catches my eye, there's a smirk on his face, but then he winks at me as he passes, following the stage manager out onto set.

Of course Billy's interview is a hit. He has the studio audience in the palm of his hand the whole time, telling funny stories about shooting his latest movie and then being so charming during the commercial breaks, taking pictures with fans in the crowd.

After the show Billy stays to sign a few autographs for crew members and visitors with backstage access. Because he's always polite and endearingly modest, I can see why everyone around Billy feels loved and important. As one woman fairly swoons over him agreeing to pose in a picture with her, he meets my eyes and gives the faintest eye-roll, which the fan doesn't notice as she helplessly rambles on about all of his movies she's seen. Finally, the mob in his dressing room thins and I walk him out to where his limo is waiting.

"Are we still on for dinner?" he casually asks as we pass from harsh studio lighting into the early evening light. I didn't know if he even remembered his offer. He hasn't said one thing since we talked about it earlier.

"Sure." I sound way more relaxed than I feel.

"Cool." And he walks past me to the driver's side of the limo. I'm only waiting a few moments when he comes back around the car toward me. And then the car starts to pull away.

Reading the confusion on my face, Billy smiles.

"Well, he's not really hired to wait for me to eat dinner, right? I figured you could give me a ride home afterwards. That's okay, isn't it?" He reaches over and takes my briefcase, and with his other hand now at the small of my back he starts leading us through the main entrance to the guest parking lot.

Well, that was a tad presumptuous, but somehow Billy is pulling it off. I unlock the Beemer by remote when we're a few steps away. Billy aims for the passenger seat and I rush to help him toss some empty coffee cups and papers left on the seat into the back. *Good impression, Sophie. Now he thinks you're a shameless voyeur* and *a slob.*

Getting to the restaurant is easy. It's truly around the corner, but in LA everyone drives everywhere, however close. Billy uses the short ride to check his voicemail messages, so I have a couple moments of quiet to gather myself together. But I don't have any great realizations or anything. All I can think about are ridiculous things like should I reapply my lip gloss or is that trying too hard?

Inside the dimly lit bistro, the hostess asks Billy if we wish to sit up front by the small jazz band or somewhere more quiet and intimate in the back. Before my head can vote for music's welcome interference, the hostess is leading us through the restaurant to a small table for two all the way in the rear. It's hard to ignore that we are in a really private, dark—dare I say, romantic—area of the restaurant.

Billy orders a round of celebratory champagne and with only a cursory glance at the menu asks that a few appetizers be brought to the table right away. I look slowly over my menu, focusing on the lyrical French phrases, trying to quiet my nerves. I can't help thinking about how Jacob always orders things from the menu that he knows we both like, so we can sample each other's meal.

"Sophie? Know what you're gonna have?" He has that smirk again on his face, as if he can tell that I'm hiding behind my menu.

"I always think I'm going to order something different when I come here, but then I end up getting the exact same thing."

His smirk becomes something bigger, like I just told him my favorite sex dream.

"I always get the filet. It's the best," I defensively explain, so he realizes I always get the best thing, not because I'm boring.

"So tell me about yourself, Sophie Atwater. What do you do for fun?"

"Um . . . well, I love my job." At his non-reaction I quickly continue, "I do! I know it sounds lame, but it's fun, exciting, and there are a lot of perks." Eek. I didn't mean to imply *him*! "You know, like going to great concerts and shows . . . and stuff."

"Yeah? What was the last band you saw?"

Put on the spot, I try to think of a band people are talking about in the office. Who did Tru say she went to see recently? Some random ska band—no, that's not the impression I'm trying to make. I think back on all the talk shows I visit—I see musical acts perform all the time. Why am I trying so hard to impress him with the "right" answer?

"Last time I had a client on *The Tonight Show*, Prince was the musical guest. He performed outside, and the NBC PR chick invited me to stand with her at the front of the audience. He totally had the whole crowd in the palm of his hand. That was pretty cool."

"Prince, huh? So you're a classic eighties kind of girl?" I wasn't sure how to take that. I mean, I totally love eighties music. But maybe that's a bit cliché. He's from Texas . . . if I say country music, that's too obvious . . . I don't want to seem like I'm trying too hard *or* have an immense desire for acid wash and big teased hair.

"I love Kid Rock." Okay, maybe I don't "love" him, but I do like his music. I try to think of some actual songs to add validity to my claim. Why didn't I just say Springsteen?

"Now we're talking." He effortlessly deepens his good ol' boy accent. "He's doing a concert here next week for the new album."

"Oh yeah, I've heard it's an insane tour—that he totally rocks." I don't know, it seems like a safe enough thing to say. I'm trying to keep up my enthusiasm here. "We rep him at the agency. The music division is always raving about him."

"Really? You think you could get me tickets?"

"Definitely. No problem. I'll email someone now." Which I proceed to do while he gets the waiter's attention and orders us another round of drinks.

A couple hours later, I am slightly more than pleasantly stuffed on delicious food and definitely buzzed off a pair of martinis. Billy has been keeping the conversation light and easy, but there's a little hum through my nerves at the way he occasionally brushes my fingers with his as he makes a point. And the ridiculously sexy way he keeps eye contact with me, like he's never going to let me out of his sight.

I wish I could've enjoyed the feeling of Billy's complete attention without the nagging at the back of my brain—never letting me fully forget that what I'm doing is wrong. I had two more drinks than was wise just to try to get Jacob out of my head. And I'm starting to feel a little bipolar here. Because when Billy excuses himself to use the restroom, I can practically see the devil on my left shoulder and the angel on my right, each begging me to do the "right" thing. Devil-Sophie reminds me of how neglected I've felt the last several months. That it's not like Jacob has asked me to *marry* him or anything. And that I haven't done anything bad anyway. It's not like Billy and I have had "sexual relations." Yet. And then Angel-Sophie pleads with me to leave, reminding me that I am in a committed relationship, that Jacob has been nothing but honest with me from the beginning, that I owe him the same. For the record, Angel-Sophie, in her prudish *Little House on the Prairie* smock, is not gaining any ground on Devil-Sophie, in her Pussycat Dolls getup.

Yes, I've got myself a well-deserved guilty conscience. Even two strong dirty martinis can't completely eliminate that feeling. Because, believe me, I try. As we get up to leave, and I feel the weight of Billy's unfamiliar arm over my shoulder, I am reminded of a faint drowning sensation. Being with Billy is exciting, sexy, and thrilling to my toes, but the fact that I am cheating on Jacob makes me feel cold and clammy all over. But wait—I am not "cheating" on Jacob. I am having a work dinner with a client. It happens all the time. For that matter, Jacob has work dinners with females all the time too. This does not qualify as cheating.

Or so I try to unsuccessfully convince myself.

Distracted, and only half-listening to Billy deal with the valet, I wait in the passenger seat of my own car. I turn to my "chauffeur," about to protest as he pulls out onto the road. Without even looking at me, he says, "It's easier for me to just drive than explain the directions." Which frankly, I'm relieved to hear. I would hate for him to think I'm so hammered that I can't drive. Not to mention how embarrassing that would be. But obviously, he doesn't care how much I drink, a lovely relief from the judgment I feel from Jacob. Happy to have found one clear weakness in Jacob—his constant harping on my intake of alcohol—I can finally relax a little, the Devil-Sophie encouraging my feelings of righteous indignation. Who is Jacob to tell me how to live my life? He makes me feel like I'm an alcoholic, for God's sake. I mean, seriously, it's not like I wake up at 8 A.M. and start gargling with vodka.

All thoughts of Jacob, alcohol, and injustice flee from my head when I feel Billy's hand brush my thigh as he reaches for the radio. Okay, maybe that was an accident. But after he adjusts the dial, he brushes it again . . . and lingers. I sense my blood pressure start to climb. My whole face and chest are now flushed, and butterflies are performing *Riverdance* in my stomach.

So for the second time in a week, I find myself in the confined quarters of a car with Billy Fox. But this time definitely feels different. Equal parts alcohol, recklessness, and lust. Shaken not stirred. The interior of the car practically shimmers with sexual chemistry. And after the champagne and martinis, I really don't care. Billy, at this point, probably perceives Jacob as a borderline negligent, definitely inattentive, absent boyfriend. Perhaps I've been highlighting all his worst faults, and maybe I've been painting a totally one-sided version of our relationship. All to impress the gorgeous man sitting mere inches away.

I guess, semi-subconsciously, I figured if Billy thought I was in an unhappy relationship, it would be almost like I wasn't in a relationship at all. I was going for the vulnerable weak girl approach. As he steers the car up the windy roads toward his home in the Hollywood Hills, I look around and realize it's going to be a bit complicated to find my way back to the freeway. Billy squeezes my leg, and again reads my mind.

"Why don't you come in? I'll draw you a map of how to get out of here." His eyes size up my condition. "Maybe get you a bottle of water too."

"Sure," I say, only because I can't think with his fingertips grazing my thigh.

We get out of the car, and I can't help but stop in awe of his elegant designer home. It's breathtaking. Neither ubiquitous Spanish Villa–style nor Mid-Century Modern exactly, Billy's "crib"—a sprawling ranch-style mansion that appears at the twist of the hill—is uniquely him and worthy of *Architectural Digest*. That's me—always thinking like a publicist. He takes my hand and leads me up the front steps. I touch the beautiful limestone columns on either side of the entryway and delicately step inside. A richly colored Moroccan rug invites you to kick off your shoes in the sconce-lit foyer. Down the hall, I catch a peek of charcoal-gray couches and a Bauhaus-style leather armchair with a Wii game controller resting on its seat. A bachelor obviously lives here, because it's neat but not hospital clean. While I'm still poised in the doorway, Billy uses his grip on my hand to pull me closer. Without really thinking about it, I let him.

And knowing all the million reasons why this is such a bad idea, when he leans in to kiss me, I do absolutely nothing to stop myself from kissing him back. And, holy crap, I am kissing him back. And I am loving every second of it.

Before the kiss escalates, Billy draws back, offers another irresistible smile, and says, "Come on . . . come in. Did you want some water? I'll show you around. Give you the tour." He tugs me past a formal dining room—the vast windows of which reveal LA's twinkling glow below—into a perfect chef's kitchen of brushed stainless steel, industrial pendant lighting, and seemingly miles of sleek blue-gray slate countertop. More than half my apartment could fit in this single room. I lean back against the gorgeous counter as he opens a hidden refrigerator door and pulls out two bottles of chilled Fiji water.

For some reason just looking at the sweating water bottle in my hand revives the buzzed Angel-Sophie.

"You know what? I should go."

"Really?" Billy seems sincerely caught off-guard. I see the initial look of surprise on his face before he covers it with another mischievous smile, and it seals the deal.

"Yup. I've got work tomorrow." I take a fortifying swig of artisan water, letting its coolness focus me. "I'll come take a tour some other time. Definitely." I mean, I don't want to burn my bridges here or anything. I just know that right now I have to get out of here before any line left is crossed.

"Let me draw you a map, then." Billy steps away and starts to open a drawer.

"That's what the GPS is for. I'm good." He shuts the drawer and leans back against the island, his arms crossed, and he's staring at me curiously.

"Sophie. What's up? Are you okay?"

"Yeah, yeah." I want to be subtle, but I can't seem to slow down. "I just realized what time it is." I slide past him on my way back to the foyer. His footsteps echo behind me as I reach the front door.

"Sophie. We're cool. Right?" He's not touching me, at all, but I feel him just behind me. His mouth is so close to my ear, and immediately, my fingers clench on the doorknob. I know if I turn around, I'm not leaving here tonight.

"Good night, Billy. I'll call you tomorrow." Still holding the doorknob, I turn my head enough to kiss him quickly on the mouth. Before he can get traction, I pull away and take the stairs back to my car two at a time.

"Good night, Sophie. Drive carefully." He stands at the door and watches until I am driving away.

8

I AM SO GRATEFUL TO HAVE A WORK EVENT EXCUSE TONIGHT.
Honestly, at this point, three days after "the kiss," I would have
made up an event and then hidden inside my apartment with
the lights off to avoid facing Jacob. We haven't spoken since our
heated phone call. I recognize how crazy I sound, but maybe
I'm actually protecting him from my company until I get my
head straightened out. My heart too.

How positively "noble" of me.

Tonight's event is the LA premiere of a quirky independent romantic comedy that Bennett/Peters is in charge of
organizing—arranging the carpet, managing the press, pro-
viding publicists to handle talent, and corralling big stars to
turn out for the screening to garner maximum media coverage.
Think of it like party planning, but with a twist. Even if the
movie itself is terrible, our job is to make the evening an Event,
complete with a star-studded red carpet. And guess whose
newest client is going to be on said red carpet? Billy specifically brought it up, indicating that he planned to attend. For a
second I had thought he was asking me on a date. But before I
embarrassed myself, he clarified that the director happens to
be one of his good friends, and he wanted to show his support.

Striding toward the office elevators with purpose, I am fantasizing about what Billy will be wearing when I see him in a few hours, and I barely notice Tru rushing around the corner after me until she practically skids to a halt.

"I'm so glad . . . I caught you before you left," she says, nearly out of breath. You would think I'd been running.

"What's up?" I say, sort of wishing she hadn't caught me. I'm not in the mood for any more problems. I hit the call button again.

"You just said you were going to walk Billy Fox down the red carpet at the premiere tonight, but I think you forgot about the meeting for Tribe of Hope's fund-raiser. It's been on your calendar for weeks."

Crap. She's right. Without a personal client attached to the film (and thus doing interviews), I hadn't planned on working the indie's premiere. The more junior agents would have it covered. But now that Billy's going to be there, I'm determined to pitch in.

With Tru's earnest face looking at me dead on, I feel my eyes darting from the elevator door to the hall where she came from. I can't even meet her sincere stare. I mean, this is exactly the kind of thing she is supposed to catch. And Normal-Sophie would right this second be effusively thanking her for saving my hiney once again. But not this time. Normal-Sophie has left the building, and right now we're dealing with Maniac-Sophie. But M-S is clever enough to disguise herself as N-S.

"Thanks *so much*, Tru. I'd totally forgotten. I'll just get Billy set up on the press line, and then I'll head straight over to that meeting." Where Jacob may very well be. Sure I will. "Thank goodness you reminded me!" I add for good measure as she walks away satisfied. "See you tomorrow!" Maybe the final yell as the elevator doors slide closed is a bit over-the-top, but what the hell. Before the elevator reaches the lobby, the problems of the day are gone and I am already in the now familiar dream-world where no one exists except me and Billy Fox.

THERE SHE GOES AGAIN is all I can think, as I watch Priscilla ignoring clients to schmooze every executive on the red carpet. Not to say that socializing isn't a crucial part of this industry. Because it definitely is. I just spent the last five minutes comparing life in Chicago versus LA with *E! News*' Giuliana Rancic, in between celebrity arrivals, as I spied Billy mingling with the director twenty feet away. But seriously, if Priscilla can't do her job, it shouldn't matter how many people she knows. I say "shouldn't" because, let's face it, tons of people, in every industry in the world, only got their job because they are so-and-so's son/cousin/wife/mistress.

But if "forced" to point fingers, I'll say that Priscilla is clearly not helping any talent or executives walk the red carpet—God forbid, *doing her job*. Instead I watched her graciously chat up one of the movie's producers, and now she is oozing charm all over a network executive. Our eyes meet briefly as she shifts position to block the sun's glare. It's still bright at 7 P.M. and the photographers are going mad with the perfect light to capture the actors strutting the red carpet. Priscilla lowers her perfectly manicured hand from her eyes and laughs at something Network Guy says.

My BlackBerry buzzes to notify me that Megan Keef has arrived. I reluctantly say good-bye to Billy, who lands a quick peck on my cheek before he heads inside the theater. With so many photographers still gawking at him, I appreciate that he was completely professional and didn't give them anything gossip-worthy. The warmth of his hand on my shoulder disappears too quickly as I rush over to the will-call table to meet my soap star. With all the heady drama and forbidden romance, I feel somewhat like a soap heroine myself.

Halfway through the screening I know there's no way I'm leaving to go to the Tribe of Hope committee meeting. It's getting too late to make the drive across town—and frankly I'm enjoying myself. So I slip out of the dark theater and phone Tru from the lobby, asking if she'll let them know I'm caught at work and regrettably unable to attend. To my surprise—and increasingly guilty conscience—Tru enthusiastically volunteers to go in my place. "Don't worry, I take *amazing* notes," she promises. There's nothing I can do but thank her profusely and then return sheepishly to my seat.

After the movie, I find Billy and Megan in the crush and make sure they both are escorted to the after party, right across the street. Again, Billy allows me to play the cool professional, but just as we slip past the velvet ropes and cross the threshold into the club, he brushes his hand across my butt. Not really a slap, but definite contact. For an instant I think it's an accident, until I see the adorably cocky grin on his face as he passes me to meet up with friends at the bar. He knows exactly what he is doing. And clearly enjoys every minute of torturing me.

Billy and I part ways once again, but somehow I find my

eyes drifting around the crowds in an effort to spot him, and once twenty minutes or so pass, I assume he's left. At one end of the room sushi chefs are meticulously preparing gorgeous rolls and sashimi, while across the space a rather loud Italian is offering three different styles of homemade pasta. A large, fully equipped bar is smack in the middle. While there are definitely lulls in the food station lines, the six bartenders I see mixing drinks and skirting the ice sculpture/martini spout are working nonstop.

I spend the next hour or so avoiding Priscilla and keeping Megan Keef company. I decide to ignore the handful of cocktail swizzle sticks I see jammed in her clutch. Sometimes you have to pick your battles. We chat at the bar for a while, share a few drinks, and neither of us can resist the incredibly decadent brownie bites and mini crème brûlée on Chinese soup spoons the servers later bring out on trays. I introduce her to some of my favorite colleagues at Bennett/Peters. Megan is totally down with just hanging out; she's not always trying to mingle with other celebs. I swear, another martini and I'm going to unload the whole Billy/Jacob problem on her. Glancing over at her now, listening to Jeff vent about a situation with his meddling parents, she has this really compassionate look on her face. I bet she can keep a secret. Well, actually I know for a fact she's pretty, ahem, discreet.

But as the evening wears on, the perfect opportunity never presents itself. Which, as I see her off at the valet, I realize is probably a good thing. I can't be confiding my personal problems to a client. What the hell is the matter with me? Things are finally starting to feel back to normal at work. The day after

my Nintendo meeting screwup I came in extra early, toting
Elle's one nostalgic carb indulgence—the best NY-style bagel
with cream cheese I could find—and left it with the handwritten
note "Sorry I was a schmuck. Never again. —Sophie." Elle's assistant, Lucas, said she smiled upon reading the apology and then
took the peace offering into her office, wherein he later spotted
its empty and meticulously cream cheese—free wrapping.

I should definitely get out of here before I blow it. I give my
ticket to the valet and figure I'll call it a night. My work is done.
It's better if I don't see Billy again anyway.

But obviously my subconscious has summoning powers.
Because I'm just thinking about him, and suddenly I feel a
warm body at my back.

"Are you sneaking out?" he whispers in my ear conspiratorially. He leans into me a little, encouraging me to press my
body up against him. Which feels way too good to stop, even
though I know I should. I mean, we're right out in front of the
party. Anyone could see us. Or maybe they can't, since his back
must be mostly blocking me. Except that I wouldn't even attempt basic geometry right now.

"Yeah, it's time for me to head home. I still have to work tomorrow. If I can dig out my desk."

"Oh really." He has such a sexy laugh. "I didn't peg you as a
pack rat."

"I'm not!" I hastily rush to get any unattractive image from
Hoarders out of his mind. "Since I took on Billy Fox as a client . . . I can't help it."

"I see. And how is this new bad habit my fault?" He is now
inches from my body. A little shiver shoots up my spine.

"People keep sending me stuff for you. Like, there's the gift bag from the event last week. All sorts of stuff gets dumped in my office for you. It needs to be sorted through and then I can . . ." I lose my train of thought as he puts his hands on either side of my waist, on the pretense of keeping me warm. But, at this point, I'm so hot I'm likely to spontaneously combust.

"When am I going to see you again?" His voice is a low whisper, and I can feel the vibrations course through me.

"Um . . . I don't know." *There's a clever answer.*

"Really? Aren't you in charge of my schedule, Ms. Publicist?" he asks straight-faced, but it's clear he's toying with me. He leans down, and I sense his lips getting very close to my left ear . . .

Just as my car pulls up.

I don't know whether to be relieved or royally pissed off. But either way, I leap from Billy's arms and head around to the door the valet is holding open for me.

Billy's steps echo as he follows me. He hands the valet a folded bill and takes ahold of the door. I slip past him and ease into the front seat. Billy's hand covers mine as we both reach for my seat belt. He pulls it confidently across my front and, after the telltale *click*, delivers a very gentle kiss on the mouth.

"Call me. When you know." And then he's gone.

COMFY ON MY SOFA AT LAST, I decide to waste a mindless hour on Facebook, catching up on others' lives. The Internet is the perfect way to forget about tonight's premiere and Billy's parting words. But after smiling over Izzy's recently posted shots of little Charlie chasing seagulls on the beach, I find myself Googling "Billy Fox" and clicking straight to Images. Rows and rows of his now-familiar face appear.

There's a sharp knock at the door.

What the hell? It's nearly ten-thirty.

Pulling a huge sweatshirt over my pj's I look through the peephole.

It's Jacob.

I wish I could say I had a feeling this was coming. Or some sort of omen that something was going to happen. But that would be a complete lie. I am totally blindsided to find his distorted face illuminated under the hallway light. More than anything, I want to sink down on the other side of the door and pretend not to be home. But the lights can be seen from the street; he knows I'm here. And he has a key. The knock was a courtesy. In the space of a few breaths I already feel nauseous.

I search for something normal to say as I unlock the door. Jacob stands in the doorway, an indecipherable look on his handsome face as his eyes search mine. What's he waiting for?

"Hi." I lean my weight onto my hand, which is locked in a death grip on the doorknob. But I feel I've achieved a relatively neutral tone.

"Hi." He still hasn't moved.

"Come in." Whatever it is we're about to say, I definitely don't want all my neighbors to hear.

"It was nice to see Tru at the meeting—though not quite the same as having you there." Jacob seems confident as ever as he paces past me into the living room. He doesn't take off his jacket but goes right for the sofa and sits down. I follow and sit beside him as he leans forward with his arms braced on his knees. My eyes follow his absentminded glance at the Billy Fox gallery on the open laptop. There's a sudden stab of regret. "Sorry. I had to work . . . ," I mumble, shutting the laptop and moving it to the side. Jacob is so focused he doesn't appear to notice my flushed embarrassment.

"We need to talk, Sophie." He looks directly at me, and I feel like he's staring right through me.

"Okay." Understand that I'm not playing some sort of control game here, making him talk first. I am just so scared shitless that I can't form a complete thought. Jacob doesn't jump right in to fill the awkward silence. We sit there not talking for what seems like forever but is probably less than a minute.

"Look, I'm not sure what's going on lately," he finally says. "There's been this weird tension between us, and I'm not sure why."

"How about the horrible things you said to me last week? Maybe that's caused some of the 'tension' you're feeling." Flashback to Girls Junior Basketball—the best defense is a good offense.

"You know it isn't just that. Sophie, I'm sorry if I hurt you, but I *am* concerned. And I know you don't want to hear this, but you have been drinking a lot lately. And I think it's affecting our relationship."

"You make me sound like a freakin' alcoholic. Jesus. I like to have a few drinks to unwind. Big deal. And, you know, just because I've had a couple doesn't mean you get to talk down to me all condescending." I can't just sit here like this, so I get up and start pacing around the room.

"I don't think you're an alcoholic. Look, I just think there's some stuff here that we're not saying. We have to get it out. We have to talk about what's really bothering us or we're not going to be able to work through it."

"What the hell does that mean?" I turn back on him. "If I don't admit to having a problem, you're going to break up with me?"

"That's not what I said." Jacob is still looking plaintively at me. His calm tone hasn't changed once. Part of me wants to take his hand and reassure him that everything is all right. We are good together. But then anger and doubt creep back in.

"I heard what you said. You want to know what my problems are? I've got a problem with you being judgmental about me wanting a glass of wine at night. That's my problem." *And I'm afraid that I've spent the last two years waiting for something that's never going to happen.* But of course I'm too afraid to actually say that.

"Okay, look. I'm sorry if you find me condescending when you drink. I didn't realize I was doing it. But I really didn't come here to talk to you about that or fight. We need to figure out what this distance is between us. Sometimes lately I get the feeling that you don't want to be around me."

I snort disgustedly and turn away from him. Leaning against the back of the sofa, I take a deep breath. Should I tell him about Billy? How ridiculous would that sound: I'm falling in love with a movie star. Am I "falling in love" with him? Or is it just a stupid phase and in a week I'll be dying for Jacob to come back? Oh God, I am such an idiot.

I go with a half-truth.

"I want to be with you, Jacob. It's not that. I've just been really busy at work. I have a million things on my plate right now, and I mean, your work gets crazy sometimes too; I would have thought you'd understand being swamped. I try to be understanding when you're busy."

I just want this conversation to end. I can't tell him about Billy or my doubts and fears of our own stalled relationship; I realize that now. But I'm not just going to back down either.

"Okay, you're busy. We're both busy. But we've always made time for each other in the past. Look—Sophie. I'm laying it all out here. Tell me what's going on. I want us to work through this."

Silence again. I think of a hundred things to say, none of them right. And Jacob being so nice only makes me feel worse. But I can't help myself.

"Please, Sophie. Just talk to me." His intensity spurs me to fight back.

"Jacob. Listen to me! There is *nothing* to work through. Nothing to talk about." I grip the back of the sofa as I stare into his hurt and concerned face. "I just need some space. That's all. It's no big deal."

"I'm sorry, Sophie. Our relationship was a big deal to me." Same quiet, intense voice. He gets up and goes to the door. "Call me when you want to talk." Since I'm not looking, it's just the low click as it shuts behind him that tells me he's gone.

Was.

I'VE BEEN LYING IN BED in the dark for hours now. I look at the clock again. 2:13 A.M. Two minutes since the last time I looked. I can't sleep. I keep replaying the conversation with Jacob over and over in my mind. What have I done? Did we break up? Do I want to break up with him?

I don't know.

I just don't know.

9

ELLE CALLS ME IN FIRST THING TO REVIEW LAST NIGHT'S premiere. It's a tad unusual protocol, but I'm not really focused on the subtleties of work right now. I keep replaying last night in my head. Is it really the end for Jacob and me? I keep waiting to feel panicked or sad, but mainly I feel numb. I don't know what's been happening to me lately. I used to be able to separate work from personal life. Of course, until now, I've never really had a lot of personal "problems" per se.

So I find myself sitting in Elle's comfortable office, reciting how the evening went as if I were some junior publicist on my first red carpet. I tell her whom I walked down the press line, what coverage they got, and then we gossip a little about the after party.

"Anything else I should know about?" Elle asks as the chat is winding down.

"Um . . . nope. Everything went well."

She nods and then turns back to her computer, my signal that the meeting is over.

As I walk back down to my office, I dismiss the nagging question mark in the back of my mind as being overly sensitive. Elle's chat didn't mean anything out of the ordinary. The premiere *did* go well. She probably just wanted an excuse to catch up since everything has been so hectic lately. Except I am pretty high up on the totem pole around here to be doing Tuesday morning quarterbacking for a little indie film premiere. Unless it's because I *was* a little off my game at the Nintendo meeting. When did I start getting paranoid?

Having logged on to my computer, I lose a couple hours catching up on the ninety-three emails I received since last night. Responding to the crucial ones and organizing the rest requires only a portion of my concentration, which is lucky because Jacob's parting words keep echoing in my head.

He definitely used the past tense. He said, "Our relationship *was* a big deal to me." No matter how I look at it, it seems clear to me that we are broken up. You don't use the past tense when discussing a current relationship.

I search my innermost thoughts for heartbreak or relief or any identifiable emotion. But all I find is the disappointed look on Jacob's face that I can't shake. He hasn't called me or sent a message since the blowup.

I'm not going to be the one to call him.

A reminder for tonight's bimonthly book club pops up and I'm relieved. I need a nice distraction. I'm trying to remember what book we were assigned and whether I read it, when a recap email from Tru about the Tribe of Hope meeting I missed appears in my inbox. Well, *that's* not going to help distract me from thinking of Jacob. I scan the meeting's minutes, embarrassed to notice that quite a few discussion points were aimed at me, not to mention that several labor-intensive duties were heaped on the shoulders of the girl who didn't show up. Great.

Now I feel even guiltier than before. Let's face it. I am not going to be able to work if I don't figure out this whole Billy/Jacob debate. Right now.

I bring up my AOL instant messenger and look for Izzy's screen name. But it's nowhere to be seen. The clock says 11:30, so it's 2:30 P.M. in New York. Izzy often takes late lunches, but usually she puts the "away" message up first. It's like she never signed on this morning . . . And then it hits me. If I weren't so preoccupied, I'd have remembered she's taking some time off in Connecticut with her family. I mean, I could still email her, or call, but the reception is terrible. The last time I reached her there, we had one of those absurd conversations where we got disconnected in the middle of a sentence but I didn't realize she was gone until I heard the recorded "If you'd like to make a call, please hang up and try again" . . . and felt like a self-absorbed fool. Not to mention that she is on vacation and deserves uninterrupted family time with Simon and Charlie. I know Izzy would selflessly call me back in a heartbeat, but I refuse to have her spend her holiday dealing with my romantic crisis.

Okay, so what would Izzy say if she were here? Probably that I'm an idiot and Jacob is the best thing that's ever happened to me and I can't throw it all away on a fickle movie star, whom I don't even know that well. Not to mention that he's a client, so it would be completely unethical for me to start dating him. Or maybe not . . . Maybe she'd understand that it is *Billy Fox* we're talking about here, and it's not so easy to just say "no, thank you." And you can't deny that the two of us have a strong attraction. That counts for something, right? Or maybe the fact that there even *is* a Billy Fox incident happening means something important is lacking in my relationship with Jacob. I mean, if I were totally happy with Jacob, would I even be tempted by or notice Billy beyond the usual appreciation of eye candy? So maybe Billy's not the problem. He's a symptom. Or have I been watching too much *Grey's Anatomy*?

Also, I can't forget my fight with Jacob last night. He has no right to act like I belong in freakin' AA meetings. Or like I don't care about our relationship as much as he does. Because that's bull. I hate how he's always so calm, saying stuff like that, leaving me all freaked out and upset while he's still Mr. Cucumber. He has no right to dictate to me like that. And then, he just walked out. And he hasn't been in touch at all. Maybe he doesn't love me as much as I thought he did. Maybe he's "just not that into me," which would explain why he hasn't proposed and recently stopped staying over as much. Maybe in fact he's *glad* that this is happening and he's going to use it—making me the "bad guy"—to finally get free of me. Even just thinking that gets me stirred up and angry, which mostly just hides the growing pit in my stomach.

Tru buzzes to let me know the Nintendo people are ready for our conference call. I've wasted too much time and energy dwelling on my star-crossed romance yet again. Clearly I'm not going to get this figured out right now after all, but at least this time I'm prepared for my meeting. I rally my focus and jump on the call, placing a temporary Band-Aid on my deeply bruised heart.

I TAKE IN SADDLE RANCH, the distinctive "rock 'n' roll meets Western barn" chophouse and bar. Normally this crowd favorite, with its exposed rafters, giant oval-shaped bar in the center, mechanical bull ring, and red felt–lined pool tables, is comforting, seeing as my girls and I have been regulars for years and I met Jacob here, but given what's going on, tonight it's bittersweet. I look around and note that I must be the first person to arrive for book club. Yes, we are the kind of book club that meets at Saddle Ranch. For once my BlackBerry is stowed away in the pocket of my purse and not an unnatural extension of my hand. Jacob would be proud. But immediately I push further thoughts of Jacob to the back corner of my mind. We're broken up—I better get used to the idea.

However, I've decided *not* to tell my friends tonight. That would make it all too real. And I don't want to spend the evening with everyone feeling sorry for me.

Lost in thought as I am, it takes a minute for me to feel the stare of the annoyed chick bartender. I order a vodka martini and, wonder of wonders, actually find an empty bar stool to sit on while I wait for my girlfriends. I glance around the bar, aware that my first instinct is to immediately break out the BlackBerry to get work done, or at the very least to seem to be in communication with someone. But as my eyes focus on a cozy couple clearly new to "true love," I forgo my "don't talk to me" defense mechanism and lose myself in a fantasy of what the sappy couple's life is like.

"Whoa . . . If it isn't Sophie Atwater. Where's your posse?" I don't even turn my head as Damon's voice draws me out of my too-sober trance.

"Hey, Damon. The girls will be here soon. So, good game on Saturday, huh?" Damon and I are natural enemies on every level, and any chance I have to get a dig in, is just, well, Darwinian. And my SC team did kick Bruin butt—Damon's rival alma mater—last weekend. We get one game a season to thump them down, and I have relished it just a little bit deeper since meeting Damon.

"Give me a break. The refs were ridiculous. The playback showed he was clearly off-sides. The BCS is a joke." Initiating an attack about football has the added benefit of distracting this supercilious jerk from the "I told you so" smugness I'm sure is just lurking beneath the surface if Jacob already told him of our breakup. Even so, I don't risk meeting his eyes. "Sophie . . . look . . ." For a second, I think I hear compassion in his voice. Like I said, I'm not looking directly at him, so I can't be sure, and I sure as hell am not about to check. Pity from him would be unbearable.

He starts to lean into me, and for a crazy second I think he's going to hug me or something. Every muscle tightens up in fight-or-flight mode. Jacob must have told him about our breakup and he's ready to gloat.

"What, Damon?" I snap in the bitchiest snobby voice I can muster.

Without any hesitation he carefully reaches past me and grabs a handful of the bar mix in a bowl. He straightens back up, still silent. He crunches a few nuts, never taking his eyes off me. I am totally withering under his stare, but try not to let it show.

"Nothing, Sophie. Nothing." He walks away and somehow it feels like he takes any hope I had of making up with Jacob with him. Weird, like I can see my happy ending with Jacob following Damon like a shadow as he leaves the bar without talking to anyone.

I down my martini and order another immediately. No more daydreaming for me.

Tina, who was once my freshman roommate, arrives first, and we make small talk at the bar, waiting for our friend JoAnn and the others. Tina, with her sweet pixie looks, takes forever to order her drink because she's flirting with the cute boy bartender, who of course rushes up to help her, while I spent ten minutes trying to get the chick bartender's attention a second time. While Tina is doing her thing, out of the corner of my eye I catch sight of someone who looks exactly like Billy from behind. I guess I was wrong about quitting that daydreaming. Now I'm hallucinating Billy Fox everywhere I go? But of course I have to get a better view of this look-alike. I tell Tina I'm going to the bathroom and edge around the bar, taking the long route to the back hallway.

There are three guys playing darts along the rear wall, in sort of a private section, but several girls are watching and cooing, blocking my view, so I make kind of an obvious beeline to get a better look.

And then the doppelganger turns his head, and it's him!

We lock eyes, and Billy's surprise and pleasure at seeing me shows immediately on his face. I can't say the same for mine. I have in fact no idea what expression I have on my face. I am thinking a million things a second as he approaches. *What are the chances? First I break up with Jacob and then I happen to run into Billy, in a town as big as LA. Is the universe sending me a sign?*

My head is spinning, but the fact that for the first time since we met I am truly "available" seems to be the only thing I can hang on to. I feel practically naked with the knowledge.

"Sophie Atwater. What a surprise to see you here." He doesn't spare a backward glance at the women in their group, which makes me feel like the only attractive woman on the planet.

"I'm meeting my girlfriends. My book club." I want to make sure he knows I'm not stalking him, or that I'm pathetically here alone.

"Impressive. A book club at a rowdy country bar on Sunset. That must be a first." His teasing relaxes me to the bone.

"Yeah, well, that's how we roll." I smile, feeling like it's the first real smile I've had in ages.

"I like how you roll, Sophie. But then, you already know that." He doesn't move closer, but he is totally turning on the charm. I can feel it like that electricity endurance game at theme parks. You hold on with both hands and see how long you can stand the pain. Whose dumb idea was that game? Anyway, the sparks are jetting through me right now, that's for sure.

"We broke up." I manage to not entirely blurt it out, but it is pretty direct. Way to play it cool. Also, *did we?*

"Really?" He doesn't smirk, but there is something new in his eyes. "I can't say I'm sorry." He pauses. "How are you doing?"

I can't bring myself to dismiss it verbally, but I try for a casual hair toss to communicate my point. "I should get back to my friend." I gesture toward the bar.

"Weren't you heading that way?" He points correctly to the

back hallway. We all use the bathroom, why is it embarrassing to have him know?

"Um, yeah."

"I'll walk with you." It's like ten steps.

"Okay." He falls in line with me but remains silent. We enter a smaller, more intimate hallway. The bathroom doors are at the end, next to an exit to the employee parking lot and smokers' patio. We are alone. I stop outside the women's restroom door and prepare to say a clear good-bye. I can't have him waiting for me, that is just beyond uncomfortable. But as I turn to face him, he presses me back against the wall. Before I know it, we are kissing outside the women's restroom. And it is an amazing kiss, even hotter and less self-conscious than on his doorstep. I forget everything for a second and just relish the moment.

His hands come to my waist and slide up under my arms. Not quite taking things to the next level, but not staying still either. The men's bathroom door swings open, but he doesn't stop. Keeping his head against my neck, he pulls me out the back door. In that instant my publicist instincts kick in. *He was protecting his face—he didn't want to be recognized . . . Oh my God . . . he could be recognized making out with me in a bar on Sunset. What the hell am I thinking?*

Forgive me for taking a second to put this all together. It's incredibly difficult to concentrate as Billy slides his delicious lips down to my collarbone. Now both hands are under my shirt and he is confidently easing them up my back. God it feels so good. He's smooth and confident and gorgeous. I so want to keep going, but we are now making out in the parking lot like a couple of idiot teenagers. If nothing else, I have to think about his image.

"Billy, we can't do this. Not here. It's too public. We have to stop." I'm not sure if I got all the words out, or just some of them . . . I'm not exactly riddled with conviction here. And he completely ignores me. Let me just say, he is an excellent kisser. But my PR instincts are still screaming at me. Regrettably, it's what he hired me for.

We both jump at the sound of an alley cat scurrying out from behind a Dumpster. In the distance there's the faint hum of traffic.

"Billy. Stop." I grab his hands and hold them still. With a lot of regret.

To his credit, Billy doesn't try to change my mind. He is still breathing heavily in my ear, but he seems to understand without my having to say it again that this is definitely not the time or place.

"I'll take you back inside." He looks me in the eyes for a second, kisses me again on the lips, and escorts me. Thank God for smokers paving the way to keep the back door from locking us out. We totally got away with this little episode.

Billy and I don't even say good-bye. I duck inside the restroom and straighten up. In the mirror, while I see that my lips are a bit swollen, I think I actually look quite collected. I do a few minor touch-ups and then keep myself in there for another minute or two. As long as I can stand it. I don't know whether he'll still be at the dartboard, or gone, or what. And I'm not even sure which I'd prefer.

I finally muster up the courage to leave the ladies' room and head back toward the bar. Billy and his friends are not at the dartboard, or any other nearby game area. I can't look too obviously, and I immediately spot Tina coming toward me.

"Where the hell were you? Was that *Billy Fox*?" I can't disguise my gasp. Did she see us? Oh God!

"You saw him?"

"Uh, yeah. Everyone in the bar is talking about how he was here, and then he walked with you down the hallway. Is he a client? Did you help him sneak out the back to avoid TMZ? What's he like? You have to tell me the whole story!" She keeps peppering me with questions long enough for me to sort out that she didn't in fact see anything and I am in the clear. And she's also given me a good cover story. Though I do wonder for the rest of the night, *Where* did *he disappear to?*

Now on my fourth extra dirty martini, I look around at the table of girls I've known since college and smile fondly. The book discussion aspect of our gathering was short-lived, especially once almost half of us confessed to barely cracking the more highbrow (read dense) selection. I am seated between Tina and JoAnn, a corporate lawyer I've know so long she bought me my first legal beer. I don't talk to them every day, or even every week. But when we do get together, it's as though no time has passed.

I order another round of drinks, thinking we need a toast "to friendship."

As our server brings over the crowded tray, it fuzzily occurs to me that the animated conversation has been flowing for some time without much of my own participation. And I drunkenly realize—these are my friends, my chosen family, who love me for who I am. Once Izzy left for the east coast, some of these girls became my lifeline. I decide I should confide in them after all. They will know just what to do. I put my arm affectionately around JoAnn and squeeze, the unexpected gesture startling her enough to tip her fresh wineglass over.

"Whoa . . . watch it! Sophie, these are my favorite jeans."

"Oops," I say, rushing to blot them with a pile of cocktail napkins. As I'm trying to help, I can't stop the spontaneous tears creeping into my eyes. "Sorry, JoAnn. I didn't mean to ruin them. Let me pay for dry cleaning. Shit."

"Sophie, it's fine. It's not that big a deal." JoAnn's voice has softened as she grabs the napkin mound I'm holding limply and lays it down on the table. She rotates in her seat to face me better. "What's going on? Is everything *okay*?" Nothing gets past my girlfriend.

I lean in and say, "I think I'm falling in love with someone else." The rest of the table is too distracted to overhear. But in truth, I'd take advice from any of them right about now.

"What do you mean?" Liquid courage loosens my tongue, and I backtrack and tell her the whole story. The charity event, the stolen kisses, the fights, the breakup—everything.

"But I always thought Jacob was good for you. He's so level-headed and kind. Have you tried talking to him?" Sensible JoAnn didn't even blink at the name Billy Fox. Unlike Tina, celebrity doesn't faze her. Ever the lawyer, she cuts to the heart of it. Hearing her say Jacob's name brings the tears back.

"No. I haven't said *anything* to him. But it's over. I'm free and single and can do whatever—or whoever—I want. There's a gorgeous movie star chasing me. Desiring *me*. I should be here celebrating my luck . . . yet it sometimes feels like a rebound. Or unreal. I don't know how to feel or what to do." I grasp the delicate stem of my fresh drink like a lifeline.

"Sophie. You did stuff behind Jacob's back. You're feeling confused and guilty. Figure out what you truly want and then honestly talk to Jacob. But promise me you'll really think this through. Obviously you are crushing on this *actor*." She clears her throat. "But we're talking about two different things here. If you want to break up with Jacob for good, you have to decide that based on what's going on between you and Jacob, not because of some other guy. And then you can figure out if you want to date Billy Fox. But don't abandon a *real* relationship, one that means so much to you, to both of you, for some fling with a guy you just met."

I take another swallow of my drink and try to process her words. Is she right? Am I really throwing away something so important on a "fling"? But how does JoAnn know it's just a "fling"? She hasn't met Billy. She has no idea what it's like between us. You can't put into words that kind of chemistry.

"JoAnn, I can't believe you think I'm throwing Jacob away for a 'fling.' Is that really what you think of me?" I hear my voice rising, but I can't help it. The more I think about it, the more horrified I am that she would even say that to me.

And the more terrified I am that she might be right.

My outburst gets the other girls' attention. The table suddenly seems very quiet.

"Calm down. I just meant that you should really consider this before everything's final." JoAnn tries to take my hand, but her soothing voice sends me over the edge.

"I wouldn't expect you to understand. When was the last time—"

From behind, a hand slaps over my mouth, but I am still trying to have my say as I am pulled away from the table and nearly dragged to the front door. I trip over the uneven concrete driveway and fall to my knees. Immediately, Tina is at my side helping me up. As the valet runs off to get her car, she dusts me off.

"What was that all about? You're officially worrying me."

"I'm fine," I mumble unconvincingly. All the fight has gone out of me and I am starting to feel a little nauseous. "I'm sorry, I'm so sorry."

And I am—for everything. For the entire mess I've created. And all the alcohol I've consumed to forget.

"It's all right, Sophie. Come on, let's get you home." Tina doesn't press for any more explanation. Instead, she eases me into the front seat of her Toyota, buckles me in like I'm a child, which I guess I am tonight, and together we pull onto Sunset, heading west. I'm grateful for the silence, the sisterhood, and the cool feel of the passenger-side window against my cheek. Rocked by the car's gentle vibrations, I finally close my tired eyes and for at least a few merciful minutes escape.

I GENUINELY DIDN'T CONSIDER that my car wouldn't be there in the morning until I am standing in front of my empty parking space in the garage. I even look around for a split second, seeing the cars of my neighbors, before it all hits me. Like a ton of bricks. This is what I imagine it must feel like to have your life flash before your eyes. I picture drinks with Billy, kissing him on his doorstep and in the back hallway and yet again outside the bar, walking up the steps to my condo and collapsing on my bed, thankfully alone. And then my mind zooms in on the "kissing Billy" part. And I must replay it in my head a million times.

Suddenly and without warning, I find myself sinking to my knees in the middle of the underground parking lot and crying. At first I can't imagine what's hit me so hard that I would be weeping like this. But as I continue sobbing, hot tears mixing with antifreeze on the pavement, I begin to realize why I'm crying.

Amazingly, it's not because of Billy, or my throbbing headache, or the major screwups at work, or being so stupid as to leave my car in West Hollywood. I'm crying because of Jacob. Pure and simple. And it took one insane night, and one too many drinks, to lead me to this epiphany. I don't want him. Billy, I mean. What I want—what I've always wanted—is Jacob. Kind, loving, handsome, loyal Jacob, who would never intentionally hurt me. Who I know loves me and would be devastated if he ever knew what had happened. It's not control but solidity that he offers. He's not flawless, but then again, clearly neither am I.

I've made a huge mistake.

Like I'm having one of those breakthroughs they often talk about on *Dr. Phil*, I suddenly find myself thinking totally lucidly about the whole obsession with Billy Fox. And I see that it *is* a symptom of a problem with my relationship with Jacob. But without a doubt I know in my gut that I want to fix that problem. That I want to make it right with Jacob. That *he's* the man I want to spend my life with, and I'm not going to just give that up because it's tough, or because some hot cowboy makes me feel good. A real relationship is so much more than that, and here I've been secretly wishing that Jacob would fight harder to keep me. But how could he? I haven't even told him that he's losing me. He has no idea how I feel, or that I'm questioning him.

I'm the one who needs to fight for our relationship right now. And that's exactly what I'm going to do.

Just as suddenly as they started, the tears stop. Now I'm completely focused on my plan. I've got to find a way to make things right with Jacob. Out comes the BlackBerry, but as I'm about to dial his number, it occurs to me that I don't really know what I'm going to say. I've got to figure out a strategy, so he knows how serious I am. And I can't let him know I'm stuck in my garage with no way of getting to work.

And, yeah, how *am* I going to get to work?

RIDING IN TRU'S VW BUG, I'm entranced by the fake flower on the dash. I can't stop staring at the plastic petals as she veers in and out of traffic on Wilshire. I still have no idea what I'm going to say to Jacob. But one thing is clear, I am going to have to tell him the truth. You'd think that would make it easier to figure out what to say . . . just tell him what happened and how you feel, right? That's your advice? Well, that's the stupidest thing I could do. Think about it! I have to figure out how to spin it, so that I tell him everything—because I do realize I have to tell him everything—but I've got to present it in just the right way or I really will lose him. Forever. And this is too important. I just wish I knew what way that "right way" is.

As soon as I arrive at the office, knowing Jacob won't be at his desk yet, I leave a message for him to call me, then I distract myself from willing the phone to ring by working on the upcoming Nintendo launch party. I didn't realize just how much my personal life had been preoccupying me, because now that it's settled—in my head at least—I am 100 percent able to focus and be the publicist extraordinaire I once prided myself on being.

My simple but genius idea for Nintendo is to get the two stars of the summer's breakout teen action movie to host a "tournament" of the new 3D game system at the launch party. The pretty cool setup will include a score-keeping tree following all the hip celebs competing. Obviously we'll be giving away great gift bags to all the celebs for attending, but in addition the winner of the tournament gets to donate $5,000 to their favorite charity. A nice altruistic touch.

After getting that all wrapped up, I look at the clock. 12:30 P.M. Why hasn't Jacob called me back? That's not a good sign. But I hesitate to leave another message. I don't want to seem like I'm stalking him. I settle on a short email, just so he knows why I'm trying to reach him. I didn't tell his assistant all the particulars—I mean, I don't want everyone in his office to know that we were fighting.

From: Sophie
To: Jacob
Subject: call me

Hey, I left a message with your assistant earlier. I just want you to know how sorry I am. You're right. We need to talk. S

No point in getting into all the gritty details in writing. He knows what I mean. Staring at the sent emails list will get me nowhere, so to distract myself while I wait for Jacob to get my messages, I shoot a due "email of shame" to Tina and JoAnn, apologizing for my behavior, and then round up a couple girls from the office for a group sushi run. Afterward one is kind enough to escort me to Saddle Ranch so I can pick up my car.

Over the afternoon, tons of accounts require catch-up. I make several calls on Billy Fox's account too. And surprisingly don't feel all that weird talking him up to magazines and talk shows after what's happened. Bottom line, he's still a smart, sexy, successful actor, and it's not difficult to promote him. No problem.

I keep myself so focused that it's not until after six-fifteen that I notice how unusually quiet the office seems. When I poke my head out, the mostly empty desks and dark offices confirm my suspicion.

"Tru, where *is* everybody?"

"There's an event downtown tonight and they rallied extra volunteers to set up," she says, the unmistakable industrial beat of Nine Inch Nails emanating from the unplugged earphone in her hand.

Ten minutes later I sense Tru lurking in my doorway. I look up—only it's not Tru.

"Billy!" Okay—I knew I was going to have to reach out and set the record straight. But I was hoping to do it outside the office. Possibly after the courage of a stiff drink. And certainly not until I have the chance to speak to Jacob. "Um . . . what are you doing here?"

"You said there was a bunch of stuff in your office for me. I thought I'd stop by and pick it up."

I glance around my cluttered office. There are boxes of stuff on the floor, Xeroxes and press kits and photos strewn everywhere from days of inattention.

"Yeah. Your gift bag from the premiere the other night is here, and . . ." Billy looks at the obscenely overflowing canvas bag, but his next words reveal his real motivation.

"I expected to hear from you." In its surprising vulnerability, I detect a stronger hint of his true Southern accent. Pretending not to hear, I begin sifting through the papers on my desk. Finally I uncover a FedEx package. "Ah, here are the tickets you requested to the Kid Rock concert. Do you want to take them now or should I have them sent to Wanda for safekeeping?"

Billy glances at the envelope in my hand and offers me a sheepish grin.

"You take them."

What? Major favors were pulled to get Billy these seats—with a backstage pass no less—two days before the concert, and now he doesn't want them?

"Well," he shifts his weight, and leans one slim hip against my desk, "remember you said how much you love Kid Rock? I asked if you could get tickets because I wanted to take you to the concert." Oh my God. "So . . . want to go with me?" Okay, Billy Fox is an expert in the "bedroom eyes" department. Completely against my will I feel my knees weaken. Billy's cologne drugs me a little as he leans in closer.

And then I remember Jacob.

I hadn't planned on having to spell it out for Billy so suddenly.

"Listen, Billy . . . here's the thing . . ." I sort of figured if I distanced myself from him over the next couple of weeks, he'd get the picture. I mean, he's that kind of guy—he's got women all over the place, he's not going to be that upset losing me, right?

For a start, I take a determined step back . . . and walk right into my rolling desk chair. Off-balance, I fall back—only catching the seat's edge—and feel the chair scooting away before the back of my head hits the ground. Billy instantly reaches out to catch my fall, only to end up sprawled with me behind the desk.

"Ow!" Okay—no subtle or graceful exit for me. I have to humiliate myself and then beat myself up on the way down.

"Sophie! Are you okay?" Billy, of course, still sounds cool and collected. Nothing throws this guy off his game. I whimper as he gently runs his hand through my hair to check for injuries. "Any excuse to play doctor."

"What the hell is going on?"

All of a sudden time stands still. At the sound of Jacob's angry voice, I literally feel the blood drain from my face. Think of the instant guilt and panic when a police car turns its siren on, regardless of how fast you're going. Well, multiply that by a million and you will begin to understand how I feel in the long seconds that crawl by as I gently push Billy off me and pull myself to my feet.

"Sophie." Jacob's voice is utterly void of emotion now. He doesn't sound angry, hurt, anything. But his jaw seems so clenched I can only imagine the horrible thoughts running through his head.

"Hey, man. It's no big deal." Billy's suave tones are like nails on a chalkboard in the brutal silence. He's clearly one of those types who have to fill uncomfortable silences with chatter. "She slipped, and I—"

"Sophie, what's going on here?" Apparently Jacob is not interested in Billy's version of events. And the horrible thing is I can't summon the courage to tell Jacob the truth. The truth that Billy was hitting on me, and that I was tempted to respond. That I *was* attracted to him. I can't plead innocent when I wasn't.

"Jacob, right?" continues Billy. "Look, she's a good girl. She told me all about you actually."

And that's when I finally see Jacob lose control.

"*Get out.*" Jacob's harsh, low growl or his firm step forward finally succeeds in antagonizing Billy. And to my horror he steps in front of me—to *protect* me from Jacob. I am mortified to realize that I am frozen. And honestly, I don't know if it's fear of what Jacob might do or the entire embarrassing situation of this coming to a head at the office. But as this all is unfolding in front of me, I feel like a spectator, like those people who have near-death out-of-body experiences. Only, clearly, I am here, and my lack of response is only making things worse.

In the moment, I am unable to form words or move any part of my body. And Billy clearly misinterprets my fear and decides to play the hero. "Look, I don't know what you think has happened, but you're wrong. And I am not leaving until we clear things up." Billy turns to me and touches my arm. "Sophie . . . you okay?" In frame-by-frame slow motion I look down at Billy's hand on my skin. It takes me what seems like hours to notice how weird it is that I am so numb I can't feel it. I am staring at his hand and I just can't feel the pressure or the heat or anything. And then I lift my eyes to Jacob. He is standing in the doorway, his eyes glued to mine.

"Sophie." All he says is my name. And all of a sudden I completely lose it. All the pressure, the guilt I've been feeling for weeks, and the embarrassment chokes me. I haven't cried so hard in public since I was twelve. I feel the tears overflowing, pouring down my cheeks, again as though this is all happening to someone else. And believe me, if I were in a movie theater watching this scene I'd be scoffing to my companion because of how ridiculous it was that the girl would just flee the moment. "*Please*," I'd say. "Why didn't she just say that nothing happened? No one would just leave like that!"

Well, as humiliating as it is to admit, that's exactly what I do. I can't meet Jacob's eyes. My arm slips from Billy's grasp—probably because me running is the last thing he expects. I leave them both standing in my office and I run. Straight to the ladies' bathroom, always a reliable safe haven. After throwing up, I wash my face and try to avoid my reflection, resigned to staying in there for the rest of my life.

10

NOT KNOWING WHAT ELSE TO DO, I SLOWLY HEAD BACK TO MY desk. I've no real sense of how long I spent hiding, but it was significant enough for any remaining witnesses to steer clear and depart. The empty cubicles and desks around me are a relief because I wouldn't know what to say to Tru or any other concerned coworkers anyway. But when I arrive at my office, it too is empty. Both Jacob and Billy are gone. I don't know what to make of their disappearance. I sit down at my desk and stare at the computer screen. Microsoft Outlook's help icon blinks back at me. Does Bill Gates have a help menu for this? For completely fucking up your life? Could I search that under topics?

Before I can talk myself out of it, the phone is in my hand and I'm dialing Jacob's number.

"Hey. You've reached Jacob's cell. Leave a message." The easygoing tone is like a time capsule of better, uncomplicated days. I listen to his familiar deep voice, trying to formulate what to say. Should I just apologize and beg forgiveness? Minimize what happened? Try to explain? *Beeep.*

"It's me. Sophie." Oh yeah, that's good. Like he doesn't recognize your voice. "Right, you know it's me. Listen, we have to talk. I can explain. Please call me." There is so much I want to say. My brain is literally stuffed with things to express, things I wish I had faced earlier, but none find their way out. "Please." And I hang up.

There's nothing else to do but wait—and frankly, I could use the extra time to collect my thoughts. I'm emotionally exhausted. Even workaholic me can see there's no way I'm focusing on any other task this evening. Time to close up shop. Sophie Atwater's Day of Destruction is officially closed for business. And not a moment too soon. A strong pour and then soaking in the world's longest bath is all I can think about.

The tough thoughts can wait for the morning.

Habit takes over, and I gather my things, log off my computer, grab my purse, and am about to switch off the overhead lights when the office phone rings.

Jacob. The pit of my stomach tightens. I'm not ready.

But the caller ID shows not Jacob, but Elle. And it's her direct line. Apparently someone else is working later than usual.

I reach for the receiver before voicemail intercepts. "This is Sophie."

"Would you kindly come up and see me before leaving tonight." Elle's formal tone is—as always—the Mona Lisa smile of aural interpretation. But it's definitely a summons, not a casual request. After seven years, I know her well enough to realize this isn't a social call. Great. Now what? Did word somehow get to her about the scene in my office? Doubtful. Tru's not one to gossip. Or did Priscilla already mess up the Wrestling account? Of all days, I'm not in the mood to deal with her incompetence and any managerial blame.

Better to get it over with. "I'm on my way."

Lucas is also gone for the day, so I announce myself at Elle's open doorway. She's standing with her back turned, gazing at a tableau of framed photos. The wall of grinning Bennett/Peters clients, their trainer-toned arms draped chummily over Elle's shoulders, is a virtual who's who of Hollywood. It's an impressive testimony to her outreach and reputation.

"You wanted to see me?" I say.

Despite the assumed damage control to address, a visit to Elle's office suite tonight is almost comforting. She's of the tribe of hard-edged former New Yorkers who readily took to the abundant sunshine and casual chicness of Southern California. In sharp contrast to my cluttered and comparably chaotic workstation, hers always reminds me of a cozy boutique hotel, complete with its inviting sitting area of facing ultra-suede couches, with an assortment of trendy throw pillows, that sandwich a vintage coffee table. I swear the air even smells faintly of jasmine.

If this little dose of Zen is my future, I'm on the right path.

"Yes. Please close the door."

Okay, *something's up* because at this early evening hour only the cleaning crew might overhear. *Oh Priscilla, what have you done . . . ?*

I shut the door, my curiosity piqued.

Elle turns around and motions for me to take a seat. I try to read her face, determined to judge the category of shitstorm ahead, but she's far too Sphinx-like—or possibly Botoxed—to decipher. "What's up?" I ask neutrally, running a finger across the nubby texture of an adjacent pillow.

"We've been working together now for what, seven years or

so?" I nod, still trying to piece together where this is going. "You've proven yourself repeatedly to be a valuable asset of Bennett/Peters. I'm not always the most effusive with praise, but I want you to know that I've come to highly respect and trust you."

Wow. This is so *not* what I was expecting—however nice to hear—and I can feel my shoulders relax and sink back more comfortably into the cushion. Despite my recent tardiness and slipups, I *am* a great publicist. And to be recognized as such by Elle, especially at the end of what felt like the worst day ever, is a sign of hope. Somehow everything—the current mess I've made of my life—will work itself out.

And most remarkably, am I about to get promoted or something?! Why else would she ask me to shut the door to start singing my praises? After all the earlier tears, it feels amazing to crack a smile. After the day I've had, this is really incredible timing.

"Thank you, Elle. You don't know how good that is to—"

"And now you've put us—*me*—in a very uncomfortable position."

Wait. What?

Only now do I notice that Elle isn't smiling at all.

"I'm worried about your judgment, Sophie," Elle continues, now restlessly pacing in front of her desk. "I'm concerned about your recent lack of focus." Each sentence hits me like a rock thrown in the dark. "And I'm very disappointed by some client interaction."

In an instant, I'm on my feet, cheeks flushed, ready to defend myself. "Elle, once again I'm *so sorry* about the Nintendo meeting and any other seeming lack of focus lately. That won't ever happen again, I promise. You know I'm one hundred percent committed to my job and would never—"

"Do we need to discuss Billy Fox?"

Billy. All the incited fight in me evaporates. *She knows.* I take a step back and sit on the edge of the couch. I feel light-headed. How could I be so stupid?

And it only gets worse.

Elle stops pacing to join me on the couch, at the opposite end, a small cluster of pillows between us. There's nowhere to hide as she peers at me wistfully. "Understand, the inappropriateness is not the issue. These things happen."

I meet her gaze. She's a woman. She understands.

"Initially there were rumors. But gossip is like smog in this town—everywhere, and you simply learn to ignore it. But then photographs—*extra steamy* photographs shot in what looks to be a back alley—of Billy Fox and his new 'mystery paramour' surfaced, ready to circulate in the gossip columns and on the websites."

Oh my God.

"Luckily a media contact of Priscilla's got advance word of the photos' existence and she was able to forewarn us of the imminent scandal."

The potential repercussions were clear. If the truth got out, it might damage Billy's *and* the firm's reputation. Given that, Elle explains, she and Billy's manager, Wanda, paid off the source.

I am horrified on so many levels. *How* did anyone know about Billy's and my budding romance? We were careful. I'm

erratic emotion at bay) and update my outgoing messages. Elle's taken it upon herself to notify my clients and their management. As with many troubled starlets and pop stars before me, the absence will be attributed to inscrutable "exhaustion," as if I simply overworked myself into a corner, which in a way I did. I force thoughts of Tru, Jeff, and the rest of the team's private reaction to my little breakdown and sudden departure out of my mind. It's all too humiliating to consider.

On the corner of my desk a small framed photo catches my eye. I pick it up for a closer look. It's of Jacob and me from our trip to San Francisco. We're nestled close in a rowboat at Stow Lake in Golden Gate Park, Jacob's left arm around me, his right extended out of frame to work the camera. I remember laughing with the unbalanced boat's rocking, and the trial snapshots chopping off our heads or capturing clouds. There's simple joy on our faces. I barely recognize that girl of half a year ago. What happened to her?

To *us*? To lead me here?

The happy memory has been staring at me—just to the left of my computer monitor—for months. And yet I'm looking at it now as if for the first time. When did it—*Jacob*—fall into my blind spot? I slip the slender frame into my purse and without a look back head to the elevators.

Only to encounter a barracuda in Balenciaga.

"Sophie, darling," Priscilla says, her skinny ass blocking the call button. "It's such a relief to hear you're taking a well-deserved break. Good for you."

We're alone at the elevator bank. I should have sensed her circling—like a buzzard.

As if for the benefit of a nonexistent audience, she continues. "I can't imagine how *exhausted* you must be." The most condescending smile cracks her face. "Don't you worry. I'll take good care of your clients." She moves aside and calls the elevator for me. "Well, maybe not quite as much *personal attention*."

If I didn't think it would force Elle and HR to make my break permanent, I would have readily decked the smug bitch that helped "save" my job.

Lifesaver, my ass. It worked out too well for her to be coincidental. There's no doubt in my mind that Priscilla somehow played a major role in my ousting. If it's my last business at Bennett/Peters, I will find out how and take her down.

Throughout the hour-long drive home, I check my phone incessantly. There's no word from Jacob. Or Billy, for that matter. And now I'm suspended from work, the place that was even more "home" to me than my condo. To this workaholic, I might as well have been fired. It *feels* like being fired, the void of the days ahead unbearable. And then there's the self-disgust. I can't even look at my BlackBerry in dread of the sure-to-come collective advice of bed rest, boosting vitamins, and homeopathic treatments from those sincerely wishing me a swift recovery.

What am I going to tell Izzy? My parents?

It's a fine mess.

That's when I realize I do have a plan. My plan is to curl up on the sofa, drink a bottle of wine, and die. My plan is to stay in the fetal position until someone calls the landlord about the smell from my apartment. And then the police can come collect the body.

Tonight, all I want to feel is numb.

I drop my bags inside the front door and march into the kitchen. I stare at my nearly depleted wine rack. Two bottles? How did this happen? But if I ever deserved wine, tonight is the night. So with complete righteousness, I bypass the Riesling and grab the bottle of Opus One that Jacob bought me when we were touring Napa wineries one romantic weekend. The prized bottle we talked about opening ten years later. It was the first time we really made plans, as a couple, for a shared future.

I remember how exciting that moment felt. Its promise.

And then I recall the hurt look on Jacob's face as he said my name just hours ago. The foil can't come off fast enough. The corkscrew may as well be embedded in my heart. I just want to dull the pain. Overcome with grief, I jerk the cork too strongly and it breaks in two, half-trapped in the neck of the bottle.

Of course.

I dig around my seldom-used kitchen drawers for something, anything, to poke it back into the wine. And then I stop.

I don't want to be that girl anymore, drowning her problems.

If I resist the heavy pull—at least tonight—then I've done *one* thing right.

And really, I've got to start somewhere.

I return the wrecked bottle to the rack, peel off my shoes, and curl up on the couch. It's *Survivor* night. I wonder if Jacob is doing the same across town and if he's thinking of me. I resign myself to watching *Survivor* solo for the first time, determined to find immunity from my own troubled self.

11

WITH PLENTY OF TREPIDATION AND VERY LITTLE APPETITE
I'm on my way to meet Jacob for Thai. Though left unsaid in his
texted invite and my even briefer acceptance this morning, we
both know "The Talk" is on the menu.

No wonder I feel nauseous.

He finally texted just after *Survivor* ended last night:

MEET ME TOMORROW AT TUK TUK AT 6:30?

Short and to the point.

Now here I am walking into a restaurant that thinks it's one
velvet rope away from being a trendy nightclub. As if pad thai
required its own DJ. But the establishment is roughly equal
distance between our homes, and at 6:30 P.M. we're meeting
early enough to ensure it's near-empty and the house music is
at a more ambient than tabletop-dancing level. Still, is *this* to
be the climax of our romance and culinary quest—a generic
Thai joint? The thought is too depressing.

Jacob's already inside, nursing a Singha beer as he reclines
against the tufted white leather banquette. He's still in work
clothes, but the tie has been put away and his shirt's top few

buttons left undone, revealing bare throat and a glimpse of chest hair. "Mr. Steady" looks good—maybe not "model pretty" like Billy, but in the short seconds I get to take him in before he notes my arrival, my pulse quickens.

Once I'm seated in my chic yet not all that comfortable plastic chair, his eyes on mine reflect a familiar carousel of conflicting emotions. We may look like any couple on Date Night, but there's palpable tension radiating from Table Twelve. And it's more than a Singha and the smiling Buddha figurine in a neighboring alcove can assuage.

"I don't even know where to begin . . . ," Jacob says, his fingers absentmindedly tugging at a corner of the beer bottle's label.

If only I could reach over and kiss him, reassure him there's nothing to discuss. We're all good. Let sleeping dogs lie and all that. But I know it can't be so easy.

"We're meeting and talking. That's a start." I place my hand over his restless fingers. He doesn't pull away, but he doesn't exactly take my hand.

"I know things haven't been perfect between us lately," Jacob continues, "but . . . okay, I'll bite. What the hell was that all about yesterday?"

With impeccable timing, the clueless waitress arrives to fill water glasses, list the specials, and take our order. A part of me wants her to never leave us, as if her orderly presence could forever keep any messy conversation or consequence to my relationship with Jacob at bay. But collected menus in hand, she leaves me to my fate.

Now it's my turn to fidget, tracing the soft marigold petals in the center bud vase. I can't lie to Jacob. But I don't want to hurt him either. Or lose him . . . if there's any hope of fixing us. What's the truth without being *too* truthful?

"Yesterday—in my office—was a huge misunderstanding," I blurt out. "You've got nothing to worry about with Billy Fox."

"That was a whole lot of tears over nothing."

How do you refute that? Jacob's no fool.

Deflect.

"For weeks now, something's been off between us," I say. "You must have felt it too. We were in a rut." And then I madly just blurt it out. "And then sometimes I think about the future."

"I knew things were off. And I tried to get you to talk to me that night at your place. But what are you saying?"

"We've been together for nearly two years and I still don't know where we're going. You never discuss the future. I love you, Jacob. But I'm terrified that you're comfortable with the status quo. And I'm . . . not."

"Are you talking about marriage? Haven't we both seen enough relationships fall apart over a piece of paper? We had something great here. Together. I don't want to mess it up for some technicality." I'm dumbstruck by his words. My gut was right—Jacob doesn't want to marry me, as I feared all along. Obviously the word "marriage" is just not in his vocabulary, and I'm so hung up on hearing the void of it, I almost miss the next part. "I want to be with you and only you, Sophie. But let's let the future be what the future will be."

Happiness left to c'est la vie. It isn't enough.

"I didn't look for it," I say, the words tumbling out, no matter how much I wish to protect him. And us. I know the truth will harm him, but keeping it inside is perhaps more unfair to him. "I didn't even believe it at first when Billy flirted with me. But the fact that I let myself be charmed . . . means something."

"Yeah, that you'll fall for a cliché." *Ouch.* "Was George Clooney or Bradley Cooper unavailable? Why, Soph? And of all people . . . *him?!* Billy Fox? Is that even a real name or something they manufactured in Hollywood?"

Exit Easygoing Jacob. I know all about hurt pride.

"Look, I get that you're upset . . . but nothing really happened. We made out. It's not like we slept together. And I felt you and I had broken up."

"Oh, well I guess everything's great, then."

"It was a mistake. I realize that now. Jacob, I want things to work out. I want you."

"Well you have a funny way of showing it. Instead of being mature and, I don't know, *talking about it*, you're out test-driving, kissing other men—"

"*One man. Once.*" *No time to be a stickler.*

"Whatever." He bitterly laughs, signaling the waitress for another beer. "If you'd had a ring on your finger, would that have made a difference with Billy Fucking Fox? And you're asking *why* I haven't proposed. Doesn't that answer your own question?"

"That's not fair . . ."

"No, what isn't fair is that you decide our relationship is over without consulting me."

"*You* spoke of our relationship in the past tense. The message was clear. Am I supposed to wait for the official press release?"

The fragrant food and Jacob's second beer arrive, signaling

the end of Round One. The clued-in waitress can't leave our table fast enough. In fact all eyes around us are conspicuously averted, the clearest indication that our heated row is tonight's main entertainment. We pick at our meals in steely silence, becoming that dispassionate couple we used to privately point out and smugly whisper, "What's *their* problem?"

Finally Jacob pushes aside his plate of Panang Curry. "I called you at work today to reconfirm, but Tru said you were 'on leave.' She seemed kind of surprised that I didn't know."

Round Two.

I put down my own chopsticks, searching for any way to prevent a deepening crack from shattering. Why can't we get to the "other stuff" later?

"Yeah. I'm taking some time off," I say as if it's nothing. As if Jacob doesn't know any voluntary absence from work on my part would involve a serious medical condition or act of God. "Mental health day" isn't exactly in my vocabulary.

"Oh really? Hmm. Finally making time for your scrapbooking?" Jacob says, and actually cracks a smile. Even with all the preceding tension, we share a laugh at the absurdity of the scenario. I'd sooner take up needlepoint or knit sweaters from cat hair.

"Belly dancing lessons actually," I banter back, relieved to have some humor in this conversation. "Great for the core." For a moment, we're back to our old selves, exchanging sophomoric jokes. Relaxed and in tune with each other. My error is getting swept up in the easy flow. "I got screwed at work."

The look on Jacob's face makes me realize the incredibly poor choice of words.

"No! I mean I got in trouble with Elle. She heard about . . . the whole Billy thing." I'm floundering, drowning in my own confession. "That was bad. But when the photos surfaced—"

"*Photos?!*"

"Yeah. It's weird. I have no idea how someone managed to capture the kiss—"

"That's what bothers you most? How you got *caught*?"

What a fool I am. Again. "No." The respite we found, the welcome reminder of our chemistry, drops away as if we confused a tiny ledge for solid ground. His hazel eyes go blank and distant. "Jacob, please say something."

"I think you should go."

"Jacob."

It can't end like this.

"Just go," he says flatly. "Please."

There's no arguing. I remove my wallet, drop some cash on the table, and reluctantly agree to his wishes.

"And just so we're clear," he says, as I take my first step away, "we're done."

I walk out with my head up even though I'm dying inside.

"Thank you! Have a good night!" chirps the miniskirted hostess on automatic pilot as I exit the restaurant.

Outside, the evening lights and traffic sounds on San Vicente Boulevard are disorienting. I pause under the gray-and-white striped awning, watching others go blithely about their lives. That's when I realize I'm still clutching my wallet. As I return it safely to my purse, my hand brushes something cool and metallic.

The framed photo from my desk. I'd forgotten all about it.

It's my wake-up call. I love Jacob, yet if it was meant to be— the *right* relationship—wouldn't I have fought stronger? Refused to let it go? Wouldn't he have gotten over himself months ago and proposed, determined never to lose me? Maybe he's right. *C'est la vie.*

Keep telling yourself that, Sophie.

And maybe, eventually, I'll believe it.

EVERYONE KNOWS, like it or not, that life is full of surprises. But it still takes us off-guard when the unexpected comes from within, when we find that the unpredictable stranger is ourself. Why else would I be huddled here, in the telltale self-help section of my mom's store, with a half-asleep cat in my lap?

"Do you want to tell me about it?"

"Do I have much of a choice?" I ask resignedly, peering up at my mom, whose tortoiseshell reading glasses hang from her neck.

"You're here," she says perceptively, moving aside the little tower of books I pulled and joining me on the carpet tiles. "I'd love to imagine you dropped by just to say hi and support an independent bookseller, but I sense you could use a shoulder."

She's right, even if my unannounced visit is as much a shock to me as to her. I got in the car after my disastrous dinner with Jacob, but instead of driving home, I found myself headed in this direction. The bookstore's warm glow against the surrounding night was nearly magnetic. I wanted the comforting smell of books, the relative hush of evening browsers, the melodic jingle each time someone entered.

I wanted my mom. There, I said it.

"Oh honey, what's wrong?" she asks, placing my head on her shoulder, a reassuring gesture from long ago that still feels instantly natural.

"What *isn't*?" I tell her everything. Well, almost everything—she's still my mom. My troubles with Jacob. The PG-13 trouble of Billy. My affected job. Tonight's fight and the end of a relationship. Remarkably, the only interruption is when she has to excuse herself to ring up or help an occasional customer. By the time I'm done unloading, the front door is locked, CLOSED sign turned, and it's just the two of us plus Libro, who slowly crawls out of my lap, stretches, and then returns to his window-seat bed. A rough life that one keeps. *I'll trade lives. I could use eight more shots at this.*

"*Do you* have a drinking problem?" my mom finally asks, as neutral as one can.

"No. It's more a *thinking* problem, though too much alcohol doesn't help." And that's the truth. I won't blame booze for my problems. Yes, I've overindulged lately. But take it away and everything won't be better. It's the symptom of a bigger problem. An escape. I accept responsibility.

There's something I have to ask. "Do *you* think I made a mistake?"

"Who's to say? In matters of the heart, no one has all the answers. To be fickle is to be human. We have to embrace—and learn from—some trial and error. Your father and I just want you to be happy."

"How did someone so wise as you end up with a daughter like me?"

"Switched at birth?"

"Mom! That was a rhetorical question."

"Oh sweetheart, I'm kidding." She kisses the top of my head. "You know, we two Atwaters are more alike than you imagine. Certainly more than you give yourself credit for. It's why we sometimes butt heads."

I look at her skeptically.

"For instance, you inherited my stubborn gene—though I suppose you got some help there from your father too. And you've got the drive, which is a wonderful thing . . . but it can be blinding if you're not careful."

"Oh, I've got plenty of time to ride it out right now," I say, the thought of sitting at home insufferable. Now that I'm not buried in work, I don't know what to do with myself. It must show on my face.

"Tell you what. Let's surprise your father. Come home for dessert. Or dinner if you're still hungry. We'll take you any day of the week."

I did barely manage to eat earlier. And the alternative is mentally replaying my conversation with Jacob in a despairing loop. Choice made.

"We're on," I say. "What's for dinner?"

A VERY WELCOMING LIZZIE waits with me on the den's couch, head resting in my lap, as my parents confer in the kitchen. Technically they're discussing dinner options, but I know my mom is bringing the other half of the household up to speed on my developments.

I'm a grown woman but the enduring child in me irrationally fears she's about to be grounded.

After a few minutes my dad sits down next to me, takes the remote from my hand, and mutes the TV I was only half-watching.

"How you doing, kiddo?" he asks in his straightforward way.

I know he's not comfortable with lengthy discussions on feelings, but he's never been one to back down from a challenge. And as I contemplate his question, I realize I'm okay. I mean . . . not really. I got suspended from a job I love; I'm heartbroken over losing my boyfriend. But actually, I'm okay.

We've been silent for a while and he's still waiting for an answer.

"I'll survive," I end up saying. Not because I can't talk to him about my problems, but mostly because it's true. Right now, I'm just figuring out that I will survive. Not in a Gloria Gaynor way. Not yet. But I'm getting there.

"Okay, hon. Okay." My dad is not the one who will push me to open up, or force me to discuss and rehash stuff to death. As a teenager I thought he was being obtuse or borderline neglectful because I wanted him to drag stuff out of me. I didn't want to just answer the question. I wanted him to work for it. Now I see that he doesn't miss a beat, my dad. He's reading between the lines, and he knows me so well that if I have a serious problem, something I really need to get out . . . he's let me know he's available. And it's up to me to take the next step. He can't do that for me. So he'll accept a vague answer, knowing that it's either true and we can move on, or he'll be hearing more about it when I'm ready. Have I mentioned that I love my dad? I do.

"Sophie?" my mom calls from the kitchen. "I could use your help in here."

That's doubtful, as my mom is anything but deficient in the kitchen. But tonight I welcome the gracious invite, the opportunity to hang at her side. And true to her word, she puts me to work. Watching me butcher garden tomatoes for the salad, she silently takes the paring knife away and hands me the serrated bread knife. The simple switch takes the task from bruised and messy to perfect and painless. What did she say earlier? Trial and error. I get it now. In her own way, that's my mom; leading by example, leading through love.

There's no quick fix for my heart. The visit doesn't erase the pain. But it does feel a teeny bit more manageable.

Hours later, I return home with a full belly and a doggie bag of optimism.

Little do I know how soon my resolve will be tested.

12

IT'S BILLY WHO BREAKS THE NEW PROTOCOL. FOUR "WORK"
days into my Bennett/Peters exile, I wake up to find his text
message:

> HEY S. NEED YOUR EXPERTISE.
>
> WANDA NEEDN'T KNOW. BF

Yes, I should have immediately deleted it, per Elle's decree.
Going directly against her wishes isn't exactly the surefire path
to restoring faith. Let Priscilla handle it. Walk away.

But . . .

I am going stir-crazy in my condo. The place has never been
neater, and I'm up on all the *Real Housewives* and cupcake competition shows. I'm not under house arrest, but minus the struc-
ture of my old life, I'm too listless to take real advantage of the
unaccustomed freedom. And what if a peer or client spots non-
exhausted me? Staying in is my form of denial—as if the office
is temporarily closed for fumigation.

I've been dodging Izzy's calls for days.

But even I have my limits.

The request for my "expertise" stokes dormant publicist pride.

I'm curious. I'm bored.

Besides, Billy already knows the truth of my "exhaustion."

And as Jacob made very clear—I'm single.

I make the call.

As it turns out, Billy's message is a request for my "trusted female opinion" on potential wardrobe for an upcoming audition. I'm flattered that—of all people—he thought of me. Certainly I know enough about wardrobe—I work side by side with stylists for photo shoots and red carpet events to make sure my clients look exactly right in each appearance. I agree to help him out—and me in turn—appreciating the excuse to look presentable and get out of the condo.

It's not a romantic rendezvous, I remind myself.

"So I was thinking you could come over to my place," Billy suggests over the phone. "I never got to show you the back deck, pool, and hot tub. It's perfect. We can hang out after maybe. And you can relax. Short of a helicopter ambush, the fence and landscaping keep it paparazzi-proof."

Maybe *I'm* not the one who needs reminding.

In truth, this wasn't our first communication since last week's disaster. From my personal account, I'd immediately emailed Billy with the bad news before Elle or Wanda could initiate damage control. And I let him know I felt it's not going to work between us. To his credit, he was understanding and, after a marathon text-messaging session, reluctantly agreed that we should try being friends. Once Billy discovered just how much our budding "relationship" had cost me, he honestly felt awful. I barely dissuaded him from talking to Elle, figuring it would only make things worse. I knew better and need to accept responsibility.

It's not that I'm not into him. But after realizing too late that Jacob was "the one" for me, I need a romantic time-out, a solid step back to determine my next move. Joining Billy at his Hollywood Hills home is a bad idea. His pheromones alone are intoxicating; I don't need an entire house of possibilities. And if we're spotted together, there has to be at least a shred of plausible deniability. Otherwise I may as well kiss my job 100 percent good-bye.

But I'm tempted in spite of myself.

"Maybe we can we meet somewhere . . . a little less intimate?" I say. "If Elle learned I was at your place . . ."

"Say no more. You're helping me out. The last thing I want is to get you in trouble. Or *any more* trouble. Hey, I've got an idea. You know Clutch on Melrose?"

I do. It's a stylish boutique à la DASH, owned by Missy Tyler, a former child actor turned reality TV star, who successfully spun her fame into retail versus rehab.

"Missy and I are old friends," Billy says. "Well, old for this town at least. I'm sure she wouldn't mind us taking over the VIP lounge a half hour or so before they close. If anyone spies us, you're just out shopping. As you said when we met—stick as close to the truth as possible. Easier to remember." Even across town, I can instantly picture his disarming smile.

Everyone wants to be famous, but as I've witnessed from the sidelines, the end of anonymity is no joke. We're told, "Stars—

they're just like us," but it's not like Billy can offer to meet up undisturbed at the local Starbucks or Coffee Bean. So compared to the literal hotbed of his reclusive mansion, a visit to Clutch sounds ideal. Maybe I'll even score a discount.

"I'm in," I say.

"Great. Let me give Missy the heads-up and I'll text you the details."

I'm about to disconnect and start pulling myself together, when he continues.

"And Sophie?"

"Yeah?"

"It's good to hear your voice," he says. "And for the record, I'm sorry about, well, everything."

Me too.

A QUICK PEEK at Clutch's tucked price tags reminds me why the chic spot is not my go-to. But the covetable collection of clothing and accessories is incredibly well curated and meticulously displayed. It's a richer girl's candy store of fashion. The vibe is pure Hollywood Regency glamour, with antique mirrored storage, a bold sixties-inspired graphic rug underfoot, tailored white wingback chairs for lounging, and a cascading crystal chandelier. Imagine the love child of Kelly Wearstler and Rachel Zoe. The space smells divinely of fresh grapefruit and mint. Ella Fitzgerald is singing "Love for Sale." Just try to resist.

There's a small but gorgeous selection of men's clothes toward the back. Any of them would fit perfectly into Billy's versatile good looks.

At this hour there are only a few other shoppers present. I'm leaning against an ample table covered in perfectly folded tops in a range of gemstone colors.

There might have been less temptation at Billy's.

"Sophie?"

I turn to a waify salesgirl with an enviable blowout. "Yes?"

"Your friend is already waiting in the lounge. Please follow me."

Very discreet. I'm impressed. Thank you, Missy.

I follow my guide through a curtain and down a short carpeted hall separated from the other changing areas. She gestures to a closed door, nods, and leaves me.

Am I supposed to knock? I don't want to barge in unannounced if Billy's in there changing. I'm about to knock when the door suddenly opens and once again I'm face-to-face with the delectable Billy Fox.

"There you are," he says, flashing his megawatt smile. "I thought I heard footsteps outside. Come in. I was worried you got lost."

He looks good (surprise surprise) dressed casually in a white V-neck tee, Diesel jeans, and black motorcycle boots. A less tortured James Dean, with a tan. We embrace—or rather I stand there in the doorway, a little self-conscious in my teal DVF wrap dress and heels, as he hugs me, planting a brief kiss on my cheek, and draws me into the chamber.

I wasn't sure how I'd feel seeing Billy again. On the ride over, I promised myself nothing had changed. My choice of Jacob arrived too late, but the rationale stands. I just need a distraction. And if it's a gorgeous slab of blue-eyed demigod, who's to argue? But now more than ever, around him, I'm a whirlpool of emotions. It's like my insides are a frozen yogurt swirl of lust, guilt, regret, and curiosity.

The intimate environment isn't helping.

Clutch's VIP lounge is predominantly a coral velvet circular settee. Thick brocaded drapes wrap a private changing area. An enormous framed mirror with a few shirt options hanging casually from the frame leans against the damask wallpaper, reflecting my bemusement. It's definitely not Starbucks.

Way to stick to your guns, Soph. Does he have to wear a shirt at all?

I can't decide if Billy is the most devilish Don Juan or I'm just utterly clueless.

"Take a seat. Get comfortable," Billy says, moving aside a set of scripts topped with his sunglasses. "Can I offer you a drink? There's vitamin water or chilled Sancerre in the mini-fridge."

It takes all my willpower to request the sensible water. Billy helps himself to a glass of wine, resting the stem glass and open bottle at his feet as he joins me on the upholstered seating.

"What's new?" I ask, pretending it's just a casual catch-up.

"Other than losing my favorite publicist? I know I said it before but I feel really terrible about what happened." He turns to me and winks. "Well, the fallout at least."

"I prefer to see it as a sabbatical."

"Just hurry back, will you? If I have to listen to Priscilla's haughty voice much longer, I'm hiring a personal assistant just to take her calls. What's her deal anyway?"

"Vampire blood, I suspect." It feels good to laugh, to release some of the bottled frustration.

"Did you, um, catch my Malibu beach 'date' with Eva Mendes in the papers? That's purely Wanda's handiwork."

This nugget *is* news to me. I'd self-quarantined all entertainment media the past few days, partly in fear of finding myself in a blind item. Or Priscilla lurking in the background with any of my clients. The era of studio "matchmaking" may be over, but it's not uncommon for crafty agents and managers still to pair up their clients for publicity or deception. There's no better guaranteed attention than when a fresh pair of shiny stars align.

"Eva's pretty amazing," Billy continues, "but she's not my type."

"Yeah, she's awfully heinous," I deadpan.

"How are things with Jake?"

No pussyfooting around.

"*Jacob.* Over." I close my eyes but still see Jacob's crushed expression, hear the angry parting words. "I don't want to talk about it."

"Well, if it helps, anyone who accepts losing you is a fool."

"Says the man who shrugs at Eva Mendes."

Billy laughs, raising his palms in surrender. "What can I say? The heart knows what it wants—even if it sometimes confuses the hell out of us or others."

"You know, I *will* have a glass of wine." *Just one.* Billy gets up to fetch me a stem glass as I ponder his last remark, connecting it to Mom's words. *In matters of the heart, no one has all the answers.* Why has everyone but me gotten the memo? "You are a very wise cowboy."

With a pretend tip of his hat, he responds, "Why, thank you, ma'am."

"So . . . you needed my fashion 'expertise' for . . ."

"Oh yeah, sorry." Billy retrieves the scripts, but instead of handing me a copy, he holds them to his chest. "Promise you won't laugh."

That gets my attention.

"You know how the whole zombie craze won't die?" he continues.

"Undead, so to speak," I say to tease.

"Well my agent and Wanda think I should do one. A horror project. Connect with a younger demographic—particularly teen boys. Raise my Q Score."

I'm not an agent or a manager, so I'm not supposed to have an opinion on projects . . . and as of just recently, I'm not supposed to have any opinions at all when it comes to one Billy Fox so . . . "Aha. Okay." I demur. "So this is . . ." I peel back the stack of held scripts and even upside down can't mistake "BRAINS FOR BREAKFAST" emblazoned across the title page. It's impossible not to laugh. *"Seriously?"*

Now he's laughing too. How could he not? "Hey, it's only the working title!"

"But I thought your next project was the one you were so excited about? Where you get to go all Meryl Streep with the new accent . . ."

"Still happening, but schedule-wise there's an opportunity to squeeze in this other shoot first. Screen tests with potential costars are next week and I want to bring my A-game out of the gate."

"Well you know what they say: breakfast *is* the most important meal of the day. And if they're serving—"

"Yeah yeah," Billy says, playing along. "Keep it up and someone won't get to borrow my future Teen Choice Award surfboard." He holds up a stunning, easily $300-plus blue button-down. Then swaps it out for a gray T-shirt. "Which shirt should I wear to meet the producer? I need to seem . . . you know, capable of saving the world, but I didn't really dress for it."

"Well, what does your character do? I mean . . . what were you doing before the zombies arrived?"

"Actually I have to work on memorizing the scene too. You want to help me with that? Then you can make a more educated decision."

"You win. Hand it over," I say, indicating the script. "Who do I get to read? And please don't say Zombie number forty-two."

"Nah. You're playing Emily."

Emily. I test the name out, ready to become this mystery girl. The lean script can't be more than a hundred pages. I quickly flip through my copy, pausing at the presumed audition scene, tagged with a Post-it.

"She's kind of my girlfriend," Billy says.

"Oh." I take a deep sip of wine.

CUT TO:

INT. HOSPITAL EXAMINING ROOM – NIGHT

MAX huddles with EMILY, a very sexy young nurse in uniform, on the edge of a paper-lined examining table.

A hanging curtain shrouds the far side of the room.

They're staring intently at the room's closed door.

MAX

It's okay. I locked it. No one's getting in.

EMILY

(quietly)

Are you sure we're alone?

"Wait, what *kind* of movie is this again?" I say, interrupting the scene.

"Relax. It's strictly R. Although there's always the Director's Cut."

"Mhmmm."

"It's nearly a family movie," Billy says, clearly enjoying messing with me.

"Yeah . . . one where they get eaten."

"For real, this is an important, character-building scene. Okay?"

What the hell. I nod.

And then Billy—or rather Max, my "boyfriend"—takes my hand. It seems silly but the sudden intimacy is startling, even if it's plainly scripted. I'm very aware of his close physical presence, the crisp trace of deodorant, the buffed manicure of his nails, the rise and fall of his breathing—and that we're alone.

Billy turns my face toward his and looks deep in my eyes. His own eyes' intense shade of pale blue is positively hypnotic. "When we get through this," he says calmly, *"and we will* . . .

everything's going to be different. We're going to go somewhere safe and warm—just the two of us. And have our chance to start over. Can you picture it?"

Yes. And there it is echoed on the page in black-and-white. I read on. "Yes. Where there's no more pain. No regret."

"And life is simple again. The open beach. Smell of salt in the air. Cry of gulls circling overhead. The sun on our shoulders. Toes in baked sand. Your hand curled in mine."

Despite my parents' and Izzy's standing ovation for my fevered performance in sophomore year's production of *The Crucible*, I don't consider myself a particularly good actress. But in *this* moment, I am practically Method. Emily and I are one.

I grip my script tightly. Emily doesn't have that many lines.

"Everything happens for a reason—even this," Billy/Max says. "And as long as we stick it out together, we'll survive." His hand runs tenderly through my hair. "I was a fool to take you for granted. It's taken all this—the chaos around us—to understand how I feel about you. Surviving isn't worth it alone."

Yes, even in my rhapsody, I can tell it's a little cheesy. But it's exactly what I need to hear . . . from someone . . . and the affirming words resonate inside.

I believe him.

Billy/Max leans in and we kiss. A passionate, open kiss that leaves me a bit woozy.

"Oh Billy." *Oops. A little off-script.* But Billy, ever the professional, doesn't break character.

"Shhh."

"Sorry!" But again I'm off-script, the two worlds confusedly overlapping.

"Did you hear that?" he whispers urgently, eyes now wide, his fingers gripping my forearm. He silently edges off the settee and stalks toward the changing area. "I thought I heard something."

My heart is in my throat as Billy grips the curtain folds and, without warning, flings it open. *"Oh my God. Run!"*

Billy's horror is so convincing that I nearly dive off the settee, tossing my script to the floor. I'm half-expecting to find the walking dead shuffling toward me, a willowy salesgirl with dead eyes and a blood-smeared mouth craving my flesh. A beat later, I don't know whether to laugh or be humiliated. Either way, my pulse is still racing.

"It's ridiculous, right?" Billy says, referring to the script, but his words—and their larger truth—trigger an epiphany.

The "love" between Billy and me isn't real.

Or at least it's very different than Jacob's. I can see it clearly now. This isn't *Romeo and Juliet* or *West Side Story*. We're not star-crossed lovers. The only tragic ending may be my reputation and stalled career.

And the fact that I hurt Jacob, losing the one guy who loved me most.

I wanted a future, a commitment with Jacob. And when it didn't happen on my own timetable, insecurity twisted into frustration. Instead of exploring *why*, I left myself open to the exciting yet totally unexpected possibility of Billy.

I got swept up in the moment—seduced by the easygoing charm and sexy attention Billy embodies.

But there's no real future with Mr. Fox and me. And so, as with poor promised Emily, the happy ending isn't guaranteed—or, let's face it, even likely.

With all I've seen in my job, why didn't I realize sooner that I was beholden to make-believe?

Now, Billy isn't a bad guy at all. He may even care for me. But this exercise puts my infatuation—because ultimately that's what it is—into belated perspective.

"You okay?" Billy says. "You seem miles away."

"I'm good," I reply. "You're going to nail the audition—screen test—whatever. Really. I totally bought it. But I've got to get going."

An escape *is* in order. And I know just the place to help clear my head.

But first I've got to do something long overdue.

Back home I boot up the laptop and log on to my personal email account. Lots of unread or unanswered messages. I'm too ashamed to simply pick up the phone and call.

Dearest Izzy,

I'm sorry. As I'm sure you guessed, I've been avoiding you.
A LOT has happened lately—much I'm not proud of.
Unfortunately I'm not coming to New York next week.
Please tell Simon I'll sorely miss him and "the Boss."

Where to start? I suppose the beginning . . .

13

ON THE OPEN ROAD, FLIPPING THROUGH RADIO STATIONS, I'm amazed to discover just how many country music stars relate to my current situation. Whether they're losing at love, not knowing how they'll get through another day, or enduring the unemployment blues—I find myself totally nodding my head, grateful that at least Keith Urban and Lyle Lovett understand what I'm going through.

The drive east to Palm Desert usually takes about two and a half hours from Brentwood. Given that I "cleverly" decided to make the drive during peak hours, it will be closer to four. Luckily I brought some good company. In the passenger seat, Lizzie alternates between poking her head out the half-cracked window—pink tongue blissfully lolling out of her mouth—and curling up to nap in the increasingly warm sunshine. The old girl may be light on conversation, but she offers plenty of comfort and unconditional love.

It's only fitting that she joins me on this getaway. My family originally picked Lizzie out at a breeder's house on our way home from the desert one winter. I remember knowing immediately she was the right dog. It's not that she was the only one who came running up to me with wishful puppy eyes. Nor was she showing off or trying to get her brothers and sisters to play with her. Instead, Lizzie had a rope chew toy in her mouth and wouldn't let go. As an only child, I related to how self-sufficient and independent she was. And knew for certain we were meant to be together.

This morning my parents were gracious enough to loan me Lizzie and the keys to my childhood vacation home. After seeing things for what they are with Billy and belatedly confessing all via email to Izzy last night, I need a little off-the-grid time. And visiting Palm Desert, a city in the heart of Coachella Valley, approximately eleven miles east of Palm Springs, in the arid early summer, is definitely going against the grain. Dry heat or not, once the average high temperature settles in at triple digits, only the year-round aging Baby Boomers, sun-loving die-hards, and absolute masochists stick around.

But I'm not worried. In fact I welcome the relative quiet and easier parking of off-season. Besides, I've been coming here since I was eight and gracelessly swung my first golf club, so it's not like I'm going to be surprised or bowled over by the intense subtropical climate.

Plus I miss it. The open blue skies and namesake palm trees seemingly lining every road and all the plentiful golf courses. The city has hosted many of my favorite memories.

Regrettably it's been years since I last spent any time there. After college, once I started working, freedom was scarce and what few breaks I had generally weren't spent accompanying my parents out of town. No, there were always friends, boyfriends, or the demands of work to keep me preoccupied. Now with all three cornerstones of my prior identity on hold (or at least out of reach, in Izzy's case—I symbolically turned my Black-Berry off), I'm experiencing the first true—if very disorienting—break from all my old routines.

For better or worse, I'm 100 percent free—even if it feels a lot more like adrift.

Past Moreno Valley, I leave CA-60 East to take the exit onto Interstate 10 East, signaling we're more than halfway there. I adjust the BMW's windscreen visor, helping to block the direct sun, and put my sunglasses back on. Even with the satellite radio now tuned to "Nineties Dance Party"—the B-52s "Roam," fittingly enough—my mind starts to drift as the sameness of the road and surrounding scenery lulls me.

I wonder what Izzy's reaction was to my email. Is Billy declaring his love right now to another "Emily" at the audition? What's happening with my projects at Bennett/Peters? Does Elle regret her decision? Or am I simply office gossip, a cautionary tale? And what of Jacob? Does he miss me? Or is he already moving on to someone kinder and less complicated? Perhaps a pretty peer in finance, who will cherish talking about . . . whatever it is they do, exactly.

The downside of this road trip may be a little *too much* time to analyze.

Okay, I'll think positive. *The Secret* and all that. What's the first thing I'm going to do when I get to Palm Desert? Lie by the condo association's pool and finish every paperback romance and mystery novel I can get my hands on. It's hardly a long-term solution, but it's a plan.

I'll take it.

As the miles rack up, so does the outside temperature. We're definitely entering desert territory. I raise the automatic windows. "Sorry, girl. Time to switch on the AC." Lizzie looks up at me quizzically, all deep brown eyes and two tan dots punctuating her eyebrows, but happily concedes once the cool air is blowing.

I've got nothing but time to figure things out. There's no reason to go back to LA right away. I mean, there's no point, right? No job to wake up for . . . no red carpets to organize or phone calls to make. No relationship. I can stay in the desert for as long as I want. My parents are cool with it, and at this time of the year the condo otherwise sits empty. A little caretaking is in order.

This trip is about slowing down. During the few vacations I've taken since I started my career, I have never been able to really relax. I check my email compulsively, like an addict with a twitch. I am always high-energy, mid-story, and on the go.

But this is certainly not like a holiday. And as it turns out, it's a lot easier to not check my phone when I know the only people who would be contacting me are the people I don't want to hear from. Over the last week I have accepted that I won't be hearing from Jacob. That Elle is not going to call, begging me to come back, because her firm is not crumbling down around her without me. When I saw Wanda von Kingstead's number on my missed call list the day after my suspension, I realized two things: There are some calls you just don't need to return, and self-preservation overrides a person's habitual, borderline obsessive message-checking trait. Wanda's remains the one and only voicemail I've ever erased without hearing one word.

Outside Beaumont, I pull over for some gas and the boost of

a fresh Diet Coke. It feels good to stretch my legs and back. The strong dry heat hits me, baking the asphalt, yet its nostalgic familiarity is comforting. It's only the cold (which for me is anything below forty degrees Fahrenheit) or heavy humidity that makes this SoCal girl miserable. Just ask Izzy, who humors my "softness" whenever I visit New York in all but its most mild seasons.

Lizzie's content to keep her serial nap going, so I leave her momentarily to man the vehicle.

An electronic chime announces my entrance at the convenience mart. It's one of those overlit places—day or night—with more blinding fluorescents than Hollywood's shorthand vision of the afterlife. An exhausted-looking mom tries to wrangle her pleading kids out of the snack aisle, shaking her head at each air-plumped bag or can of Pringles. In the rear at the beverage coolers, an acne-scarred teenager pretends to admire the range of bottled iced teas while cagily eyeing six-packs of beer. *Been there, my friend.* I grab my soda bottle plus some water for Lizzie and head to the checkout, happy to spare my corneas.

And that's when my old life catches up to me.

Up front, next to the impulse gum and candy, sit the usual tabloids. Without a pause, the entertainment publicist in me automatically scans the headlines. And there in the top right corner of this week's *In Touch* is the headline BILLY AND EVA BUILDING DREAMS above a shot of the striking pair hand in hand beside a meticulous sand castle on a beach somewhere.

Gotta hand it to Wanda.

The picture-perfect sand castle is a giveaway that—whether

Eva was in on the ploy or not—this caught date was intended to be anything but private. Just the ridiculous thought of Wanda demanding an extra turret makes me laugh.

"You've got a great smile."

Caught off-guard, I look up to find a super-cute—if barely legal—Hispanic clerk with enviable lashes and a black faux hawk behind the register. He's flashing me his own killer smile.

"Thanks," I say, paying for my purchases. "You too."

I leave the innocent flirting at that, but the unexpected compliment couldn't have had better timing. It reminds me that there's a whole future of possibilities. Change in hand, I catch myself grinning again in the automatic door's reflection.

Sure, that one was more baby than babe. But I won't lie. For the first time in a while, it felt good to be me.

Arriving at my parents' place in the desert is like traveling back through time without a flux capacitor, though it would've been nice to go eighty-eight miles per hour. I feel like a young girl again pulling into the driveway of the sweet bungalow-style condo with its one-car garage, concrete tiled roof, sage-painted plantation shutters, and sentinel palms flanking the front walkway. In the distance, the majestic San Jacinto Mountains spread out as if embracing the entire fertile valley.

Lizzie perks up, recognizing the home as well. Seconds later she's racing me to the front door. Seems someone else feels like her younger self.

Once inside, Lizzie scooting out of sight, I deactivate the security alarm and then turn around to get my first good look.

The two-bedroom condo was originally decorated in the

mid-eighties and, other than looking a little worn at the edges, remains remarkably the same. It's like stepping into the past. Long forgotten high school golfing trophies (my elegant swing disappeared years ago with my pre-cellulite thighs) maintain their place of honor in the den. There's the mirrored wet bar with its glass shelves that adolescent Izzy and I once raided, smugly replacing the pinched booze with water and later learning the hard way not to mix our liquors. The flat-screen TV is new, but I recognize the oversized cream-colored sofas, the framed watercolor paintings (from Mom's *artiste* phase), and the corner game table that hosted many a competitive round of Uno, Monopoly, and Pictionary. Combined with the wallpapered bathrooms and kitchen straight out of *Family Ties*, it all makes me keep waiting to hear my parents announce it's time for me to go brush my teeth before bed.

Nowadays my parents could afford to buy something new and modern, but it's clear that they're equally sentimental about the idyllic shared past.

I find Lizzie lounging on the ceramic tile floor beside the sliding door that leads out to the back patio. Just beyond the simple patio lies the deep green fairway of the 8th hole. Yes, our "backyard" is a meticulously maintained golf course—one of roughly thirty in Palm Desert. I sit down beside Lizzie. Does she remember Dad and me heading off with our clubs to play? Or how Dad would barbeque out on the patio while Mom tried to teach me the "pleasures" of cooking, when all I wanted was to be searing steaks outside.

One thing's for certain: I'm glad I came.

After taking Lizzie for a walk and starting to get the house cooled, I retrieve my light packed bag and the not so light container of special formula dog food from the car. I'll pick up groceries for myself tomorrow because, even taken by surprise, my supermom whipped up and sent along a small cooler of goodies for dinner tonight. Reheating a delicious home-cooked meal in the microwave sure beats scavenging the pantry's limited canned goods or hitting the closest fast-food franchise. And now I'm feeling extra grateful because pressing a few buttons is about all the energy I can muster. The long, monotonous ride and climate adjustment have left me wiped.

Soon after dinner, I don't need anyone to tell me it's time for bed.

I decide to pass over the more comfortable master suite to reclaim my old room. It just feels right to be in *my* space again. And it's just as I remember it. The décor grew up with me from purple-loving, imaginative child to too-cool, impulsive teen, but there's the same twin bed I slept in nearly every Friday and Saturday night of my defining years. High school achievement ribbons and more trophies line the bookshelf, and most amusingly, the walls are still tacked with posters and clippings of past teen music idols and "Billy Foxes" of their day.

Be careful what you wish for.

Lizzie takes her usual spot at the foot of the bed and in no time is snoring.

Following her example, I change and climb into bed, pulling the sheet and thin coverlet up to my chin. Lying there—coming full circle—brings on the strangest feeling, both uncertainty and Goldilocks's *just right*. On the bedside table is my old Sony "Discman," batteries long drained, with an Alanis Morissette CD still inside.

You, you, you oughta know.

I'm working on it.

Lights off, I rediscover the faint constellations of plastic glow-in-the-dark stars on the ceiling. For years, they comforted and inspired me. Eyeing them again, I no longer wish I had the power to stop time or even return to the past. I want to fast-forward, to move beyond the sadness that returns when I lie still at night. Those wishful gifts are all fantasy. I'm stuck in the present with a mess of my own making.

But as exhaustion pulls me into a deep slumber, I'm more hopeful here that, somehow, I, Sophie, will find my way out.

14

I WAKE TO THE SOUND OF LIZZIE'S INCESSANT BARKING.

"Lizzie, no . . . ," I murmur, pulling the sheet over my head in a futile attempt to go back to sleep. To my side, the desert's powerful sun is already threatening to push through the closed blinds. Lizzie's wake-up call crescendos, which is weird because she only gets super-excited these days . . . if someone is at the door.

And that's when I catch the underscore to Lizzie's fanfare—a faint yet steady knock.

Whah? I'm not a morning person. I'm really in no mood for any cookie-pushing Girl Scout or Jehovah's Witness. Who else still knocks on people's doors unannounced? I haven't been here a day and the Neighborhood Welcome Wagon has already arrived? Maybe if I lie still and close my eyes, Lizzie will calm down enough so I can go back to—

"Sophie?! Are you in there?" I distinctly hear from outside.

No way.

I know that voice.

Jumping out of bed, I scramble to the front door, hair wild and half-dressed. Lizzie's deliriously running back and forth in the foyer. I turn the deadbolt, unlock the door, and then throw it wide open.

Please don't let this be a dream or some heatstroke mirage.

Arms crossed, she cocks her head and says, "Did you have to pick the hottest day ever to sleep in?"

"Izzy!!" I throw my arms around her. My best friend who's remarkably here, twenty-seven hundred miles away from New York. Picture one of those Publishers Clearing House winners, stunned and then weeping joyful tears at the invasion of TV cameras, balloon bouquets, and an oversized check at her doorstep, and you have an idea how I feel right now. "How did you ever—"

"Dennis and Jeanne tipped me off when I called looking for you. *Someone's* been impossible to get in touch with lately."

It's true. I've been avoiding her and, well, everyone. Talking to others would make my situation too real, even though I knew I was denying myself their support. Sending the belated email to Izzy only thirty-six hours ago was a major step forward, but I still feared her immediate reaction enough to skip town and consciously stay offline.

Lizzie, finally chill, joins us out on the front porch, nuzzling her old friend, little stub of a tail wagging furiously.

"You do know I'm always here for you?" Izzy continues, crouching down to ruffle Lizzie's fur but never taking her deep almond eyes off me.

"Of course," I say. She's the closest I have to a sibling. "And likewise." But here, across the country, on my doorstep?

Only Izzy.

"Good. So invite me in. I'm baking."

While my unexpected guest cools down and hydrates, I hurriedly shower and get dressed. Minutes later, hair still damp, I find Izzy walking around the living room, reliving her own memories of the place.

"Seems like yesterday, right?" I say, taking a seat on one of the sofas. Lizzie watches from the floor of the foyer, worn out from all the earlier excitement.

"It's been, what, ten years since I was last here? And yet I feel totally at home. Though I'd be happy to never see *that* again," Izzy says and laughs, pointing at the wet bar. "Just the thought of our high school bartending 'skills' makes me queasy."

"Izzy, it's *so* good to see you." I still can't get over the fact that she's here. If you didn't know better, you'd never guess that she's originally a SoCal girl herself—even though she was always of the rarer dark-haired and stubbornly pale variety that was more interested in catching esoteric punk bands at claustrophobic clubs than rays at the beach. I made peace years ago with the fact that the east coast—especially New York City—suits her. And it never hurts to have an open invite to the Big Apple. Okay, there's no getting around the real reason she's suddenly back in California. "If you're here for the intervention, you're a little late," I say sheepishly.

"But not the restoration," Izzy says, offering an optimistic smile that would give anyone hope. "When I got your email, everything clicked. I'm so sorry. You must be devastated. I started to write back . . . but then impulsively booked a direct flight to LA instead. Thankfully I thought to call your parents first."

"But what about your job? And Charlie and Simon?"

"Eh, they're fine for a couple of days. Simon sends his love. And work will survive without me. Felt like you needed me most now."

Sometimes I really think she's psychic. It thrills me to have my best friend again.

"On the flight over, I concocted an entire body-mind-spirit recovery plan," Izzy says. "Or simply put, I'm here to distract you until you feel better."

If my life was a movie, the next ten hours with Izzy would be a cheesy montage set to your absolute favorite pop song. Time flies by and, true to her word, I laugh more than in the last couple of weeks combined. We stroll the mile-long, lushly landscaped El Paseo shopping district, "The Rodeo Drive of the Desert," sampling its high-end boutiques and abundant art galleries for both a little retail therapy and welcome shade.

El Paseo's numerous restaurants usually offer the best people-watching, but since the summer heat has considerably weaned the crowd, we opt for a different trip down memory lane. Juanito's, a kitschy little Mexican restaurant we always enjoyed before Sunday evening rides back to LA, has been there as long as I can remember. And inside we discover that, like the condo, it hasn't changed much in the last two decades. We follow the golden-skinned hostess, who clearly lives in the desert because her only alternative would be to live inside a tanning bed, to our table and order a round of margaritas on the rocks—an upgrade from the virgin daiquiris of our past.

Finally, stomachs full, we consider a scenic drive out to Joshua Tree National Park but, with a shared knowing look, elect to indulge in some last-minute spa treatments at The Spa at Desert Springs Resort Hotel. One date scrub, mineral spring wrap, and deep tissue massage later, I practically float home.

For a whole day LA isn't even on my radar.

Somehow Izzy is still awake, but I can sense that the long day has finally caught up to her jet lag. As she checks in with Simon, I bring in her black Epi leather Louis Vuitton carry-on from the rental car and then direct her to the master bedroom. "You get my parents' room since clearly you're the more adult of the two of us," I say, ending any further protest.

Minutes later, when I'm sure Izzy's passed out cold, there's a soft knock at my bedroom door.

"You asleep?" Izzy stage whispers.

"No. Come on in," I say. Izzy enters, dressed for bed. How is she still standing? "Aren't you exhausted?"

"I've got a two-year-old, remember? It's amazing how little sleep I need."

I scoot over, thinking she's come to join me for a nostalgic slumber party chat, but the surrounding time capsule proves too distracting.

"Oh my God," Izzy says, admiring the poster of Leonardo DiCaprio from *Titanic* tacked next to the closet. "Nice."

"If you think that's special, tomorrow you should see what treasures I found stored in the closet—including the old Ouija board, photo albums, journals, and my dog-eared copy of *Let's Go Europe*."

"How could I forget that priceless tome we carried everywhere. Hey, remember in Copenhagen when we met that girl from Orlando—"

"At the hostel without any hot water and—"

"She told us she traded her copy of *Let's Go* for some hand cream."

We laugh at the ridiculous memory. I tell you, send two clueless friends overseas together at an impressionable age and they'll be bonded forever. The stories never get old.

"Wait. I almost forgot something," Izzy says, going back to her room and soon returning with a bright pink and blue herringbone-patterned box. "All the talk about Europe reminded me of the little gift I brought you."

In my hands the square box is fairly light. A pink banner atop reads: LADURÉE PARIS.

"They're macarons imported from Paris via Manhattan's Upper East Side," Izzy says, removing the box top to reveal two rows of variously hued decadence. "They're all the rage."

"And here I thought cupcakes were still trendy." I can't resist sampling one of the vibrant meringue-based cookies, sandwiching sweet ganache, jam, or buttercream. And then I select another flavor to try because, well, I don't want to be rude. And devour another. "Wow" is all I can mumble between bites.

"Whoa, *mademoiselle*, save some for me," Izzy says, joining me on the bed and mock-wrestling for the box. "Actually, eat away, because after today's gluttony, we're getting some exercise tomorrow. A little sweat therapy."

I look at her skeptically. It's not that I'm unathletic per se. But I haven't stepped foot in a gym for several weeks now, and admittedly it's not near the top of my to-do list. Plus I know Izzy, who miraculously finds the time and motivation to regularly work out or swim laps during her lunch hour. There's no way she's going to let us simply pedal a bit as we watch CNN or syndicated sitcoms on the TV monitors.

But I hold the trump card.

"Sounds great," I say, channeling drama-club-skill sincerity, "but I didn't bring any workout clothes." *Shucks*.

"Nor I," Izzy says. She surveys the room, a mischievous smile dawning on her face. "But I have an idea."

WE MAKE QUITE A PAIR. In matching red high school gym shorts, complete with a white racing stripe down each hip, there's Izzy, sporting a The Cranberries tee, and me, non-ironically rocking a Hootie & The Blowfish concert tour T-shirt. I don't know who should be more humiliated. Probably me because I once wore each proudly. Thank goodness for elastic waistbands and the very relaxed sizing of the mid-nineties.

"I forgot you were once so badass," Izzy says slyly, checking herself out in a wall-to-wall mirror at the Fitness Kickboxing gym.

We're waiting for the preceding class to finish. Remember, in the past I *dated* a would-be ninja and that sport-of-the-future kickboxer, but I've never tried kickboxing myself. From what I see, it doesn't look so bad. I'm even a little ashamed of my initial resistance.

Other than the front desk and adjacent beverage cooler, the matted room consists of nothing more than two parallel rows of ten heavy hanging bags and some jump ropes to the side. There's no potentially embarrassing one-to-one combat arena.

It's just you and a can't-miss bag, waiting to get pounded. To the chirpy beats of a Katy Perry remix, the cute and very flexible male instructor calmly leads his class through a series of wind-down stretches. Basking in the sheen of hard-earned sweat, everyone's all smiles. There's even a round of spontaneous applause at the finish.

I'm actually looking forward to this new experience.

My favorite Rihanna song, "Umbrella," comes on. I excitedly nudge Izzy with my freshly purchased and rather comically padded boxing gloves. Compared to the fingerless variety on most others in the room, they make it seem downright advantageous to be a newbie. As if I'm off to bowl with the bumper rails up to prevent any chance of gutter balls.

And then, the ol' bait and switch.

Mid-lyric, Rihanna is replaced with something like speed metal mixed with the dregs of hip-hop. A stern hipster guy in his early twenties, with a shaved head and a beard with no mustache, Amish-style, picks up the instructor headset.

Oh no.

"Okay, people, I don't want to see anyone standing around," our confirmed drill sergeant barks. "Grab a jump rope and start warming up."

"Did you sign us up for the *advanced* class?" I ask Izzy as we claim neighboring bag stations and select jump ropes off the wall.

"No. There's just one general class each hour."

Great. So long, inspiring pop princesses.

"Less talking, more sweating!" Amish Beard announces. "Sixty more seconds of jump roping and then we're going right into jumping jacks . . . Fifty seconds . . . I want that heart rate up. We're just getting started here."

This is going to be the longest hour of my life.

Finally after the jump-roping, jumping jacks (a first since PE class), and far less fun push-ups and thigh-burning squats, we're warmed up enough to pull on the gloves and start taking it out on the bag. In rapid fashion, there's a whole new language of moves to absorb: jab, cross, hook, uppercut, front kick, roundhouse kick, raised knee, and more. I get it. Sorta. But there's a bit of a mental pause between moves as I recalibrate which arm to use, where to hit the bag (upper, lower, side), and how my feet are supposed to be positioned. Instead of a fierce warrior, I feel more like a marionette in shaky hands.

I try to keep up—pantomiming the instructor and my class-mates, terrified of being called out. Shouldn't there be some kind of beginners' orientation?

To my left, Izzy's laser-focused. But she's done this before.

Next are the combinations, and if I thought I was a little off before, I'm now practically left on the side of the road as nearly everyone else marches by.

"Jab-hook-jab—double cross—uppercut—front roundhouse kick!"

Or as I like to reinterpret: "Blindly punch or kick to your liking!"

Sweat is dripping into my eyes, and my T-shirt is sticking to me. Hootie and I are getting very intimate. The few fifteen-second catch-your-breath-and-get-some-water breaks are fleeting. When we're told to jump, arms stretched, as high as we can, then squat, walk out on our hands to push-up position, perform ten, and then repeat—twice, I catch my own mumble echoed on the lips of the heavyweight African-American girl directly across from me. *Oh hell no.*

You try to do push-ups while exhausted and wearing giant leather mittens.

And then we get to crunches—the apex of cruelty. Teeth clenched, I work through it. My endorphins are on overdrive.

"Come on, is that it? Give us more sets of crunches!" shouts the most annoying Amazon in an electric blue sports bra and matching hot pants. "I'm just getting started! Whoo!"

There's a special place in hell for such people.

"Oh give it a rest," Izzy mutters. I'm not sure if anyone else heard, but it makes me adore her even more.

Finally, we get another breather and I sidle up to Izzy.

"How do you do it?" I say, tearing off the gloves to grip my bottled water. "How do you push through?"

Izzy's an equally sweaty mess. "I use this to work out my frustrations, my stress, with sweat and direct sand contact. Picture your problems and then beat away. It's *very* therapeutic."

"In thirty seconds get ready for a final full-power round!" the instructor commands.

"Pain is the great equalizer, trust me," Izzy adds, as I tighten the second glove's Velcroed strap with my teeth, preparing for battle.

Over the next ten minutes I take Izzy's advice. The gung-ho instructor drones on, his terrible choice of music playing, but it starts to feel more like an out-of-body experience. Everything falls away until it's just me and the bag facing off.

A parade of "motivation" appears in my head like a private

PowerPoint slide show, exposing all my bottled-up frustration. Each becomes a satisfying bull's-eye and I let loose. There's smug Priscilla. Take a roundhouse kick. The solid smack of the impact feels oh so good. There's Jacob *for being so stubborn*. Jab-cross-jab. There's Billy *for being too damn cute*. Left hook—upper cut—raised knee strike. And, ultimately, there's myself *for getting in this mess*. I show no mercy.

I'm winded. My arms and legs burn. I wipe a glove across my sweaty brow.

But Izzy's right. It *is* incredibly cathartic—an almost primal breakthrough.

A fresh start.

After a round of blissful showers and a change to clothes from this decade, Izzy and I spend the remainder of the day lying around the condo with Lizzie. We watch a *Top Chef* marathon, comb through old photo albums (laughing over regrettable hair and wardrobe choices), take a short field trip to the condo association's pool to commandeer prime lounge chairs, and then return home at dusk to grill burgers, since we burned enough calories earlier to eat whatever we please.

The embarrassing lecture I feared from my far more sensible friend never comes.

That evening as we're washing plates and rinsing empty beer bottles to recycle, Izzy offhandedly remarks, "It feels kind of odd to be back in California and not see the ocean."

An idea—befitting our rebellious teenage years—hits me.

From the linen closet I grab two bath towels. Lizzie's ears prick up as I open the sliding glass door. "Sorry, girl, you gotta stay. But you," I say, pointing to a puzzled Izzy, "follow me."

Outside it's still hovering around eighty degrees. Beyond the back patio, the rolling green hills of the golf course are softly illuminated by a half-moon overhead and the glow of other houses dotting the perimeter of the fairway. I must have a peculiar look on my face because Izzy is at my side whispering, "What are you up to?"

"I can't offer the ocean but there's a private 'beach,'" I say.

A hundred yards away is the pale, amoeba-shaped outline of a sand trap.

"Sophie Atwater. Rule-breaker." Izzy pats me on the back. "I take it back. You are *still* badass."

We leave our shoes behind on the fairway. The sand is warm from a day in the blazing sun but comfortable enough to enter barefoot and select a prime spot to lay out towels. When we're on our backs, gazing up at the stars, with toes in the sand, the illusion of open beach—however mute the surf—is complete and peaceful. I should have thought of this retreat years ago. In the relative dark, no one takes notice of the intrusion. I mean it's not like we rolled a keg and a DJ out here to party, interrupting my older neighbors' *CSI* viewing.

"I forgot how much I've missed this place," I say. "Everything is simpler here."

"You certainly don't see stars this clearly in Manhattan," Izzy says, tracing constellations with her fingertip.

"I kind of wish I never had to go back. With my job in limbo and Jacob done with me . . . Maybe I *can* just stick around longer."

Izzy props herself up on her elbows and then flips to her side, facing me. "Okay, Sophie, let's get serious. We both know you'd be bored out of your mind here in no time. You belong in LA. It's where you thrive."

"Thrived," I correct.

"I don't believe that. Yes, you've had a setback—okay, a major one. Or two. But everything is going to work out. You know how I know? Because I know you."

"I wish I had your confidence. Hell, sometimes I wish I had your life. It's all come together just like you imagined."

"My life isn't perfect, Soph. *No one's* is. I still fight with Simon sometimes. There are nights I'd sell my soul for a solid eight hours' sleep. And work is, well, lots of work. A busy career, long days, two working parents, and a two-year-old aren't exactly so ideal and stress-free. I envy *you* sometimes."

"*Me?*"

"Yes, you. Now I wouldn't trade my life for anything—Charlie and Simon are my world—but you're at a moment of unlimited potential. The future is just waiting. And you don't even see it."

"I've made some bad decisions."

"Perhaps. But you've got to stop kicking yourself. Learn from mistakes and move on. Look, you know I'm a huge fan of Jacob. But if he can't step up or understand how you feel . . . Who wouldn't fight to commit to you? You're Sophie Atwater, Badass Extraordinaire. If there wasn't Simon, Charlie, and our irrepressible fondness for men, *I'd* scoop you up."

"Technicalities," I say, and we share a laugh.

In my heart I know she's right. I need to pick myself up. A break from LA was necessary, but hiding out is just another form of denial. I can't change the past, but I can shape my future.

"What would I do without you?" I say to my best friend.

"Let's never find out. But I'm sure it would be awful."

"Unimaginable."

"Or, come to think of it, college."

"An expensive reminder that we're best stuck with each other." There's really only one other thing to express. "Thank you."

Izzy takes my hand and squeezes.

Two big city girls lie back and resume stargazing in the desert. No other words are needed.

Early the next morning I see Izzy off to the airport. We hug good-bye, promising to keep in close touch (okay, *I* promise to do better), and then Izzy's off to rejoin her family. Waving from the driveway, I realize I too am ready to go home. And very very sore from yesterday's workout. Rubbing my arm, I head inside to pack up my own stuff. I wish I knew where life will take me next. But with renewed faith and confidence, I'm going to be all right.

15

WHILE AN AMBITIOUS JUNIOR PUBLICIST AT BENNETT/ Peters, I witnessed one of Elle's A-list clients—a three-time Grammy Award—winning performer of a certain age—utter something so audacious it became an in-joke between Izzy and me. I was at the late Virgin Megastore on Sunset assisting Elle with her legendary client's *Greatest Hits* CD release signing. Several hundred ecstatic fans stood in line, their numbers snaking through the roped aisles and out the front door, patiently awaiting precious seconds of basking in the diva's greatness.

My role was to pass out Post-its for fans to pre-print a name if they wanted their newly purchased CD personalized, and to remind them—again and again—that absolutely no memorabilia or albums would be signed except the latest one. There simply wasn't time for each superfan to pull out a half dozen promotional photos, magazine covers, boxed sets, and random sentimental objects—and *they would* if allowed—to have signed and still keep the line moving.

Plus, signed teddy bears aren't Nielsen SoundScan—counted and thus won't boost the all-important *Billboard* ranking.

Elle gestured to me from the roped-off atrium, where she stood behind her seated client, monitoring the scene. At the time I was still in awe of all-access status, relishing the jealous glares of others as with a wave of the laminated pass around my neck I sailed past jaded salesclerks, stressed-out event coordinators, and enormous security men.

"I need you to take over photo duty," Elle said, handing me the next-in-line fan's digital camera. A single posed photograph was allowed, but *we* snapped it and it was a clockwork affair. The fan was not allowed behind the table or even to touch the star. Instead, he or she leaned into the frame to capture a flash of beatific smile as the star signed her increasingly illegible name. There were no do-overs.

I soon got into the rhythm of the process. Some overwhelmed fans were literally speechless when they got to the head of the line, shyly nodding when addressed and almost fleeing from the table with their signed CD. They were the easy ones. Others were determined to make their moment count. While the star autographed or posed for the requisite photo, the über-fan regaled her with praise, trivia, personal anecdotes, and even bids at being Barbara Walters. They were the ones we had to move along, playing "bad cop" to the star's generosity.

But after two hours even I felt a certain exhausting sameness. And the line was still going strong.

Up next, an excited male fan rushed the revered diva, but before he could open his mouth, she held up a bejeweled hand and plaintively said, *"Please, anything but 'the Story.'"*

From that moment, whenever I wanted to defuse a situation, I'd utter those unforgettable words. Too much of anything is insufferable. You reach a point where you just don't care.

These days I'm taking the command to heart—no longer wallowing in the mire of the last couple of weeks. What's the point of rehashing past mistakes in my head, wishing I had done things differently? Feeling sorry for myself isn't going to get my job back. And if not Jacob or Billy, *someone* worthy will enter my life. But opportunity is not going to find me sitting in old sweats at home watching cable.

Ever since my return to LA a week ago, I'm starting to feel like my old self—more or less. Even the rare restless day I don't, it's better to fake it, to push through—because there's really no acceptable alternative. Like Izzy said, I'm *Sophie Atwater*. Enough with the moping.

It's time I regain some control.

And I'm going to approach it in the way I do things best—as a highly skilled publicist. Yet this time the client in need of a makeover is myself. Bring out the color-coded checklist.

First up, I'm getting back out there socially. Otherwise a life of relative solitude at thirty-one is the gateway to an existence of microwaved dinners in the cherished company of several cats. The perfect opportunity arrived while I was off in Palm Desert. Amid the usual bills and junk mail, I discover an official invite from Travis's parents to his thirtieth birthday blowout at their home in less than three weeks. Jacob will likely be in attendance, but Travis is my friend too. I refuse to lose him in the "divorce."

I RSVP yes.

Speaking of Jacob, there's been no word from him other than coming home to find his copy of my house key slipped under the door in an envelope with the simple note:

I figured you'd want this back.
Hope you're well.
J

Instead of uncorking a bottle of wine, I went online and researched local kickboxing classes. My ten-class card is now nearly up for a renewal. Izzy, my ever-cheerleader, has been sending fist pumps from remote. I'm still not begging instructors for more crunches, but I do feel like I belong among my sweaty classmates. And I've got some fancy fingerless gloves to prove it.

Jacob's old key is now in my kitchen junk drawer. Somewhere out there, a guy doesn't know it yet, but this key—to my home and my heart—is awaiting his arrival. Or so says my mom . . . and I've chosen to believe her. It's that or stocking up on kitty litter.

With my newly adjusted attitude, I fill my days helping out at Mom's bookshop and taking classes or catching up with friends. The next book club is held poolside at Tina's Spanish-style apartment complex on Melrose. I'm not only prepared—having "read" this month's selection via book-on-tape on the ride home from Palm Desert—I bring *notes*. Since my usual contribution is to ask, "Another round?" JoAnn nearly chokes on her mango margarita when I volunteer to lead the discussion.

"I don't think we've met yet," jokes Tina to the new me. "But I've got a hunch we're going to be tight."

"Must be a psychic connection because I was thinking the very same thing," I say, as we tap our plastic cups together in tribute.

The upside to my former workaholic nature at Bennett/ Peters is that I acquired several weeks of unused vacation time— in addition to the usual personal and sick days—so *for now* I'm at least financially solvent. I've been putting off contacting a headhunter or even networking because there's only one place I truly want to call "home" again. Elle's well aware of my intention—and financial time line—and we've set up a future meeting "to discuss." This state of limbo can't last forever. Short of being Priscilla's assistant, I'm prepared to accept any terms if it means I'm back in business with my sorely missed clients.

As for Priscilla, the only contact I have is when she regularly appears on my punching bag. I know in my gut she's somehow responsible for my outing, but I haven't had any luck finding irrefutable proof to support it. And so, maddeningly, she's still my replacement. Per Billy, she's not exactly winning over my clients with her icy charm, but it appears she hasn't unequivocally tripped over her incompetence yet either.

To think *I'm* the one to disappoint Elle kills me.

Yes, I've stayed in contact with Billy too. Through a semi-daily text exchange, I've gotten the chance to know Billy the person versus Billy the star. I'd go so far as to say we've become actual friends. He now hilariously relays disastrous dates and the latest on-set fiasco. In turn I find the humor in my own life. Yes, he's still a big flirt, but I've learned to take a compliment and realize it doesn't have to mean anything. It's his very nature to charm. On one hand, it's weird. I am not Facebook friends with any of my exes. But Billy isn't really in that category anyway. He's in his own league, and frankly, his friendship has meant a lot through this unsettled period. I know if it weren't for him maybe I'd still be with Jacob. But that isn't Billy's fault. I know now it's my own.

With total freedom—and all right, to stave off boredom . . . and maybe a little guilt too—I throw myself into the Tribe of Hope benefit gala planning. It feels good to have a purpose. And without all the previous drama and distractions, I'm great at it. As Izzy foresaw, I'm truly starting to get my mojo back.

Tonight, for instance, I'm brainstorming with a handful of other publicists and talent agents generously volunteering their time and service in a corner of the foundation's loft-like office space. The celebrity gala event—the foundation's critical annual fund-raiser—is rapidly approaching. Over the past several weeks, my subcommittee has been diligently garnering prizes for the popular silent auction, enlisting media contacts to promote and cover the event, and securing use of A-list names for the "hosting" masthead. It's shaping up to be a huge success, but any publicist worth her salt keeps upping the potential till the end.

Irene, a fortysomething talent agent in a very expensive-looking cream pantsuit and towering heels, offers up lunch with the notoriously germaphobic comedian/host Howie Mandel as a possible prize for the evening's live auction finale.

"No disrespect but the guy's most comfortable with fist bumps," Brian, a fellow publicist, counters. "Any winner wants to feel special, not contagious."

"Speaking of special, *I'd* be most inclined to bid if it was more of a fantasy date scenario," says Tanya, a striking African-American agent from CAA. "Think champagne, strawberries, and dark chocolate with some ridiculous hottie. *That* gets checkbooks out."

Hmm. I know a certain "hottie" who performs good deeds.

"I can ask Billy Fox," I say. "He's a client . . . and a friend."

All eyes turn to me.

"Billy Fox?" Irene says incredulously, her wide, cougariffic smile combating with dermal fillers. "Can you guarantee I'll win?"

"Highest bid and he's all yours," I say with a wink.

"Can't think of any better use of my 401(k)," Brian says dreamily, "although my husband may disagree."

"Then it's settled," I say, retrieving my cell phone. "If you'll excuse me, I have a favor to ask."

I'm preparing for voicemail when Billy picks up. "Greetings from the Apocalypse."

Huh?

My dramatic pause must have registered. "That's right, I forgot to tell you," Billy continues good-humoredly. "I got the part—the zombie movie. You helped me get the gig. Can you believe we're already in production? These indies move fast. You caught me trying not to get fake blood all over my trailer."

"That's great. Congrats!"

He's not letting me off that easy. "The elusive Sophie Atwater. To what do I owe this pleasure? I always believed the rumors of your disappearance were greatly exaggerated."

"Well you know . . . I'm keeping busy, even volunteering my publicity services. In fact there's an auction coming up benefitting Tribe of Hope's commitment to breast cancer awareness and—"

"You need my amazing emcee skills again?"

"Not exactly. I'm calling to see if you'd agree to, um, be a prize. In a 'bid for a date with Billy Fox' auction. You know, a shared dinner and some chitchat." I'm not embarrassed to ask if he'll support the charity, but I do play down the cheesy fantasy element. "That is, if you're game. And free. I'll make sure you're, you know, chaperoned the whole time of course. If you can't, I totally get it. I know you're busy fighting off the undead."

"Are you pimping me out, Sophie?" Billy says, mock-offended. "What kind of a gentleman do you think I am?"

"One who can help raise a lot of money for a worthy cause."

"Well if a 'date' with me can help cure cancer, I'm all for it. Count me in."

No arm wrestling necessary. No list of conditions—coy or demanding. Or "let me discuss it with my manager first" run-around. Just a simple and sincere yes.

"Billy Fox, you *really are* a good guy," I say and mean it.

"I'm just me," Billy replies, and I can easily picture the twinkle in his eyes that effortlessly manages to charm us all. "But thanks. Your stamp of approval genuinely means a lot. I gotta run. They're calling me back to set now." He makes a ghoulish roar.

After promising to relay to Billy all the pertinent details, I return to the committee and take my seat.

"He's in." I am grinning, picturing his phone covered in slime or goo or whatever the makeup department uses to create open wounds.

There are actual cheers.

Irene puts down her iPhone. "Well I just checked my bank balance. Looks like I'm going to have to settle for a mere mortal. *Hello.*" Something over my shoulder captivates her complete attention. "Now *that* will do just fine."

Curious, I turn to see what's got her all enraptured.

Across the room sits an incredibly sexy man, rolled up sleeves exposing strong arms below broad shoulders, studying what looks like a pile of spreadsheets. A pin-striped suit jacket hangs on the back of his chair. His face is largely turned away, but I'd recognize that fall of soft chestnut-brown hair anywhere.

Jacob.

"Wonder what's *his* story?" Irene says, joining my stare. "I don't think I see a wedding band. Surely he can't be straight *and* available? The truly eligible are as common as unicorns in LA."

Thankfully Jacob is engrossed in his work, seemingly oblivious to being on display. He must have arrived after I left to call Billy. Maybe with my back turned and across the room he hasn't even noted my presence. Of course I knew he was still involved with the foundation, but in our very distinct roles we'd yet to cross paths.

Seeing him now *is* like encountering a unicorn. Surprisingly unreal.

And the first coherent thought that comes to mind is: *Hands off my man.*

I thought I'd moved on. Punched it out. Shut it away in a drawer.

Yet here now with Jacob I find myself feeling territorial.

Unlike with Billy, there was never much of a reaffirming epiphany that it wasn't right. Or real. Jacob and I ended things over disappointment, stubbornness, and hurt. But never from lack of love.

The rest of the planning meeting continues around me. I nod along and lightly participate in the final details, but my mind is elsewhere. I refuse to turn around and see if Jacob ever spots me, shielding myself from his reaction. As soon as the meeting wraps, I dart for the door, nearly holding my breath until I'm seated in my car, gripping the steering wheel. I glance up at the rearview mirror and shake my head. Once again I've managed to catch myself off-guard. Why did it take Irene's appraisal for me to realize I still have feelings for Jacob? When am I gonna let it go?

16

TRAVIS'S PARENTS HAVE A STUNNING CALIFORNIA COLONIAL– style home with twin thick columns flanking a forest-green painted door, and knowing as I do the true gentleman beneath the laid-back, motorcycle-riding image, it's exactly how I pictured Travis growing up. Arriving a good half hour early to the party could have been really awkward, but Connie Harrison does not allow people to feel uncomfortable in her home. She welcomed me in like a family member, and immediately put me at ease by setting me to work. So now I'm helping organize last-minute party setup with the catering staff in the immense Carrera marble–filled kitchen. Through a half-moon wall of windows leading to the backyard I watch another small crew adding chairs and lighting votive candles as the band sets up to one side of the flagstone terrace.

I'm the first guest to arrive because there was very little traffic on the 405, and while the place is way the hell out in the Pacific Palisades, my GPS got me here with none of my usual "please make the first legal U-turn" foul-ups. Plus I'm making a renewed effort to always be on time, but with traffic's wild-card factor sometimes I overcompensate and achieve the other extreme.

But mostly I'm uncharacteristically prompt because I'm out-of-my-mind nervous about tonight. I know I will see Jacob this evening, and every possible scenario I've played out in my imagination makes me feel a little sicker. Sure, I admitted to myself how I still feel about him, but he made it very clear when we broke up that it was *over*. Period. And his kept distance since doesn't exactly indicate regret. Just as I was finally feeling confident again, old emotional vulnerability returned. *Great*. At least the simple navy sheath I'm wearing hangs ridiculously well on me—those kickboxing classes are paying off. I even went sleeveless without a second thought. But I suspect Jacob would have the same guarded reaction to me whether I was in Victoria's Secret or a burka. We're all adults here; I know he won't make a scene. But I don't know which will feel worse . . . having to make polite social small talk as if what happened between us didn't mean anything, or if he gives me the "cut direct" as in some fabulously tragic moment from Jane Austen. For him to publicly shut me out completely would be devastating.

So why even show up? Why torture myself? Because it's Travis's birthday—and one's three-o is a big deal.

Well, okay, that's partially true. I mean, it *is* true that it's Travis's milestone birthday. And Travis has always been a good friend, even through this personal and professional debacle. But that's only half of why I came. I'm here, stabbing toothpicks through prosciutto-wrapped cantaloupe balls, because I need to get this inevitable encounter over with. I can't get on with the rest of my life until I manage to face this hurdle. Otherwise the purgatory of not knowing how it will go with Jacob will haunt me indefinitely.

With nothing left to stab, I carry the elegant silver tray to Travis's mother. "Where would you like me to put these . . . ?" She told me not to call her "Mrs. Harrison," but my inner twelve-year-old is very close to the surface these days and feels uncomfortable using her first name.

"Just lovely, Sophie dear. Please place them out on the lanai." And as I walk away, she adds, "On the coffee table, dear, not the antique hutch." I love Travis's family. Originally from Greenwich, Connecticut, they are a rare and fascinating mix of gentility and accessibility. His smart and gorgeous twin sisters, Cassie and Bridget, always crack me up. His mother only looks chic and fabulous, air kissing with the best of them, but she unabashedly lights up in the company of her outgoing brood. His father, a notable architect, was once quoted in *Architectural Digest* saying that building his family was the accomplishment of which he was most proud. When Tina—my intended "plus-one"—had to bail last-minute, I knew I'd still have a grand time solo.

As I step outside and try to figure out which thing is the "hutch" so I don't put the appetizers there by mistake, the mild evening air is just perfect. It would never dare be overcast or cold for a Harrison Family Gala.

The front doorbell rings and the first on-time guests begin to file in. As only truly perfect parties do, it goes from no one to a chatty festive crowd in minutes. Released from service, I drift around, meeting Travis's family friends, some of whom I know, most of whom I don't. Cassie and Bridget, in slinky, jewel-toned cocktail dresses, stick close to my side, whispering the juicy gossip on everyone as we hang out at the inviting bar station set up in the grand foyer opposite the front door.

When Damon walks in, I am embarrassed to admit I cower and turn my back before he can see me. What is it about that guy that, even from twenty feet away, brings out the worst in me? He's with his now official girlfriend, Juliet, the makeup artist I met and liked a lifetime ago, so he can't be *all* bad. And, yes, he's old friends with the Birthday Boy and Jacob.

Jacob. Pulling myself together is no easy feat knowing that he could walk through that door at any moment.

Okay, Sophie, time to pull up your big-girl pants and grow up. It doesn't matter how he responds. You have to be mature about this. There's no alternative.

The twins luckily don't seem to notice my inner pep talk, keeping up their witty banter without missing a beat. Though there is absolutely nothing important I'm expecting, out of habit and to cover my nerves, I check my phone. And surprisingly, there is a text. I didn't even notice the buzz over the crowd.

have fun tonight. You deserve it. XO Izzy

Well, I don't know *what* I "deserve." But I couldn't ask for a better friend, and I make a mental note to text her back the second I leave tonight.

Looking up from my phone to politely laugh at whatever Bridget said to make Cassie crack up, my eyes land squarely on Jacob's face in the entry. He clearly spies me too. For a split second I freeze, but the momentum of my fake laugh actually carries me through the crisis. I instinctively draw breath when Jacob smiles back at me politely and nods in greeting. I nod back, and then he is pulled into the crowd of others arriving, and the moment is over.

It was fine. We smiled, we exchanged head-nods . . . it's fine.

"Sophie, just so you know," Bridget says sotto voce, "Jacob just got here." Cassie discreetly points toward him with the rim of her champagne glass, but I don't need to look. Their tone is hesitantly sympathetic. The twins know what went down from Travis, but I love them for not grilling me for details, for just being there with me.

"I saw him. And it's okay." It is. I mean, what am I gonna do? I realize now, I've built up this moment in my mind like it was going to be some big awakening. And it's not. I still don't have a job. I still screwed up a great relationship with a guy I really loved. And I'm still the new me—the one who loves kickboxing, has a fresh appreciation for her mother, and has big plans for the rest of her life. Even if some of the details are hazy . . .

I take a deep breath, look around, and take in the diverse gathered crowd.

"What a great party. Your mom doesn't kid around."

"Please. You should've seen their fortieth anniversary party," Cassie says. "This is nothing!" Seconds later she is deep into a description of the ice sculpture portrait of their parents when the birthday boy himself saves me with his grand entrance.

After Travis is toasted (and roasted), the party and decibel level really get going. The six-piece band is in full force. Nearly everyone—from parents' friends to the siblings' peers—is out grooving on the dance floor that was positioned over the swimming pool. I've even let myself get dragged out here by the twin terrors. And I've had just enough well-paced cocktails to think I've got some smooth moves.

The lead singer is covering OneRepublic's "Good Life" really well, and it's totally pulsing through my veins. I feel an arm brush against mine and open my eyes to see Travis smiling down at me.

"I'm so glad you came!" he shouts over the music, but really I'm just sort of reading his lips. I smile back, relieved we can't actually "talk."

"Happy Birthday," I mouth back, giving him a quick hug, which he returns in a bear squeeze before we both start lip-syncing to the irresistible chorus. We burst out laughing as we screw up the other lyrics, but still are caught up in the beat. It's so nice to let loose and simply have fun. I am just enjoying this moment, laughing, singing, dancing with Cassie, Bridget, and Travis . . . and one hundred of his closest friends.

The hours pass in a blur of cake, more toasts, and spirited dancing. I am grateful that the extra ten seconds I took to turn my simple slick ponytail into a bun is such a low-maintenance style. At some point I remove my painful shoes and hide them behind a nearby planter. Even without my heels, my feet are killing me when I finally take a break from the dance floor to wait in line barefoot at the cappuccino bar and dessert crêpe station. Eyeing the decadent options, I do the girl thing of mentally guessing how many calories I've burned sweating and wondering if it will compensate for the strawberry crêpe I refuse to deny myself. The party hasn't slowed down a bit. In fact, if anything, it's even more lively, the proverbial second (or third) wind having taken hold. And at this point it doesn't even surprise me when I see Jacob and Damon deep in conversation with several beautiful women.

It's like immersion therapy. I've now glimpsed Jacob so many times during the night that I am becoming immune to the aftershock. For instance, I watch the group chat for a second longer—even catching one pretty gal leaning in to Jacob, laughing—before the pastry chef takes my attention back to whipped dessert decisions. When I look back in the group's direction, they are gone.

"If you share, the calories don't count," Bridget says, teasing me as she sneaks a bite from my delicate powdered sugar–covered plate.

"Please. Help yourself." We sit for a beat enjoying the sugary treat in worshipful silence. I've met the Harrison family plenty of times since getting close with Travis through Jacob. And I've always gotten on well with his little sisters. But somehow tonight, maybe because I am Jacob-free, these girls have made me feel like a third sister.

"Thank you so much, Bridget. For everything tonight." I don't want to bring this moment down or anything. So I laugh. "It could've been all *Real Housewives* drama without you and Cassie to keep me in check."

"Happy to help," Bridget says, patting my arm, "but if there needs to be a smackdown tonight, you know I'm good for that too." She demonstrates her mighty kung fu moves with her fork, which gets me really laughing.

And of course Travis and his always composed parents

appear right as I'm doing my best *Karate Kid* pose. I try to tuck my bare feet under the hanging tablecloth. Mrs. Harrison, I mean Connie, still looks picture perfect—as though the party only started moments ago and she's barely left her dressing mirror. How does she do that? At my side, Bridget straightens up too. Ah, a kindred spirit, intimidated by her mother's flawlessness.

"This evening is so lovely, Mrs. . . . um . . . Connie. Thank you for including me," I tell her with absolute poise. My performance is blown in milliseconds, as Connie leans forward and with a motherly gesture wipes powdered sugar off my cheek. I blush. "And everything is delicious. Obviously."

Having been part of the party from the very beginning of the night, I don't feel at all awkward when Mrs. Harrison, I mean *Connie*, asks if I might run to the cellar to bring up a couple of reserved bottles of prized Bordeaux wine for some of the special guests (myself included).

Back inside the house, I disappear into the beautiful oak cellar, happy for the chance to escape the crowd. Everyone tonight is so, well, happy. Not to say that I'm not happy. I am. Completely. But as I drift past rows of wines, casually scanning the labels, hunting for the ones on Mrs. Harrison's list, I feel myself growing a little indignant. I've kept largely to the twins' side tonight. But just because I'm not totally into making vapid small talk with semi-acquaintances doesn't mean I'm not happy in the broad sense. I'm just not feeling "festive," that's all.

And now I'm having an argument with myself. Wow.

Eventually I find the Bordeaux section. Of course Mrs. Harrison has listed particular vintages as well as regions and wineries. No problem—I've always been good with details. Double-checking the labels, I complete the task.

"Why aren't you dating anyone?"

"Excuse me?" I could pretend that I don't recognize the voice behind me. But I do. I would know his voice anywhere. I turn around, my hands filled with wine bottles, and Jacob's stance is filling the small doorway.

"Why aren't you dating?" he says again. This time he doesn't sound so fierce, but still, there is an intensity to Jacob that I don't remember ever seeing before.

"I don't know what you want me to say." Suddenly I feel defensive and trapped, and I try to take charge of the situation. I walk up to where he is blocking my exit as if to pass right through him. But of course, Jacob doesn't budge. His stare feels like it's drilling holes through me. "Jacob, please let me pass," I say calmly.

"First, tell me why." He hasn't moved an inch since he locked eyes with me. But now he takes a step forward, backing me farther into the tiny shelf-lined room. There's an alluring hint of whiskey and cigar coming off him.

"This is ridiculous. I don't know why. I just haven't." I had been hoping to escape without answering him, but with no space between us, the words just fall out of my mouth. And now that I've started talking I can't seem to shut up. "*Why?* What is this, the Inquisition? Jacob, what are you doing?" By the last, there was a squeak in my voice.

"Travis and Izzy both said you haven't dated anyone since we broke up. Is that true?" Now my back is pressed up against the cellar wall, and the necks of a few of the bigger wine bottles are pushing uncomfortably against my spine. The gentle clink-ing of bottles settling against one another complements my short breaths. Izzy hadn't told me they spoke.

"What do you care?" I always love a good fourth-grade comeback.

"Tell me." Jacob hasn't changed his volume, but if possible he is even more intense than before. Clearly he is looking for a specific answer. One I don't know. Out of the corner of my eye I see his right arm braced on the wall next to my ear, between the exit and me. He brings his face down to meet me eye to eye. I feel like he can see into my head, and I wonder if he finds whatever he's looking for.

"Sophie . . ." This last comes out as a sigh. Did I hear regret in his voice, or was it acceptance? The room is still way too close, and with no air to speak of, I am only breathing in Jacob's breath. I can't focus. Finally Jacob ends the staring contest—he won—and his gaze travels over my face, still as intense, but now I feel the heat on my hair, my cheeks, and finally my lips. My stomach does a series of backflips.

My eyelids start to drift shut. I want him to kiss me more than anything, and I can already taste how good it will feel to have his lips on mine, and his arms coming around me. But I can feel that he hasn't shifted his body at all. I force my eyes open again and see that we are now nose to nose. His eyes are closed too. But not gently closed, he is squeezing them shut. A dead giveaway to the tension we are both drowning in.

Maybe he needs me to kiss him. Just as I get the idea, and build up the courage to make the first move, we both hear:

"Sophie! Where are you with our wine?"

"I could die of thirst waiting for you!" A giggling duet of drunken girls. Travis's sisters, whom I left what seems like a lifetime ago. Their footsteps echo in the hallway as they get closer.

And we still haven't moved.

Jacob's eyes are open again and he's back to reading my brain. But there's a slight smile on his lips as he finally pulls away from me. He doesn't step aside, but he lowers the arm he had caging me in. I feel the coolness of the room come back to me and I realize that my body is missing Jacob's warmth. I don't meet his eyes again. I just slip around his solid frame and through the cellar door. What I need is time to think, but Bridget and Cassie are upon me, and there isn't even a second for me to take a breath before they've grabbed me and the wine bottles and I'm shepherding them back to the party. I don't want them to see Jacob in the cellar.

That moment, whatever it was, is a secret I keep close, tucked away inside me for the rest of the night.

17

THIRTY-SIX HOURS AFTER TRAVIS'S CELEBRATION, I'M STILL replaying the intense encounter with Jacob. His determination. The electric sensation of our bodies nearly touching. The inscrutable thought behind his stare. If not for the twins' interruption, where might it have led? And most important, what does it *mean* going forward?

It's incredibly disorienting.

Twice I nearly phone him, to hear his voice and pry for answers. But he could just as easily call me. He doesn't need to stalk wine cellars to secure an audience. My numbers are the same. And yet he hasn't reached out. The reminder stops me each time from completing the call.

You see I too have pride.

For Jacob, nothing's fundamentally changed. It's built-up sexual tension—plain and simple. We could have kissed, even rolled around on a bed of wine bottles, but it doesn't change the underlying stalemate. Yes, it's wonderful to be desired, but mutual attraction was never our issue. I resign to the reality of the status quo.

As welcome distraction on a lazy Sunday, I choose to catch

up on last week's recorded episodes of *Black Mountain Valley*. Nothing puts my less-than-ideal life into perspective more than following the cursed inhabitants of a deceptively sleepy and incestuous little town. I may be alone and suspended from my beloved job, but so far I have eluded amnesia, an evil twin, a murderous robot resembling my deceased husband, and, worst of all, only two restaurants and three eligible men within city limits.

I'll take consolation wherever I can find it.

Less than two hours later, while I am zipping through a block of laundry detergent and home hair coloring ads in *BMV*'s mid-week installment, the apartment buzzer rings.

Now, who would come by unannounced on a Sunday afternoon?

No one I wish to talk to, I decide.

Unless it's Jacob . . .

The buzzer rings again.

What the hell. I pause the resumed soap and race to the intercom before whoever's downstairs believes no one's home.

"Yes?" I answer with a bit of don't-mess-with-me attitude in case it's a pushy pollster or a salesman.

"Hi, Sophie," says a familiar if surprising voice. "It's Tru. May I come up and talk to you for a sec?"

Now, *this* is unexpected. I deeply appreciate—and have missed—my trusty assistant, but we're not exactly girlfriends outside of work. Other than driving me to my last day at Bennett/Peters weeks ago, I can't remember the last time Tru's been to my condo building.

"Um, sure, of course. I'll buzz you in."

Moments later Tru— in retro hair and makeup, looking like a brunette Veronica Lake—is grinning at my doorstep. And she's not alone. Beside her, in "off-duty" dark selvedge jeans and a Lady Gaga tour tee, is Jeff. He's curiously smiling too. It's an impromptu office team reunion.

I'm thrilled to see their friendly faces, but the all-smiles ambush reminds me of a goodwill hospital visit. Behind them I almost expect to find a bouquet of "Get Well Soon!" Mylar balloons. Instead, I'm further dumbstruck to discover they've brought a special guest—my former client, Megan Keef, which makes the scene only more surreal because her character Annabelle's anguished face is frozen on my TV screen.

"Wow. This is a great . . . and unusual . . . surprise." When two former coworkers and a client show up unexpectedly on a Sunday, it's hard for my first panicky reaction not to be: "Okay, *now* what did I do?"

Finally remembering my manners, I deliver hugs and usher the troop inside.

I don't have to wait long for an explanation.

"Jeff and Tru told me what happened," Megan says, her eyes surveying my pad and settling contentedly on the TV screen. Then she removes a manila envelope from her designer shoulder bag and places it on the coffee table. "When I was in my *temporary* publicist's office Friday, I ran across this and figured it was yours."

Confused, I unclasp the envelope and peer inside.

I can't believe it.

"Oh my God . . ." Dumping the entire contents on to the table, I realize what this means.

I could kiss those sticky fingers.

"No? Oops." Megan winks conspiratorially.

NEVER HAVE I BEEN more excited to be at the office bright and early on a Monday.

"Good morning, Elle," Priscilla says brightly, all long legs and short skirt, as she ignores Lucas and breezes into Elle's office. "I adore that jade necklace on you."

The guest of dishonor has arrived.

Blinded by her usual kiss-ass behavior, it takes Priscilla a few seconds to even notice me in the room's sitting area. "And . . . *Sophie*. What a surprise."

"Yes, today is *full* of surprises," I reply.

"Take a seat," Elle says coolly from behind her desk, gesturing to a guest chair.

The tiniest flash of uncertainty crosses Priscilla's composed face as she complies. "Is Sophie feeling better and returning to us?" Priscilla asks. She turns in her seat to give me the once-over. "You *do* look less haggard, Sophie. The long break suits you."

I'd deliver a retort if I weren't so distracted by the open manila envelope in Elle's hand.

"Actually," says Elle, commanding Priscilla's attention, "there's something else I'd like to address. Look familiar?" She gives the raised envelope a little wave.

"*How did you* . . . I mean, what is that?" Priscilla says, a crack in her smooth veneer.

"Why don't you tell me?" Elle says. From inside the envelope, she removes a stack of photos—the aforementioned incriminating shots of Billy and me making out behind Saddle Ranch. As Priscilla's eyes widen, Elle next retrieves a digital camera's memory card, and, most damningly, an actual invoice made out to Priscilla. "Although it does seem rather self-explanatory."

The damaging photos only exist because Priscilla commissioned them. I still can't believe how low she stooped.

"I can explain!" Priscilla cries out, her unguarded voice exposing a humbler origin. "Outside the movie premiere I first glimpsed Sophie and Billy getting awfully cozy. But you didn't care or believe me. And so . . . I hired some wannabe private investigator to trail Billy and bring me proof."

"For—let's not forget—a double payday when Elle and Wanda killed the story," I interject.

Elle shoots me a look and I shut up. It's her court here.

"Sophie is not without fault," Elle says, returning her laser focus to Priscilla. "And she's been aptly reprimanded for her carelessness. As for you—I've always considered tattling childish. But to intentionally aim to *ruin* your own teammate is inexcusable. And may I add, very déclassé."

"She was sleeping with a client!" Priscilla declares, loud enough, I imagine, for the entire floor to overhear.

"Not that it's any of your business but—" I interrupt.

"You're going to lecture me on what's *inappropriate*?" Elle says sharply to Priscilla. "You let me commend you for 'saving' Sophie's reputation. But in fact you were maliciously out to destroy it—even if Bennett/Peters was collateral damage. Ours is an industry that demands circumspect behavior and prides itself on keeping confidences. In my eyes, your crime is way worse."

"Elle, surely you—"

"We're done here, Priscilla. You've got ten minutes to pack up before security escorts you out."

For once, Priscilla is speechless. She rises unsteadily to her feet, eyes blazing, and then straightens her back and strides to the door. Halfway out, she stops to address me. "Well, I hope you're happy."

"Got to admit, I'm feeling particularly good," I say. "You might want to take the stairs. It's faster." I dramatically glance down at my watch. "Nine minutes and all."

Revenge *is* sweet.

"So . . . where does this leave us?" I cautiously ask Elle once the towering tempest has decamped.

"Well, without Priscilla, there's a whole bunch of clients now without a publicist." A hint of a smile crosses her face. "I think you might be the one who knows them best. That is, if you're interested?"

Like a rocket, I leap from the couch and nearly tackle Elle with the force of my hug. "Whoa!" she says, laughing, taken aback by the unexpected display of affection, but she doesn't immediately pull away. "I'll take that as a *yes*."

Definitely.

That afternoon my ears are still ringing from coworkers'

cheers and Izzy's joyful squeal when I called on the drive home to share the good news. Tomorrow I'm officially back in business.

It's a victory.

A second chance I will not screw up.

Only one thing dampens my triumph. There are no messages on the voicemail. No missed calls. The one person I most want to share the moment with is gone.

18

IT'S FINALLY HERE. AFTER MONTHS OF PLANNING, THE TRIBE
of Hope Benefit Gala is under way. And, taking in the packed
and vivacious scene around me, I see it's on its way to being a
complete success. I gotta hand it to everyone; this is no small-
scale soiree. In fact, the black-tie event is being held inside the
Beverly Hilton's International Ballroom, the familiar site of
the annual Golden Globes Awards and Oscar Nominee Lun-
cheon. Just imagining all the legends who have graced the same
sixteen thousand square feet beneath these tiered crystal
chandeliers is truly awe-inspiring.

As if we are inside of a giant pinball machine, round tables
set beautifully for eight fill the room from the edge of the stage
to nearly the back of the house. Draped rectangular tables lining the room's borders display the silent auction prizes and
bidding sheets. An impressive crowd is clustered around each,
competitively pledging bids. Tempting as it is to get in on the
action, the last thing I need is another vacation break. I'm just
so grateful to be back to work, happily busy again, and refo-
cused on what's important. Besides, fine dining or spa treatments for two is, well, a bit overkill.

Jacob and I haven't spoken since the wine cellar incident.

Against my will, I often catch myself reliving its intensity, trying to decipher it all. But even if it proves that he too still has feelings, his refusal to admit and, most importantly, act on them is really all I need to know. We'd be back at the same frustrating place where we started. A place I'm not willing to go. Rationally I know I'm right, which makes it even more bittersweet when I inevitably spot him across the room in a dashing tuxedo. He always looks handsome in his work suits, but seeing him for the very first time in a peaked lapel tux and black bow tie conjures weak knees. I turn my eyes down to the deep maroon carpet with its pattern of vibrant blue starbursts. It's like standing on a sea of compasses, but I've got no idea which direction to follow.

"Sophie?"

I look up to find Megan looking glamorous and sophisticated in a bold red just-above-the-knee dress with a bateau neckline and cap sleeves. I bought gala tickets for her, Jeff, and Tru to attend. It seemed the very least I could do.

"Do you like?" Megan says, performing a little half turn so I can see the side drape detail and take in her updo. "It's Valentino." Very nice. And expensive. As if mind reading, she adds, "Paid in full, I promise. Got a receipt and all."

I smile back at her. We're thick as thieves. "You look amazing."

"Not too shabby yourself, Boss," says Tru, joining the conversation with Jeff right behind her, each carrying a set of champagne flutes. Tru, as only she can, took the black-tie direction literally, wearing a Steampunk-style corset dress constructed of antique lace and sewn together men's black neckties.

It's like something straight out of a *Project Runway* challenge. Or a Victorian's vacation on Mars. Jeff looks quite handsome in a simple black suit and dark tie.

"Thank you," I say, accepting the proffered champagne. After an indulgent return to Clutch, I'm sporting a flowy V-neck lavender gown that's delicately ruched at the waist. Beneath its long folds, the height and glamour boost of my favorite Jimmy Choo strappy sandals is worth every painful step. Other than highlighting my eyes, I've kept the makeup natural, and my only accessories are a charm bracelet and a small clutch. After the past weeks of not caring to leave the house, much less dress up, I feel like a debutante.

Megan raises her fresh glass in a toast. "Here's to one day curing breast cancer. To reuniting our little family. To us."

"To us," we chime and clink glasses. And she's right. We *are* a family. Maybe a little dysfunctional but what family isn't?

Tru and Jeff wander off to check out the silent auction while Megan excuses herself to catch up with a former *Black Valley Mountain* costar, whose character was last seen going into the Witness Relocation Program after helping to convict a murderous Russian mobster. Alone again, I decide to do my publicist due diligence, exiting the ballroom to check in on the adjoining International Gallery being used as the press room. Various VIP guests are busy being interviewed on-camera or photographed for gossip and fashion blogs. Brian, fellow publicist and planning committee member, salutes me from across the chaos.

In an artificially well-lit corner of the room, a female entertainment television correspondent sits almost knee-to-knee with Billy, peppering him with questions. He looks particularly hot tonight in a dapper Tom Ford tuxedo juxtaposed with a tousled rockabilly hairstyle. Watching the pretty correspondent flirt with schoolgirl-crush abandon and him give it freely back—his hand occasionally tapping her bare knee for emphasis—I'm deeply relieved to feel amused instead of jealous. Who *wouldn't* flirt with him, given the opportunity? Taking in others' reactions to him—both the discreet glances and unabashed appreciation—I see why we wisely "share" our idols. You don't date or, God forbid, hope to marry 'em. That's a sure path to paranoia and heartbreak. But best of luck, sisters.

Before Billy catches me spying, I slip out of the Gallery undetected.

Outside the Ballroom's entrance, I intercept another flute of champagne from a passing waiter's tray. But instead of rejoining the sociable crowd mixing inside or simply taking my reserved seat at one of the front tables, I wander over to the neighboring International Terrace. An all-glass wall provides access to balconies overlooking the hotel's iconic Aqua Star Pool surrounded by clusters of palm trees, white chaise lounges, and two bright cabanas. The large heated pool is lit to glow sapphire blue in the evening dark and—as proved by the handful of canoodling couples seated around it—the dramatic effect is very romantic.

Apparently love is in the air. Twenty feet away I'm tickled to see Tru coyly comparing tats with a black fingernail polish–wearing cater waiter sporting kindred spirit Doc Martens with his tuxedo pants. Go Tru.

The champagne goes down easily, lending a faintly warm

and fuzzy edge to the evening. For a second I think I'm in far worse shape than I am when the hall lights start flickering. From my clutch, I check the time on my cellphone. The program, ending with the live auction, is about to begin.

With a now-empty plate of hastily gathered hors d'oeuvres before me, I'm off the high of the initial success of the event as I sit attentively through the benefit's moving program. The foundation's chairman, two breast cancer survivors, and a young woman whose older sister passed away from the disease each give a heartfelt and compelling speech. I think of Jacob's mom's courage and his unflagging commitment that I wasn't always empathetic enough to appreciate. Despite everything that's happened in the last couple of months, I count my blessings. I've got my health, my family, and my friends who love me. Lasting romance will come one day. It's just not my turn.

The last speaker finishes to thunderous applause.

The evening's emcee returns to the stage and announces the formal close of the silent auction bidding. I turn my head and search again for Megan and my Bennett/Peters crew amid the seated crowd. Once the program begins, the lighting beyond the stage is dimmed. Single spotlights illuminate each table from above, but their limited scope highlights little more than the floral centerpieces and disembodied arms raising forks and glasses to shadowed faces. Irene, ever the negotiating agent from my planning committee, had insisted our little group be seated together at a prime front table, and at the time I didn't have the energy to resist her will.

"Thank you all for coming and making this evening a success," the emcee continues at the podium. "To conclude our

fabulous evening, it's time for the greatly anticipated live auction. At your place setting is a numbered bidder paddle. We've
got some special treats to auction off here tonight."

In thick navy font on white card stock attached to a jumbo
popsicle stick, I'm bidder #214. There's a flurry of excitement
as hundreds of people retrieve their paddles, whether they
have any true intention of bidding or not. Even I, all too aware
of my checkbook balance, am caught up in the moment, fan-
ning myself with the paddle.

"First up is a VIP private tour of the *Tonight Show* studio
conducted by Jay Leno himself, followed by two reserved front
row seats to the night's taping . . ."

Care of one reconnected publicist calling in a favor.

Yes, it's good to be back.

The auction continues with a trip to Tuscany (with ten days'
use of your own villa estate), cooking lessons from an Iron Chef,
a makeover shopping excursion with a celebrity stylist, an in-
home design consultation with Nate Berkus, and several other
one-of-a-kind opportunities. Waving over a waiter with my
paddle, for a water refill, I nearly buy myself a retreat to Tuc-
son's Canyon Ranch. Luckily the competition refuses to be outbid, so I inadvertently help raise additional money for charity.

But just to be safe I tuck the paddle back under my plate.

There's an audible stir from the audience. I look up to see
what I'm missing.

It's Billy's arrival to the stage. He climbs the few steps and
chivalrously bows to the now-blushing emcee before waving to
the crowd. The room bursts into excited applause.

"Okay, everyone, our final auction item has generously

joined us. A man who needs little introduction—Mr. Billy Fox."
He's standing maybe twelve feet away from my seat. As he scans
the immediate crowd, we lock eyes for a split second and he
winks. Irene, to my left, catches the signal and playfully nudges
me with her elbow.

If you only knew.

"Sorry, ladies, *he's* not for sale," the emcee teases, "but you
can bid this evening for his company on a memorable dinner
out. A 'date' with Billy Fox. Let's start with an opening bid of
five thousand dollars."

Two tables to my right, a thirtysomething woman in emerald-
green chiffon promptly raises her paddle.

"Five thousand dollars from number forty-three. Do we
have seventy-five hundred?"

From much farther back, someone else joins in the bidding.

"Seventy-five hundred from number eighty-seven. Do we
have ten thousand?"

I turn to Ms. Emerald, whose scrunched face is clearly cal-
culating just how much it's worth to her.

"Seventy-five hundred going once."

As if watching a tennis tournament from courtside seats,
the room's collective attention shifts to my left. A few tables
diagonally behind me, a challenger's paddle is raised.

"Ten thousand to number three eleven." The newly ener-
gized room is getting into this particular match. "Do we have
twelve thousand five hundred? Ten thousand going once. Going twice . . ."

Ms. Emerald goes bold and raises her paddle.

"Someone's got it bad," whispers Irene.

"Twelve thousand five hundred to number forty-three. Do we have fifteen thousand?"

Everyone turns in his or her seat, awaiting further volley, but number 311 is spent.

"Twelve thousand five hundred going once. Going twice." Ms. Emerald smiles triumphantly.

There's a gasp from the back.

"*Fifteen thousand* from number eighty-seven," says the emcee, relishing the drama. "Do we have seventeen thousand five hundred?"

I know Ms. Emerald is going to fold. Her crushed look says everything.

"Fifteen thousand dollars going once. Going twice. *Sold to Bidder number eighty-seven*. Congratulations."

During the polite applause, I swivel around and crane my neck, trying to pick out the lucky lady. But with the entire room buzzing now that the main event is over, it's impossible to single her out of the crowd.

Up front, Billy too seems to be distractedly searching for his winning bidder. But who *wouldn't* get an ego boost if someone wanted to meet you badly enough to part with $15K?

After short closing remarks, the full house lights return.

Irene congratulates me. "Nice coup getting Billy Fox to attend. A little sex appeal always wakes up these often sleepy affairs. Speaking of . . . you're being summoned." She nods toward the stage, where Billy stands, hands in his trouser pockets, waiting expectantly.

"Excuse me," I say, rising from my seat and then carefully climbing the steps in my ridiculously impractical heels. I've got all new respect for award trophy recipients.

"That was wild," Billy says, offering me a steadying hand.

"Thanks, Billy. I really appreciate you helping out."

"It was an honor, Boss," he says charmingly. "Besides, all I had to do was show up. Others did the bidding." He's pointedly looking over my shoulder with an expression I can't decipher.

In a twirl of fabric, I turn around with curiosity and find myself once again nearly face-to-face with Jacob.

"Jacob? What are . . ."

And then I see what's clutched in his right hand, hanging at his side. It makes absolutely no sense.

Number 87.

The winning bidder's paddle.

What?!

"You . . . but . . . ," I say, dumbfounded. *Why* would he do such a thing?

"Don't you see?" Jacob says determinedly, joining us on stage. "I'm stepping up."

Billy, never one to miss a cue, steps aside.

I'm still very confused.

Jacob explains. "I've heard on good authority that it's standard protocol for the publicist to chaperone her clients." With his free hand, Jacob brushes my bare arm, sending an electric tingle up my body. "Of course, as far as I'm concerned, Billy can simply stay home."

The grand gesture—the one I didn't even know I was waiting for—begins to sink in.

"But . . . what changed?" I ask.

"You weren't in my life. It was really that simple. My world's not the same—*I'm* not the same—without you." He gently lifts my chin toward him. "I didn't realize I was a fighter till I realized I wanted to fight for you."

"Fifteen grand. That's a lot for a date," I say coyly. "Couldn't you just, I don't know, *call me*?"

"Well, it *is* for a good cause," Jacob says. "And I consider it an investment with a lifetime of returns."

Looking into the greenish-gold of his hazel eyes, I know what I want. It's never been clearer—and mutually expressed. And he's standing right in front of me. I grab Jacob by his grosgrain peak lapels and pull him toward me. His paddle falls to the ground as he leans in, cupping my shoulders. Our lips meet and the hundreds of onlookers fade back. Here, on this elevated stage, we're on our own island.

And just like that I knew there are two survivors.

epilogue

"ALOHA" READS THE SUBJECT LINE. ATTACHED IS AN ADOR-able photo of Charlie, bundled up in a red knit stocking cap, striped scarf, and puffy snowsuit, posing next to a lopsided snowman in what must be buried Central Park.

> Will gladly trade you—the freak weather
> (TWELVE INCHES!!), not the kid :) xoxo Izzy

And there's a new message from Elle, which I can't resist opening:

> You better not be reading this until you're back,
> tanned and relaxed. Seriously. Put down the
> BlackBerry and enjoy yourself.

Busted. She does know me well.

Following the strict order, I set aside my phone and turn on the flat-screen TV. Diaper commercial. Talk show. Local news. *Seinfeld.* Infomercial. Golf. As usual—hundreds of channels to surf, nothing to watch. I'm about to give up when something on-screen catches my eye. *Grey's Anatomy* rerun? No, that's no

Seattle Grace. But there *is* a pretty young nurse in scrubs passionately kissing a civilian McDreamy.

Billy Fox.

No wonder there's a sense of déjà vu. It's the very scene we once read together. Even the great Billy Fox can suffer a straight-to-DVD release. Watching Billy declare his love again is fascinating—only this time (*Did you hear that? I thought I heard something . . .*) I stay to witness Emily's fate. From behind the dividing curtain, a gory, hospital gown–wearing zombie lurches forward, and—somewhat familiarly—Billy's love interest loses her brain.

Figures.

Jacob enters the room, sliding shut the glass door to the balcony, and asks, "Watcha watching?" Behind him, glistening blue water and Maui's golden sand beaches form a panoramic view.

"Just a distraction while I was waiting for you."

He smiles. A generous smile I pledge never again to take for granted. "Well, I'm all yours. Whatever you desire. Snorkeling? Spa visit? Helicopter tour?"

"Definitely snorkeling. Tomorrow," I say, tugging loose the knotted belt of his terry bathrobe. "*Today*, I have other ideas."

Fantasy Jake is firmly Jacob now—and I wouldn't want my leading man any other way. With a last glance at the unlucky girl now getting her heart torn out, I turn off the TV, power down my BlackBerry (after one final peek), and hang DO NOT DISTURB on the honeymoon suite's doorknob.

acknowledgments

Given that this story is all about Hollywood, I have to thank the show that gave me the insider's scoop. *Days of Our Lives* has been my home for more than half my life. The cast and crew are my family. I am so grateful every day to have such a sensational, talented, and fun group of people to spend my time with. Some of these stories may seem familiar . . . but they're not. It's all fiction. I swear.

I've been so blessed in my life to have incredibly hard-core, tough, sensitive, supportive, and dependable friends. This story couldn't have happened without each and every one of you. I love you all. I love us.

Mom and Papa, you've been so instrumental throughout my career. I can never thank you enough for your love and support.

There's an incredible team of talented, hard-working people who guide my career, counsel me, and . . . talk me off the ledge when I need that too. Max Stubblefield, you rock. Jacob Fenton, Ennis Kamcilli, Matthew Elblonk, Carrie Simons, Melissa McGuire, and Barbara Rubin: Thank you.

Patrick Price, you turn straw into gold, my friend. Thanks for putting up with my wacky schedule.

Thanks to the whole team at Hyperion Books and especially Christine Pride, my intrepid editor, who saw something special in my story and did an incredible job guiding this process and making it the best it could be.

And thanks to Dave—my teammate, my partner, my best friend, my husband.